I AM VENUS

ALSO BY BÁRBARA MUJICA

The Deaths of Don Bernardo
Affirmative Actions
Far from My Mother's Home
Sanchez Across the Street
Frida
Sister Teresa

I AM Venus

A NOVEL

BÁRBARA MUJICA

THE OVERLOOK PRESS
New York, NY

To my husband, Mauro, with love

This edition first published in hardcover in the United States in 2013 by
The Overlook Press, Peter Mayer Publishers, Inc.

141 Wooster Street
New York, NY 10012
www.overlookpress.com

For bulk and special sales, please contact sales@overlookny.com,
or write us at the address above.

Cataloging-in-Publication Data is available from the Library of Congress

Book design and type formatting by Bernard Schleifer
Manufactured in the United States of America
ISBN: 978-1-4683-0657-6

FIRST EDITION
1 3 5 7 9 10 8 6 4 2

Prologue

I WAS RECLINING ON THE DIVAN FACING THE WALL, MY BACK TO the artist. Gossamer sunbeams caressed my left shoulder and buttocks. He had posed me looking away from the window, but I could feel the fingers of light warming my body. They stretched over my arm toward the plush red curtain that hung around the foot of the bed. I lay on a maroon silk sheet that would, one day, turn charcoal-colored. The luster of flesh against the sheen of the cloth filled the scene with light and created an atmosphere of luxurious intimacy. That's what he said: "luxurious intimacy." He was a well-spoken man. He was, after all, a courtier.

Madrid is a strange city. Palatial residences stand alongside squalor. A fishmonger can live on the same street as a duke. Velázquez had a studio in the king's gallery, but he'd chosen to paint this particular piece in the private apartments of a patron. I'd snuck in through the servants' door and didn't know who the house belonged to. Perhaps Don Gaspar, as some people said, but perhaps not. Velázquez wouldn't tell me.

The morning bustle filtered through the open window.

The grunt of pack mules carrying produce to market. The throaty croon of a drunken soldier—Madrid was full of them. The curse of a scurrying servant who had slipped on the contents of a chamber pot that someone had emptied onto the street. The cry of a *buñolera* hawking her sweet, sticky fritters. The clop-clop of an aristocrat's elegantly appointed horse. French peddlers offering trinkets—glass beads, ribbons, earthenware crocks. Foreigners had flocked to Madrid after the king's father had expelled the Moriscos—Moors who had converted to Catholicism. The new arrivals filled the void—they became artisans, weavers, and of course street hawkers. The streets were full of them crying out in their mangled Spanish, "Buy a shell comb for your hair, *señora*! Buy a button to adorn your pretty dress!"

Velázquez moved toward me. I could hear the soft shuffle of his slippers against the tile floor. Even though I'd been posing for him for weeks, he was never satisfied with the tilt of my head. He gently lifted my arm and placed it over the back of the divan, then bent it at the elbow and laid my right ear on my open hand. I sensed his gaze on my back and tried not to squirm. Soon my outstretched upper arm would start to ache, but even then, I would force myself to lie very still. Velázquez—I nearly always called him Velázquez, not Diego—made a sound that conveyed neither satisfaction nor its opposite. He remained motionless a moment, then ran his finger over the nub of my shoulder. It tickled, but he wasn't being playful. He was interested in the crescent shadow on my upper arm created by the height and angle of the elbow. He leaned over my torso and adjusted the white silk that lay beneath the maroon-colored sheet. Then he tipped my buttock slightly forward in order to better capture the curve of my left hip against the intense whiteness.

"*Perfecto*," he whispered.

He stepped back to his easel. I could hear the swish of brush against canvas, and I concentrated as hard as I could on not moving.

We both knew we were taking a chance. The Inquisition forbade the depiction of nudes under pain of excommunication, which is what made it so exciting—and so frightening. Our very salvation was at stake.

Excommunication transforms you into an outcast. The bishop expels you from the Christian community in a public ceremony. A bell tolls as if you were dead, and then they close the gospel and snuff out a candle. No one speaks to you. People snub you in the street. Sometimes they spit at you. You can't receive Christ's sacred body in your mouth or drink his sacred blood, but of course, they don't take away confession, just in case you want to repent. If you show remorse in confession, the priest can help you get the excommunication lifted. But if they don't lift it before you die, you'll go straight to hell. Sometimes I close my eyes and picture myself in flames. I feel my whole body smarting, then stinging, then throbbing. I see my flesh turning red and blistering. I smell the putrid odor of burning tissue. My flesh turns purple and falls from my bones, and then I disintegrate. I hear myself shrieking, but eventually the shrieks grow weaker and weaker until they fade away. Then it all starts all over again because that's what hell is: never-ending fire, never-ending agony.

Was he worth risking hell for?

For Velázquez, I would have risked a thousand hells.

Outside, the clickety-click of coach wheels against cobblestone. The high-pitched stammer of a blacksmith's anvil. The gravelly cry of a flower vendor—*claveles! rosas!* The Arabic refrain of a kitchen slave chopping carrots.

Velázquez moved toward me and once again adjusted the tilt of my head. He wanted me to look toward the left, as though I were gazing at my reflection in a mirror. He said he was going to paint a mirror into the composition, with a little winged boy to hold it. A naked little winged boy with a pouch for his arrows and reddish-purple ribbons in his fingers to play off the reddish highlights in my hair. He wouldn't use a model for the child. Instead, he would sketch one of the many statues of cherubs you can find in any church and then copy it onto the canvas.

The child was essential, of course. Without it Velázquez could never get away with this painting. With his delicate feathers and pouch of arrows, the child would be easily recognizable as Cupid. And then the viewer would know who I was: his mother, Venus.

In Florence, not two days' journey from the seat of the most holy Roman Catholic Church, painters prided themselves on their nudes, especially their male nudes, but in Spain, preachers ranted against the decay of national morals. Vulgarity oozed out of Italy under the guise of culture, they said. Of course, this didn't mean that there were no nudes in Spain— only that they were mostly hidden away in the private collections of kings, princes, and noblemen. His Majesty Felipe IV himself had a room full of them, but nearly all of his lascivious-looking Danaës and Minervas and Venuses were painted by foreigners.

And yet now, a rich and important courtier had asked Velázquez to paint a nude. And just to up the ante, a female nude! This patron could have gone to Rubens or Furini or even to Rembrandt, but he wanted a painting by Velázquez. He was adamant about it, and I could understand why. Velázquez was the king's favorite, the greatest painter Spain had ever produced. To have a nude by him would be a feat and a triumph, especially if it were painted in Madrid, right under the noses of the authorities.

Velázquez vacillated. How would it look if he were arrested? He was not only His Majesty's protégé, but also the son-in-law of the great art theorist Francisco Pacheco, once an arbiter of good taste in painting, whose opinions still loomed large in Velázquez's mind.

Velázquez wanted to please his patron, but he didn't want to be flung into jail, and he certainly didn't want to be excommunicated. Finally, he decided to try an old trick that had worked for over a century in Italy: he would give his painting the name of a mythological figure. Italian painters knew that if they named their subjects Adonis or Narcissus or Ganymede, they could get away with anything. After all, no one expected gods to be clothed. Spaniards were much stricter than the rowdy Italians, but even so, Velázquez decided it was worth a try. He would call his painting Venus. He would say the nude figure on the canvas wasn't a human woman, but a goddess. Velázquez thought he had enough clout at Court to dare and besides, the mysterious patron had promised to keep the painting hidden away from the censors or, if it did come to light, to make sure Velázquez appeared before a lenient judge. Every region in Spain had its own Inquisitorial tribunal, and different censors judged paintings differently. Velázquez was convinced that his patron was so powerful that he could easily pull the necessary strings to keep him safe.

But where would he find a model? In Rome or Florence, plenty of courtesans were thrilled for the chance to have an artist immortalize their curves on canvas, or else a painter could find a girl through an artists' guild. And if worse came to worst, he could pick out some pretty prostitute in a brothel. In Spain, though, authorities found even clothed female models distasteful, and not even a whore would pose nude. That's why my participation in the project was vital.

"Our Venus will be different," Velázquez said when he first broached the subject. "Our Venus will be more tasteful than those Italian canvases. It will be a nude that celebrates the female form, but without shocking the sensibility of the viewer."

"Our Venus," he had said. His and mine. I was to be an integral part of a wonderful, grandiose project.

"At least tell me who it's for," I begged.

He knit his brow. Solid and swarthy, Velázquez was a handsome man despite his nearly fifty years. He had thick black hair, a robust moustache, and deep, comforting, ebony eyes. He pressed his lips to my fingertips. "It will be a beautiful painting," he murmured. His voice reminded me of cinnamon syrup.

"Can't you at least give me a hint about the patron?"

"I can't, *mi amor*. I'm sworn to secrecy." He was doing his best to sound endearing, but I scowled. Velázquez usually called me *mi amor* only when he had to implore or apologize.

But it didn't matter. I wanted to pose because I wanted to make him happy. Of course, I didn't want to get caught, to roast in hell, but he made it all sound so exciting and worthwhile. He said we would be pursuing an ideal—the ideal of beauty—something beyond the comprehension of Spain's petty, parochial conformists.

"*¿Estás cansada?* Are you tired?" He touched my shoulder and I got up and put on a dressing gown.

I *was* tired. My neck ached from holding my head rotated and still for hours, and my arm was sore from being stretched into such an uncomfortable position.

"You can't relax long. I have to work while the light is good." He was mixing colors and testing them on the palette.

"I just need a few minutes. I have a crook in my neck."

He glanced at me as though he didn't recognize me with my gown on. He dipped his brush in a pot.

"Take off your robe and lie down."

He obviously hadn't heard what I'd said. I could hear the bristles glide across the canvas.

"Can't you tell me anything about who commissioned the painting?" I asked after a moment. "At least you can tell me if this is his house, can't you?"

"Don't talk. You move your head when you talk. Now I have to position you all over again. Anyway, I already explained that I can't tell you. Someone important."

His voice no longer evoked cinnamon syrup, but dry twigs. He stood behind me and rotated my head slightly. "Pretend you're looking in a mirror. The mirror is right here." He came around to the foot of the bed and outlined the imaginary mirror in the air with his index finger so I could focus my gaze.

Outside, the fritter vendor was calling: ¡Buñuelos! ¡Buñuelos calientes!

"That's enough for today," he said curtly. "Get dressed. We're done." He tapped me gently on the back.

He didn't say "thank you." He simply put away his materials and cleaned up his workspace, then left without saying good-bye.

It was about three, time for the midday meal. I imagined he would dine with his aristocratic friends. By the time he'd finished eating and slept off the effects of the wine, the light would have changed, and it would be too late to go back to his easel. Perhaps he would saunter along the arcades of the Calle Mayor to browse in the luxurious shops, or wander over to the Prado, where gentlemen on fine horses paced smartly up and down the avenue and ladies in carriages peeped out from behind mantillas. One thing was certain: he would not go back to his wife that night.

I want to tell my story, the story of Venus, because if I don't, no one will ever know. I will tell it as though it happened to someone else, and the parts I don't know, I will imagine. After all, what is art but a play of mirrors, an illusion? After Velázquez finished our painting, a fountain of gossip spewed from the back chambers of palaces and gaming houses. "Who is she?" "Who posed for him?" Very few had seen the painting, but everyone had an opinion. Courtiers who did have the chance to see it stared at the face of Venus in the mirror—the mirror Cupid was holding—and struggled to place it. Some said the model was this woman and others said she was that woman, but who was right?

All that happened decades ago, when my skin was still smooth and white and my hair was soft and brown. But I remember as if it were yesterday. Now I'm an old woman. My flesh is no longer firm, and no one wants to see my naked body stretched out on a silk sheet. My hair is silver. My cheeks are furrowed. And yet, although I may be shriveled and ugly, I am eternally beautiful. I am immortal. I am Venus.

PART ONE

1

Seville
1619

JUANA CLENCHED HER TEETH AND GRIPPED ARABELA'S HAND. She felt as though she were caught between the jaws of a vise that squeezed, squeezed, squeezed and released, then squeezed again. She let out a shriek that caused Arabela to flinch, and dug her nails into the nursemaid's palm.

"Oh, Ara, it hurts! It hurts so much!" Rivulets streamed out of the corners of Juana's eyes and disappeared into the soft muslin pillowcase.

"Breathe, Doña Juana. In and out, in and out. Try to keep it steady."

"Give me some brandy!"

"Not yet, Doña Juana. Not until the baby is born."

Juana pressed her eyelids together. Through the window, she could hear the manic twittering of what seemed like thousands of birds. She imagined them staggering over the branches like drunkards in their euphoria, beaks turned upward, eyes closed.

"What have they got to be so damn happy about, Ara? Make them stop!"

"It will all be over soon, *niña*. By tomorrow it will be over."

"Agh!" wailed Juana. "It hurts so much! It's as though an enormous mule were kicking me in the belly!"

Ángeles, the kitchen maid, brought in a heavy pot of water and hung it on a hook over the fireplace. A moment later, the chambermaid Julia walked into the room, carrying a pile of folded rags that she placed on the night table.

"Where is Venturo? What's keeping him?" Juana felt her shift sticky around her legs, and she longed for a fresh one, but Arabela had told her that for this, too, she would have to wait. After the baby came, said the nursemaid, she would bathe her and dress her in a clean nightshift. Arabela had been Juana's own nursemaid, and now she was going to care for the new baby.

Years before, Juana's father Francisco Pacheco had spotted Arabela and her infant son on a street corner, both of them wailing in desperation. Arabela's husband had died of the plague around 1601, leaving her destitute. Pacheco took her in after doctors assured him that she was free of contagion (he was charitable, but of course not careless). She had milk, and his own newborn daughter desperately needed a pair of full breasts. Doña Leonor de Pacheco, the baby's mother, was frail and nearly dry, and anyway, it would be unseemly for a woman of her position to nurse her own child. Doña Leonor died when Juana was six years old, about the same time Pacheco sent Arabela's boy off to learn a trade. Arabela stayed on to serve Juana, and she had been there ever since. Other maids came and went, thought Juana, but Arabela was forever.

"Where's the wet nurse, Ara? When will she get here?"

"Don't worry about it, *niña*. Don Francisco has taken care of everything."

"I'm sure he has," Juana said with a tinge of sarcasm. Why, she wondered, did her father have to stick his nose into this business? Normally, it was the husband who hired the wet nurse, but Don Francisco had insisted on taking charge of all the details. Of course, Velázquez, Juana's twenty-one-year-old husband, could hardly be counted on to attend to anything. He was a well-intentioned man and a passable student, but he didn't know an enema from a crossbow.

"I still think that I should meet her first, don't you? If she's going to nurse my baby. . ."

"She's a reputable wet nurse, Doña Juana. She's an Old Christian with a brood of her own." They had had this conversation a dozen times before.

Suddenly, the vise tightened, and Juana clutched Arabela's wrist. The nursemaid could feel the girl's nails digging into her flesh, but she gritted her teeth and said nothing. In a moment, the pain subsided, and Juana began to sob softly.

"Where is Venturo? Oh God, where is he?" Juana wriggled in her shift, at once eager for the midwife to arrive and wishing that he would never come at all. Certainly, she was desperate to get it all over with. The contractions were coming harder and faster, and she was exhausted. But on the other hand, the thought of hiking up her shift and spreading her legs for Venturo Almedina repulsed her.

"Where is Velázquez? Is he waiting with my father? *Is he even worried about me?*"

"I don't know, *niña*. I haven't seen him."

Hiring Almedina had also been Pacheco's idea. Juana's

father considered himself an intellectual, and among Seville's intelligentsia, the belief was growing that birthing was a science, not just a skill to be left in the hands of ignorant females.

Pacheco and his brother had been orphaned as boys and raised by their uncle, the Canon of Seville. The Canon was an erudite man who surrounded himself with scholars and writers, and when he died, his young nephew—Juana's father—became the new head of what had come to be known as Pacheco's academy. Don Francisco was not a great intellect, but he was well-read for a painter, and his fellow "academicians" prided themselves on being up on everything. They knew, for example, that medicine was above all an academic discipline, and that doctors studied their art in medical faculties. They pooh-poohed as antiquated the old-style barber-surgeons who would cut your beard and take out your molars in a single sitting. They had all studied Luis de Mercado's *De coomunbis mulierum affectionibus*, and they had heard that in Holland and France, babies were delivered by *accoucheurs*, male midwives with diplomas in birthing. As a result, Pacheco and his friends had concluded that the midwife on the corner was now a thing of the past, which was how Juana ended up with Venturo Almedina. "A shadowy little Moor with garlicky breath," she called him.

Men-midwives were still rare in Spain, where they were called in only in emergencies. When a child was already dead and its mother was losing a lot of blood, the *partero* would appear like an angel of death, black bag in hand. No wonder that to the neighbors, he was a harbinger of tragedy, a black seraph with the stench of decay on his breath. But Venturo Almedina was an exception because he liked to assist at normal births. He had studied midwifery in the Low Countries, and although most people saw him as a sooty little Arab with blood-stained hands, more and more enlightened men were requesting his services for their wives and daughters.

At the turn of the century, when pestilence swept over Seville, Venturo Almedina had been one of the few medics willing to attend to the dying. He swabbed their sores and arranged to have them carted to isolation hospitals set up outside the city limits. Deaths diminished and people were grateful. They stopped him on the street, pressing gold coins into his palm. For the moment, at least, they forgot that Venturo Almedina's grandparents had worshipped Allah. By the time King Philip III expelled the Moriscos, Almedina had so many prominent friends that getting around the edict wasn't hard. Grateful plague survivors testified in court that for generations, the Almedinas had all been Old Christians with not a drop of Moorish blood in their veins. The judge squinted at the name Al-Medina and asked the medic to recite the Credo, which he did without stumbling once. Then he paid hefty sums to the judge, the notary, and the Court secretary, who all declared him a legitimate, pure-blooded Catholic Christian.

Almedina took to calling himself "Don Venturo," and he put a new trade tile on his door, with a picture of a man with a pink, healthy-looking baby in his arms. Underneath he placed a plaque with the words: Don Venturo Almedina, Midwife. He had seen enough bereavement during the plague, he said, and he no longer wanted to deliver dead babies. His training in Antwerp had prepared him to perform normal births, and that was what he would do. He would celebrate life, bringing healthy children into the world as long as God in his infinite mercy gave him strength and breath.

"Please, Arabela, call Venturo. I'm sure it's time."

Why can't the *partera* come instead? thought Juana. Why wasn't the neighborhood midwife good enough? Why couldn't she have her baby surrounded by sisters and aunts and friends, like other girls? Women who could rub her temples with perfumed oil and sing to her and distract her from the pain. And a mother. Most of all, she longed for a mother. Instead, she had to be attended by a rancid old Arab!

"It's time, Arabela." She groaned again.

"Not yet, *niña*. I promise that I'll send a servant when the moment comes."

Juana bit her lip and squinted until the world around her was a blur. She struggled to keep her breathing even, just as Arabela had taught her. But the vise on her womb was hindering her intake of air.

Lidia, the housemaid, showed in Doña Eusebia and Doña Sol, neighbor women who had been friends of Juana's mother. They pulled up stools and sat on either side of the bed. Arabela patted Juana's forehead with a damp cloth. Between contractions, Juana could hear the women praying softly—*Salve Maria, llena eres de gracia* . . . Lidia placed a bouquet of spray roses, asters, and miniature carnations in a vase on Juana's dressing table.

"May flowers for you, *señora*."

Juana eyed the girl. She was a slight thing, with a tiny waist, small breasts, and rounded hips. Her soft brown hair was tied back in a loose knot under her crisp, white coif. Juana wondered if she'd ever be thin and graceful like Lidia again. She was sick of her cumbersome body, her swollen ankles, and her puffy cheeks. Juana had never liked the maid. She'd noticed the coy glances the girl gave Velázquez every time she arranged the cushions in the *sala* for Pacheco's academy meetings.

"Get them out of here," Juana whimpered. "I don't want flowers! The stink is making me gag." She gasped, then let out a wail.

"I think it's time," said Arabela. "Lidia, send the kitchen boy for Venturo. Ángeles, drag the mattress onto the floor and put the birthing stool on top of it so that Doña Eusebia and I can slide Doña Juana onto it. Doña Sol and Doña Eusebia will hold her legs open while I prop up her back. We probably won't need foot stoves, but have them ready just in case she starts to shiver." Turning to the chambermaid, she ordered: "Julia, bring a pair of scissors and twine to tie the cord. I'm sure the midwife will have a catheter and an enema syringe. And don't forget to take the diapers I've been hemming into the nursery."

"If we need them," moaned Juana almost inaudibly. "If this baby even lives."

Don Francisco Pacheco sat in his study on a carved mahogany chair with a tooled leather seat and puffed restlessly on his pipe. He felt helpless. Juana's blood-curdling screams were ripping him apart, but what could he do but sit in his study and smoke?

He knew that Juana was furious with him. She hadn't wanted the male midwife, hadn't wanted her father to be involved at all. But Don Francisco was terrified he would lose his only daughter in childbirth the way so many of his friends had lost their wives. Juana was a plain little thing, with owl-like features and a pimply forehead, but Don Francisco adored her. He had given her an education that girls like her rarely received, and he had married her to his most promising pupil, Diego Velázquez, who was not only a talented artist, but a well-born young man. Naturally, Juana didn't appreciate his efforts on her behalf, but you really couldn't expect gratitude from a seventeen-year-old child with a head full of whipped egg whites.

Velázquez sat smoking in his studio, his mind elsewhere. Earlier that week, he had received a commission from the archbishop for a painting of John the Evangelist, which would hang in the Discalced Carmelite Convent of San José, along with a painting of the Virgin. The model was a local farm laborer who couldn't spare much time to pose for an unknown painter who could only pay him a few coins. The man was anxious to get back to his planting, but Velázquez had convinced him to pose for one more session. He liked the farmer's handsome ruggedness, his square jaw and high cheekbones, his full lips and thick, messy eyebrows. The commission was important to Velázquez — it was his biggest yet, and if the archbishop liked the result, he would surely put him in touch with potential patrons.

The painting was a large one, about ten hands high and eight hands wide. It showed Saint John writing the Book of Revelation in the midst of a vision, with an eagle, his symbol, at his side. Velázquez had painted the vision in the upper left-hand corner: the Woman of the Apocalypse. Maestro Pacheco was a stickler for precision, and he insisted on clean edges and crisp borders, so before he started to paint, Velázquez sketched the figure in chalk on the canvas, and then drew an outline with a small, stiff brush to delineate the principal contours. Sometimes, for hands or ears, he drew an even finer line with sharpened chalk or white lead. He built his painting up from parts, sometimes referring to the thousands of sketches Pacheco kept in the studio. He used a live model only for the finished product, which was why he needed the laborer—he had to get the details right.

Many years later, when he painted me, he used a different method. If you look at my left foot lying on the black silk, you can see that it's not precise at all. And my face in the mirror, it's blurry. But wait, I'm not supposed to be talking about *my* painting. I'm supposed to be talking about the day Juana had her baby.

But let me just say this: By the time Velázquez created Venus, he was painting in a different way. He had long before left Pacheco's tutelage. He had already been to Italy and seen the works of Caravaggio. He had learned new techniques. He had different notions of composition and color. However, that day, back in May, 1619, while his wife lay shrieking in the agony of childbirth, he was still painting the subjects Pacheco considered appropriate, using the methods Pacheco preferred.

The afternoon sun was at its brightest when the kitchen boy burst into the studio.

"Don Diego," he exclaimed breathlessly. (Velázquez insisted on being called "Don" because both his parents descended from nobility, though, I must admit, his family's credentials were a bit sketchy.) "Don Diego . . . your wife . . ."

Velázquez put down his brush and looked at the boy. "Yes? What is it?"

"Doña Juana . . ."

"Yes? Come on, out with it." Velázquez felt his hands go icy.

"Doña Juana has just had a baby girl!"

Velázquez nodded in disbelief. "A girl?"

The kitchen boy was confused. Velázquez seemed not to understand. "You know, a girl. She doesn't have a pipi," the boy ventured by way of explanation.

Velázquez continued to stare at the child. "What?"

"Yes! Don Francisco has named her Francisca. Francisca Pacheco."

His new daughter's name seemed to register more than her birth itself. Velázquez knew he owed *el Maestro* a lot, and the least he could do was allow him to name his granddaughter after himself. After all, it's not unusual for some children in a family to take the mother's surname and others to take the father's. If the baby had been a boy, Velázquez might have insisted on his own surname. But as it was a girl, what difference did it really make?

At two o'clock Velázquez put down his tools and began to clean his work area.

"I hope you're done," said the model as he put on his work clothes, "because I can't come back."

Velázquez slipped a coin into the man's palm and went to find his father-in-law. He did not stop by his wife's apartments because the parlor maid told him that Doña Juana was sleeping, and anyhow, he had more important things than the birth of a daughter to think about.

2

The virgin on the pedestal
1619

B Y THE TIME THE COOL WEATHER SET IN, BABY FRANCISCA—
they called her Paquita—was determined to stand. With
great focus, she'd grab the side of her cradle and pull herself
into a vertical position, only to fall back when the weight of her
body tipped the frame and made it impossible to balance. Plop,
down she'd come amid gales of laughter. Then she'd raise her
tiny hands, grab the rim, and begin again. Paquita had her
mother's beak-like nose and owlish eyes, but her pudgy cheeks
and bubbly disposition made her the apple of Pacheco's eye. The
child was a charmer. She shrieked with glee when her grandfather stuck his beard in her face for her to tug on his whiskers.
"Blub blub blub," he burbled cheerfully. "Blub, blub! Papi's
Paquita, Papi's Paquita!" And the baby would grab his cheeks in
her hands and plant an open-mouthed kiss right on his nose.

If at first Velázquez paid his baby daughter little notice,
one glower from his father-in-law set him on a different track.

The baby was Pacheco's first grandchild, and he expected his son-in-law to show proper enthusiasm. One morning, soon after she had given birth, Juana awakened to find three men in her suite: Pacheco, Velázquez, and Almedina. All three glowed and cooed as if they themselves had produced this sweet bundle of life. They chortled and congratulated each other, passing the baby from one to the other, none of them so much as glancing in her direction. They had forgotten all about her! Juana was furious.

"It's time for you to leave," she announced imperiously. "I'm going to nurse Paquita and put her to bed."

Her visitors stared at her in disbelief.

Juana had sent away the wet nurse, her mind set on nourishing the baby herself. Although Venturo had warned her that she wouldn't produce enough milk, to everyone's astonishment, her tiny breasts heroically churned out buckets. Yet the men were not pleased. Aristocratic women relied on wet nurses until their babies were weaned—it was simply the proper thing to do. All the duchesses and countesses of Pacheco's acquaintance did it. A wet nurse showed the world that a woman's husband could afford another servant. Pacheco was afraid that if people knew that his daughter was nursing her own child, his honor would be besmirched.

"I don't care what other women do," insisted Juana obstinately. "I'm not an aristocrat."

"Of course you are," countered Velázquez. "As you very well know, both my parents were of noble blood. Why do you insist otherwise?"

Velázquez's father, Juan Rodríguez de Silva, had given his son to Pacheco as an apprentice when the boy was only eleven years old, which proved that Velázquez wasn't as highborn as he

pretended to be. Aristocrats don't apprentice their sons to crafts-
men, especially not first-born sons, and Velázquez was the oldest
of seven. In those days painting was still considered a craft, and
painters no different from skilled workmen like carpenters or far-
riers. In Seville, most painters were illiterate, and like other artisans, they belonged to guilds and took exams to earn a license
to practice. Velázquez was an exception. He was literate and,
like his father-in-law, he enjoyed the company of lettered men.
By the time he earned his license, he was not only betrothed to
Juana but also a member of Pacheco's academy. But even so,
thought Juana, he was what he was: the spawn of the burger class
or, at best, of the minor nobility.

For once, Pacheco backed down and changed his mind—
Juana would nurse her baby. As it turned out, the academy now
opined that nursing was actually healthy for both mother and
infant—this was the new trend in humanistic circles. Furthermore, Pacheco's Jesuit friends pointed to images of the nursing
Mary as a role model not only for charwomen, but also for respectable ladies. Julia found out about Pacheco's change of heart
from his valet, but when she ran to her mistress with this intelligence, Juana shrugged and mumbled something about men's
arrogance. "Why should I care what they think? Do they have
breasts? What gives them a right to an opinion?"

The day Juana had her first serious fight with her husband
started out like any other day. She nursed Paquita in bed and
then handed her over to Arabela. Julia brought the new mother
a tray with bread and meats and beer, which she consumed

unhurriedly. Next came her morning prayers. She entered her oratory and knelt on a hassock for about fifteen minutes, then rose and considered the day's wardrobe. For the morning she chose a black, broad-shouldered silk dress with a boned bodice terminating in a point that overlapped onto the skirt. Julia helped her with the garment and slipped little cushions into the sleeves to achieve a bouffant effect. She then arranged a black velvet robe with slit half-sleeves over Juana's shoulders and knotted the sleeves of the robe to the sleeves of the dress at the elbow. Finally, she got down on her knees to catch up the hem of the skirt to reveal a red underskirt embroidered in gold. Of all her tasks, this was Julia's favorite. She loved Juana's fashionable dresses, her mantles and her coifs. She had once told Arabela that she wished she could *be* Juana, if only to dress as a lady.

It was around eleven o'clock when Juana ventured into her father's study. She knelt before him and kissed his hand. He placed his fingers on her head and gave her his blessing. Juana asked for the carriage, and Pacheco sent a kitchen boy for the driver, whom he instructed to transport the *señora* and her maid to the Discalced Carmelite convent. Pacheco was pleased whenever his daughter took the carriage. Juana's outings provided the neighborhood wags with evidence that her father was far more than just an ordinary artisan.

She's a sweet little thing, Pacheco thought as Juana left the room. *Too bad she's so plain.*

She sensed what was going through his mind. She'd heard him say it out loud often enough.

It had rained the day before, but this morning was cool and dry and fresh. A few gossamer clouds hovered in the iridescent sky. As the carriage rolled over Seville's cobbled streets, Juana peered through an opening in the curtain that covered the glass pane. Houses glistened so brilliantly in the sunlight that their whiteness hurt your eyes. Rejuvenated by the fall rain, exuberant geraniums of crimson, magenta, pink, and white bloomed in multihued, painted pots on balconies. Seville was a magnificent city, the hub of trade with the Indies. Yet it was not as great as it had been before the plague. In spite of the efforts of medics like Venturo Almedina, the city had lost a quarter of its population—some 150,000 people. Carts overflowing with cadavers, mothers weeping over expiring children, oozing sores, rotting flesh, bonfires of bloody bandages—these were the images that haunted Seville's older residents.

Yet on that that day in October, you would have never known that Seville had once been a vast morgue. In the public markets, vendors were out in mass. Piles of oranges and lemons, jugs of olive oil, perfumed soaps, brightly painted dishes, embroidered shawls—wares for sale formed dizzying patterns of rich and vivid color. Clowns and jugglers and acrobats entertained the crowds, and dancing monkeys made the children laugh uproariously. Beggars loitered in front of churches, entreating passersby to spare a coin.

By the time the carriage rolled up to the gates of the Discalced Carmelite convent, Juana was feeling a bit faint.

"*Ave María purísima,*" said the extern by way of greeting.

"*Sin pecado concebida,*" answered Juana. "I am Pacheco's daughter."

"I'll let Sister know you're here, Doña Juana."

Sister Inmaculada received them in the locutorium, where she sat in the shadows behind heavy iron bars studded with sharp spikes. Juana squinted, trying to make out the nun's silhouette. It took her eyes a minute to adjust to the dimness.

"How is Don Francisco? How is the baby?" Sister Inmaculada's voice was as raspy as a rusty hinge.

"Everyone is fine, Sister."

"What about the paintings of Saint John and the Virgin? Is that husband of yours almost done with them?"

"I don't know, Sister. I never go into the studio."

"Yes, of course not." Sister Inmaculada paused. "Still, it would be nice to have them by the feast of the Immaculate Conception."

"Oh, I imagine they'll be done by early December, Sister."

"Tell Velázquez," she pressed on, "that it would make the Virgin very happy to have them ready for her special day."

Sister Inmaculada had an intense gaze and skin like crinkled paper. Four white hairs graced her chin. Alongside her nose ran minuscule red and purple rivulets with countless tributaries. Sister Inmaculada had been spiritual director to Juana's mother, and she had been guiding Juana ever since Doña Leonor had died.

To Juana, it was clear that Sister Inmaculada was the most intelligent woman in the world. She was curious about everything, and she was always eager to know what news Juana had picked up from Pacheco and his friends; it didn't matter if it was international intelligence or local gossip—any information was welcome. Mother Teresa, foundress of the order, had always forbidden chitchat in the locutorium, but in the forty years since her death, Seville's nuns had relaxed her restrictions. They prayed and meditated regularly, of course, and they ate meat only on Thursdays, but they found nothing wrong with indulging in a bit of tittle-tattle once in a while.

Mother Teresa had been beatified a few years earlier, and would probably be canonized shortly. A large painting of her hung in the locutorium, her full, ruddy face framed by a wimple. Her penetrating eyes, stern yet tender, took in all that went on. But despite the founderess's looming presence, Sister Inmaculada was convinced that she wouldn't have objected to the feasts in which the nuns indulged on the anniversary of the convent's founding. On these days, they spent their meager resources on festive decorations and succulent dishes—stuffed squid, fried anchovies, eggplant steamed with sherry—and invited special friends into the locutorium to share their joy. After all, reasoned Sister Inmaculada, the soon-to-be Saint Teresa wanted convent life to be pleasant, and she had always loved a good party.

Had Juana heard anything about an English ship called the Mayflower? Inmaculada wanted to know. It was apparently heading for the New World, but what was it? A cargo ship? A pirate ship? "May-flower—*flor de mayo*—Just like English pirates to give their ship an innocent-sounding name."

Juana thought it carried settlers, not pirates, but she wasn't sure. Anyway, local gossip was far more interesting. There were several juicy tidbits: Juana's neighbor Doña Andrea Moreno was betrothed to Don Félix de Villaurrutia y Ponte, whose uncle was one of the richest men in Seville; and the husband of Doña María Delgado (always late for mass, noted the nun) was said to have lost a fortune in the gaming houses.

All at once, Juana felt the contours of the room go blurry. She reached toward the iron bars of the grill to steady herself, but the spikes prevented her from holding on. Julia, who had been embroidering in a corner, jumped up and slipped her arm across the young woman's back to prevent her from falling. In a moment Juana had regained her balance, and the outlines of the walls and corners of the room came back into focus.

"Are you alright, child?" Sister Inmaculada peered at Juana through the grill.

The young woman caught her breath and nodded.

Before Juana left the convent, Sister Inmaculada handed her a note for Pacheco. Ever since Doña Leonor's death, the nun had been offering him spiritual support. Sometimes she sent an inspirational thought or a prayer, sometimes an image to contemplate. Pacheco never wrote back, but he appreciated the gesture.

Juana and Julia climbed back into the carriage just as the sky took on an indigo cast and the air began to rumble. Within moments, drops like ripe, juicy grapes were splattering on the cobblestones, and a fierce wind battered the panes. Juana pulled her cape around her. Unshielded from the blustery weather, the coachman snapped the reins to hurry the horses, but the slippery, wet stones slowed their pace. Leaves, twigs, pebbles, and scraps of garbage pelted the sides of the carriage, and mud pummeled the dash. The coachman spat curses into the wind.

When at last they arrived home, Juana threw her muddy cape to Julia and hurried to the nursery to give the breast to Paquita. When the baby had had her fill and slipped into a hushed slumber, Juana dashed off to find her father and give him Sister Inmaculada's note. He wasn't in his study, so, she assumed, he had to be with his students. On her way to the studio, she noticed a black clump on the ground near the patio—something shapeless and wet from the rain. She approached gingerly and knelt over what appeared to be a cluster of glistening feathers. She shuddered. It was a dead bird, a young one. Apparently the storm had knocked it from its nest, and it had fallen to the ground, smashing its little head. Most of its blood had washed away, but its exposed brain still oozed red.

Juana felt a sudden frisson. She ran back into the house toward the nursery, calling to a servant boy to clean up the mess in the patio. Then she scuttled through the corridor and threw open the door to the baby's room, where Arabela was embroidering a cradle sheet with tiny pink flowers.

"Is Paquita alright?" panted Juana.

Arabela blinked at her, disconcerted. "What do you mean? You just nursed her. Why wouldn't she be alright?"

Juana walked over to the cradle and peered at her little girl. Paquita was dreaming peacefully, smiling in her sleep, her breathing steady and quiet. Juana started to cry.

"What's the matter, *niña*?" asked Arabela, her voice mellifluous and comforting.

"I don't know . . . I'm not sure." Juana looked down at her hands. They were trembling. Between her thumb and index finger, she still held Sister Inmaculada's note.

"I think I do," whispered Arabela, but Juana was already out the door.

Juana wavered at the door of the studio. The workspace, she knew, was unwelcoming to women, a male domain where boys learned skills essential to their craft and men produced art, a product vital to the well-being of society. The paintings created here would inspire awe in God's infinite power and yearning for His grace in everyone who would see them.

Inexplicably, Juana felt a fierce urgency to deliver Sister Inmaculada's note to her father. Perhaps, she thought, the simple act of handing it to him would calm her nerves. As she pushed open the door and peered across the room, she felt a surge of excitement. She was trespassing, she knew, but her father's rules suddenly seemed crazy to her. Why shouldn't a woman breach the threshold of the workplace? Why was it so sacrosanct?

In one corner of the studio, young boys copied studies of limbs from a sketchbook—tensed arms and dangling arms, arms bent at the elbow, arms turned upward in blessing, outstretched hands and hands grasping sticks or plumes, praying hands and fists. On the table lay books of feet, knees, noses, and ears. This was the visual vocabulary students had to learn in order to create original paintings. Although Spaniards did not usually paint from life as the Italians did, Pacheco recognized the value of live models when used judiciously. Velázquez, who at twenty-two already had a mind of his own, used models regularly. Not only that, he liked to paint ordinary people, not just biblical heroes. He painted singers and musicians, drunkards and nuns. He even painted an old woman cooking eggs! And if you could see those eggs, how they glistened and sizzled! Nobody else in Seville painted those kinds of scenes, but Velázquez saw beauty everywhere.

In those days the goal of a painting was to tell a story. A viewer had to understand the narrative—Jesus being tempted by the Devil, Saint Sebastian being martyred, Paul falling from his horse—and the narratives had to inspire. There were conventional ways of telling these stories visually, and the apprentices had to learn them. That's why Pacheco kept hundreds of prints and drawings in his archives.

In another part of the studio, a teacher was helping students stretch and prime a canvas, while an assistant explained how to mix pigments. Some boys were grinding glass to create bright blue smalt. Others pulverized dried madder root for red or pink hues, while still others crushed cochineals for carmine.

Juana looked around the studio for her father. She was fully prepared to walk right in on his lecture and hand him Sister Inmaculada's note. He would be stunned, but before he could explode, she would be gone. There would be consequences later in the day, of course, but she would argue her point forcefully, just as she had made the case to nurse her baby.

But where was Pacheco? He was not with the younger boys or with the ones already working with easels. She spied Velázquez at the far end of the room and moved gingerly toward him. Next to him, his slave and assistant—Diego Melgar, a boy of thirteen or fourteen years old—was mixing colors. Velázquez had already developed a technique. After outlining the figures, he filled in each one, giving it volume and depth. He achieved luminosity by mixing pigment with linseed oil and then applying it over a flat brown background. I loved to watch him work. It seemed a miracle the way he could bring an ancient biblical character to life with such a tiny range of colors. In those days he used only blue, red and yellow ochre, white lead, and blacks made of charcoal, bone, or vegetable dye. Of course, when he painted me, he had already developed a palate. He had broken with Pacheco's cold, conventional method of figure drawing. For example, his Saint John was so vibrant, so real, so raw and virile, with his stony cheeks and his scruffy eyebrows. Not at all like Pacheco's stiff, perfect saints.

Velázquez seemed not to notice that Juana had come in. She approached with a determined gait, striding past boys without so much as glancing at their sketches. What had caught her eye was the silky robe of the model posing for her husband. A woman! A female model in the studio! From the rear the girl looked formless and indistinct under the draping, and yet there was something about the way she was standing that Juana found familiar—and disturbing.

It was not until Juana positioned herself almost directly behind the model that Velázquez looked up from his canvas.

"I'm working," he said calmly.

"I see."

"The Virgin. A companion piece for my Saint John the Evangelist."

Juana walked around the model and turned to face her. The girl's head was tilted slightly forward, eyes lowered modestly, her hands joined in prayer. She stood firmly on both feet on a small platform used for posing.

"In the final version she'll be standing on a crescent moon."

Juana knew the story from the Book of Revelation and understood the reference, but she said nothing.

"What are you doing here?" Velázquez asked finally. He didn't look glad to see her, but he didn't seem angry.

"What is *she* doing here?"

"Lidia? She's my model."

"She's supposed to be the housemaid. Why isn't she cleaning?"

"I only need her for a few hours, to put the final touches on this. It's not easy to find a female model. Pacheco said I could use her."

Juana felt her jaws and shoulders tense. She bit her lip.

She was not going to cry. What was to be gained by making a scene? It would only give Lidia something to snicker about in the servants' quarters. She had to maintain her dignity. She was the *señora*, and Lidia was nothing but a *criada*. Anyhow, this was a battle she couldn't win. If Pacheco had given permission for the girl to pose, what did *her* opinion matter?

She stared at Lidia with a calculating eye. She ran her gaze from the girl's feet to her hair. Lidia's silken cheeks were speckled with freckles like tiny, translucent copper coins. Her face came to a soft dip beneath her mouth. Her reddish brown hair hung loosely under the Virgin's veil. Juana thought she saw a tiny, defiant smile flicker on her lips.

Juana had to hold her ground. Seville was full of bastards sired by noblemen with their housemaids, and she did not want this little schemer spending time with her husband. Doña Juana Pacheco de Velázquez would not become the laughingstock of Seville.

"She's needed in the house."

"Juana, go back to your baby," said her husband. He didn't raise his voice, but spoke firmly, with the demeanor of a mature man. After a moment he added, "The archbishop commissioned this painting for the San José Convent, and he is not a man to be trifled with. I need . . . *we* need to be in his good graces. Our fortune could depend on it."

"It's unseemly for you to be painting our housemaid," Juana replied. Anger had tinged her face with radish-colored splotches.

Velázquez put down his brush. His gaze was steady and penetrating.

"I could pose for you!" Juana blurted out. The moment

she said it she realized how absurd she sounded. A jealous hag. A resentful fishwife.

"A decent woman posing for a painting? How do you think it would make me feel to have my own wife as a model? I'd be dishonored before the whole city!" He said this matter-of-factly, and he still hadn't raised his voice. He also didn't mention that she was far too homely.

Juana was dizzy with rage. She started to cough uncontrollably. Velázquez sized up the situation and saw what he had to do.

"Juana . . . Juana," he said gently. "What do you think? That I'm going to fall in love with the Virgin Mary? No, my Juanita. You know that I love only you."

Juana had the distinct feeling that she was being manipulated, but it didn't matter. She had won. He had said he loved her, only her, and he had said it in front of the housemaid. Her position was secure—or, at least, apparent. She looked down and saw the note from Sister Inmaculada still in her hand.

"Where is my father?" she asked dryly.

"Probably in his study, writing. This afternoon the academicians are going to critique a segment of his book."

She turned and left. "*Adiós*," he called after her. Both of them were pretending that nothing had happened, and yet they both knew that something had.

3

Beyond the Moon
1619

I F VELÁZQUEZ WAS ANGRY ABOUT HIS WIFE'S INTRUSION, HE didn't show it. A few minutes after she left the studio, he put away his paints and joined his father-in-law for their usual midday meal, during which Pacheco told him that a special visitor would be attending the academy meeting later in the day. After his siesta, Velázquez put on his best velvet doublet and lace ruche.

The gathering was more animated than usual. It began with a poetry reading. Francisco de Rioja, wearing a fashionable Arab-style turban, took his place before the academicians and cleared his throat. Then, rather too dramatically, he looked out the window at some invisible garden and began:

> Lánguida flor de Venus, que escondida
> yaces, y en triste sombra y tenebrosa
> ver te impiden la faz al sol hermosa
> hojas y espinas de que estás ceñida;
>
> Y ellas, el puro lustre y la vistosa
> púrpura en que apuntar te vi teñida
> te arrebatan, y a par la dulce vida,
> del verdor que descubre ardiente rosa.

Igual es, mustia flor, tu mal al mío;
que si nieve tu frente descolora
por no sentir el vivo rayo ardiente,

A mí en profunda oscuridad y frío
hielo también de muerte me colora
la ausencia de mi luz resplandeciente.

Languid flower of Venus, you lie hidden
in sad, dark shadows that prevent you
from seeing the glorious face of the sun,
for leaves and thorns surround you,

And rob you of the pure radiance and dazzling
purple I saw beginning to tinge your petals,
and at the same time, of the sweet vitality of
the verdure, through which peeks an ardent rose.

Your woe, withering flower, is the same
as mine, for if snow fades your forehead,
depriving you of the sun's ardent rays,

The absence of the resplendent Light
of my life colors me with profound darkness,
with bitter ice, and finally, with death.

"Just as the rose wilts, so do we," murmured Pacheco mournfully.

"And who is the Light who robs you of your vitality?" snickered Juan de Pineda, Pacheco's irrepressible Jesuit friend. Father Pineda had been responsible for the *Index Prohibitorum Librorum*, the 1612 inventory of forbidden books, but his position didn't prevent him from making a suggestive comment once in a while. The men laughed like schoolboys and heartily praised the poem. Rioja was on his way to becoming a famous poet, and love sonnets like this one would soon be passed around among courtiers.

Many years after he presented it to the academy, I wrote it down and hid it in my copy of Saint Teresa's *Way of Perfection*, one of the few books I'm allowed to have here. I look down at my withered hands, gnarled and splotched with brown, and weep for my lost beauty and that of the rose, my flower, the flower of Venus. Like her, I am withered. Like hers, my face is framed by snow, although you can hardly see it beneath the wimple.

Pacheco read a few paragraphs of his treatise, *The Art of Painting*, and began a long defense of painting as a liberal art. "Painting is one of the highest expressions of man's creativity," he said, "as lofty an enterprise as poetry or philosophy. Painters should no longer be considered mere artisans, but true creators."

Velázquez had heard Pacheco's righteous harangue many times before. What held his attention on this day were not his father-in-law's impassioned words or even Rioja's extravagant metaphors, but the extraordinary creature Pacheco had invited to the gathering. The man wore an elaborately embroidered jacket of the most audacious colors: gold stitching on black panels trimmed in red, which alternated with white fluted insets. His voluminous lace collar spilled over his back, chest, and shoulders, a motif continued on his ample, flowing cuffs. On his breast hung an ornate gold medallion decorated with a reclining Venus accompanied by Cupid, attached to a heavy gold chain. His hair, ample and dark, was arranged in ringlets covered by a wide-brimmed hat with a large blue feather. He did not look Sevillian—he did not even look Spanish.

Rodrigo Caro, the academy historian, introduced him as Gaspar de Guzmán, the Count of Olivares. Velázquez had met counts before, even dukes, but this man was different. Guzmán had an air of cheerful superiority that drew people to him. He was arrogant and naughty, good-natured, but with a persistent hint of ruthlessness. He had been born in Rome, where his father was an ambassador, and had grown up among foreigners and foreign ideas. He wasn't wedded to the retrograde notions that bound Sevillians in unsophistication. He knew about art and philosophy, fashion and manners. And he knew about politics. Felipe III had appointed him to the household of his son, the heir apparent, and so at only thirty-two, Guzmán was accustomed to dealing with powerful people. He was an expert at backroom and boudoir politics, and he knew how to get his way at Court. He didn't namedrop because he didn't have to. Everyone knew he hobnobbed with men of influence. He was the prince's constant companion, advisor, and go-between. He was the sun that blinded all who looked upon him.

In my mind I can see how that afternoon, Velázquez's perceptive artist's eye never wavered far from Guzmán as the courtier nibbled on tidbits served by Pacheco's servant; lifted his goblet with a sure but delicate hand; and smiled slyly under his wide, waxed, upturned mustache. As he studied the beautiful Venus medallion rising and falling on Guzmán's breast, Velázquez suddenly saw his future clearly for the first time. All at once, he knew what he wanted. He longed to be what Guzmán already was: a courtier. But how could a mere painter, a mere artisan such as he was, get to the Alcázar of the king? How could he even approach a man like Guzmán de Olivares? Velázquez observed Pacheco's exotic guest in silence, too awestruck to venture a word.

Finally, Pacheco spoke: "Don Gaspar, my son-in-law, Diego Velázquez, the finest painter in Seville."

Velázquez bowed low. "At your service, Your Grace. If ever Your Grace needs a portrait . . ."

But Don Gaspar was already making his way to the door.

After the academicians had gone, Velázquez took off on foot toward the city's lively center, where brothels, gaming houses, theaters, and street musicians distracted men from their daily routine. As he walked through the narrow cobbled streets, Velázquez sensed the houses crowding in on him. He saw nothing quaint or picturesque about the weary façades and cracking stucco. Foreigners swooned over the Moorish arches that adorned doorways and gateways and praised the geometrical designs, elaborate tile, brickwork, and woodcarving. They loved the ornamental metals and the fancy plaster bas-reliefs. But in the diffuse night light, Velázquez saw no charm in the jumbled streets and alleys. To him, everything looked dingy. The crammed parade of wrought iron balconies was suffocating, and Seville's beloved courtyards seemed straggly and minuscule. As he crossed the plaza, a whiff of orange peels and human excrement reached his nostrils. The moon hung low and threatening over a turret, as if in mere moments, it would tumble from the sky and crush him. Tonight he realized something he hadn't known before: Seville was too small for him. He had to get out. He had to leave behind the ominous moon, the labyrinth of uneven, winding streets, and the boorishness and superstition of the people who trod them.

This feeling, he could now see, had been growing in him for a long time. In the *taller* the young artists had begun to whisper among themselves. Pacheco might be more open-minded than other art theorists, but to his students his ideas seemed hopelessly old-fashioned. How could they progress, they asked, painting only Virgins and saints from sketchbooks? A few months earlier, Zurbarán, one of the master's most promising students, had left the school to study on his own because he wanted to learn perspective. In Italy, Zurbarán argued, artists had been developing perspective for years, but Pacheco's students continued to paint flat images of the same old biblical subjects. Even as he himself branched out in new directions, Velázquez had defended his father-in-law. But now he realized that Zurbarán was right: the master was holding them back.

And then there was Juana and her jealous fits. How could he develop as an artist with a stodgy old man tying his wrists and a resentful wife telling him who could and couldn't model for him?

Velázquez imagined Guzmán's medallion dangling eerily from invisible fingers, catching the moonlight, gleaming blindingly. His temples began to throb, and a sharp pain like a jab with a burning needle seared his right eye. He leaned against the wall of a crumbling building and wept. How could he leave Pacheco? How could he leave the man who had raised him, the man who had taught him everything he knew? He loved Pacheco like a father. And he loved Juana, too. She was plain, of course, and she could be silly and petty, but she was a solid, loyal wife. She had already born him a daughter, and who knew how many more children would come? They had been playmates since childhood and they understood one another. And she would do anything for him.

Reeling, Velázquez turned around and headed home.

By the end of the month, Juana knew she was pregnant again. As the weeks wore on, she grew progressively fidgety and cross.

"How could this happen?" she snapped at Arabela. "Nursing women don't get pregnant!"

"It happens, *niña*," said Arabela calmly. "It's rare, but it can happen."

Juana fretted and whimpered. She pursed her lips and shook her head when Ángeles brought food from the kitchen. She felt woozy and ugly, and she refused to see Pacheco or Velázquez. Nor would she climb into the carriage to go to the convent, in spite of the anxious notes Sister Inmaculada sent inquiring about her health.

One night a jagged pain awakened Juana. It felt as though a serrated knife were pressing against the inner walls of her womb. Her bedsheets were drenched. She slipped her finger under her shift, and then brought it to her nose. Even before the smell reached her nostrils, she knew that she was lying in a pool of blood. She cried out wildly to Julia, who was sleeping on a low cot in the corner.

"What is it, *señora*?" whispered the groggy maid.

"Get Arabela! I need her!"

"She's sleeping," spluttered Julia stupidly.

"Then wake her up!"

In the morning Arabela sent a message to Pacheco that Doña Juana had miscarried. She herself had attended the *señora* and could assure him that this daughter would be fine. These things happened all the time. There was no need for alarm.

Pacheco lit a candle and knelt before the statue of Jesus in his study. He thanked God for not taking his daughter in childbirth and then went to comfort Juana.

In the afternoon, Velázquez appeared by his wife's bedside. Arabela was spooning broth into Juana's mouth and making soothing sounds. "La la la la, *mi niña*. You're going to get well. You're going to get well."

Velázquez took Juana's hand and massaged it gently. He couldn't think of what to say.

"I know you're upset, Don Diego," murmured Arabela to help him along. "But think of the beautiful baby that Doña Juana has already given you."

"Was it . . ." Velázquez finally stammered. "Was it a boy?"

Arabela stared at him in angry disbelief. Of course it was vital to a man to produce a son, but this was hardly the time to mention the sex of a miscarried child. "It wasn't anything," she said coldly. "Just a lifeless glob of blood."

"I'm sorry," he stammered. "It was a clumsy question."

"A stupid question," snapped Arabela. She knew that as a servant, she had no right to speak to him like that, but her concern for Juana had overwhelmed all sense of decorum.

"Yes, a stupid question," he agreed.

By the end of following year the young couple had put this unhappiness behind them. Doña Juana gave birth to a second daughter, whom they named Ignacia after Ignacio de Loyola, the founder of the Society of Jesus. Instead of a male midwife, the neighborhood *partera* delivered the baby. Another exciting thing happened that year as well: Felipe IV ascended to the throne, and at only sixteen years old, he was desperate for guidance, which Gaspar de Guzmán was delighted to provide. The dashing young man with the Venus medallion had acquired a new title, count-duke of Olivares, and, as the king's new minister, he was now the most powerful man in Spain. Velázquez was breathless with excitement. He hoped that the new minister had not forgotten his visit to the Seville academy, and especially Pacheco's promising son-in-law.

4

Secrets
1622 – 1623

JUANA SCURRIED THROUGH THE HOUSE LIKE A MOUSE IN A brushfire. Everything had to be perfect. The patio tiles had to be scrubbed so that the brightly colored birds and flowers glistened in the winter sun. The exterior walls had to be sponged and the brass door ornaments had to gleam. Juana ordered Lidia to wash every piece of pottery in the house. Cooking pots, barber bowls, inkwells, flower pots, chamber pots—nothing was too insignificant to escape Juana's attention.

"And see that you don't chip anything!" she barked at the maid.

Juana herself mopped the marble interior floors. Then she convinced Pacheco to enlist one of his pupils to sweep and dust the *sala* and fluff the cushions. She gave Julia her frilliest night shift to launder and asked Arabela to bathe the children and perfume Paquita's hair, which had grown long enough to braid.

While Arabela hung a pot over the fire to heat water for the washbasin, Ángeles, who ran the kitchen like a field commander, called out orders to the two slave girls. Pacheco had acquired both of them the year before from a Tunisian trader who was passing through Seville, and they had proven an excellent investment. There are thousands of slaves in Seville—some say over six thousand. Pacheco had been lucky to find two who were industrious and also good-natured. Both girls worked like demons, and Zulima, the younger one, had a lovely voice. Pacheco treated them kindly and was quite fond of them. "Give us music!" Pacheco would entreat Zulima. "It enlivens the house!" And melodies full of trills and *algarabías* that nobody understood would burst from the girl's lips.

"Zoraída, lay out the *mayólica* bowl," barked Ángeles. "Not that one! The one with the red and blue flowers painted on it! And Zulima, shell these peas and then pick the stones out of those lentils!"

Ángeles had purchased the peas and the lentils—and the onions and the garlic and the bacon and the hens and the rabbits—many hours earlier. The markets were open from six to ten in the morning for the midday meal, and they reopened at three so that purchases could be made for supper. In our grandparents' day, the world wasn't so finicky about the hour, but by the time I was a child, people were already beginning to live by the clock. Church bells told you not only when to pray matins and vespers, but also when to go to market, eat your dinner, and go to bed.

In the Seville sun, nothing lasted more than a few hours, which was why two trips a day were essential. The night before the big day, Juana told Ángeles to leave early for the butcher's to buy a nice piece of mutton. Beef was fine for the everyday stew, but for special occasions, Juana had to have mutton.

So at exactly a quarter to six in the morning (you knew by the peal of the campanile), when daylight was but a hint of orange in the darkened sky, Ángeles and Zoraída left for the marketplace. In her blouse the kitchen maid carried the pouch of money Juana had given her. Seville was full of pickpockets, so you couldn't be too careful. She haggled with the butcher and the green grocer, but managed to get everything the *señora* demanded for a decent price. She sent the packages home with Zoraída, then headed for the cheeses to find a nice *manchego* to be served with olives for afterward. Next she headed to the *confitería*, where creative candy-makers satisfied Sevillians' passion for sweets with extraordinary confections. Such indulgences were expensive, but this, after all, was a special occasion. Ángeles found some nice *turrones*—an irresistible nougat toffee made of honey, sugar, egg whites, and toasted almonds.

The campanile was clanging again. It was now half past nine, and Ángeles was growing nervous. Ahead of her lay hours of plucking, skinning, peeling, chopping, and stoking fires, and she cursed herself for having sent Zoraída home because she still had one more stop to make, and the package would be heavy. Spaniards—and especially Sevillians—had gone crazy for ices. Even in winter, people craved iced drinks made with juices and honey or sugar, so vendors scaled mountains for ice, which they stored in ice wells and sold to the public. The Pacheco household used about a sack of ice a day in the winter, but for today, Ángeles thought they would need much more.

Ángeles was a sturdy woman in her fifties. She had arms like corded tree trunks, and she was used to heavy lifting, but the package of ice was bulky and grew heavier as she trudged home. The day was cool and bright, a typical January day. Near

San Elmo Church she turned into an alley that cut through a maze of lanes. Her arms ached and her mind began to wander. As soon as she got home, she'd have to peel the parsnips and chop the onions. Thank God there was plenty of *aloja*—the alcoholic drink made of carob, water, and a dash of sugar—fermenting in the pantry, but she would have to remember to chill it. And then in the afternoon, she would need to buy some fruit sherbet. It was expensive—two *reales!*—so if the *señora* said no, she wouldn't buy the ambergris, but instead the cheaper kind made with jasmine or anis. And then, if there was time . . .

All of a sudden a mangy boy of about eight lunged at Ángeles from the shadows. Instinctively, she turned on her heel, but he was quick. He grabbed her from behind and punched her in the back, making her drop her packages. As he shoved her against a wall, an older boy grabbed the ice, the *turrón*, and the cheese. The ice, he knew, would bring a good price on the street.

"Thanks for lunch!" hissed the older thug. He was only about fifteen, but his teeth were already black from tobacco and disease. Ángeles slumped down against the wall, her back throbbing with pain.

"*Idiota!*" she hissed back. "Why didn't you steal my money instead? You could have bought yourself a much bigger lunch at a tavern!"

The boy stopped and stepped back toward her. "Where is your money, old woman?"

"Wouldn't you like to know! I keep it in a secret place!"

The thug squatted next to her, about to lift her skirt, but with a lightning-swift move Ángeles grabbed the ice out of his hand and thwacked him on the head with it. Seeing his friend toppled, the younger boy shot off like an arrow. Ángeles grabbed the cheese and sweets and ice and ran, leaving her assailant sprawled on the ground, dazed, blood trickling from a gash over his eyebrow.

As soon as she reached Pacheco's kitchen, she got to work. She didn't waste time telling her story. Petty assaults were common in the lanes and alleys of Seville, and there was nothing special about this one. Zoraída had already cut the mutton into chunks and chopped the vegetables for the stew. Ángeles assembled the ingredients and placed them in the huge cast iron pot that the slave girls hung over the fire. It was a quarter past ten. She had less than four hours to prepare the meal for Don Diego's welcome-home celebration.

No one had seen the man of honor that morning. On ordinary days the slave Melgar brought Velázquez an early breakfast, so that by half past ten, he would be at work in his studio. But the day before, the artist had arrived home exhausted by his twelve-day trek from Madrid on mule, and so he was probably still asleep. The trip from Court should have taken only ten days, but Velázquez and his men had run into snow and blocked roads in the Sierra Morena and they had spent an extra night in Córdoba.

Through the window, Ángeles caught sight of Julia in the courtyard and called to her. A moment later, the maid stuck her head through the door. As in most houses, the kitchen was separate from the main structure in order to prevent damage to the living quarters in case of fire.

"Still no sign of Don Diego?" asked Ángeles.

"No," Julia said. "He must be worn-out from the trip."

Velázquez had left for Madrid the previous April. He had told Pacheco that he had to get out of Seville and see the world beyond the art school's dusty halls. That day at the academy, Don Guzmán had mentioned the dazzling collections of art at Court, and Velázquez wanted to discover it all for himself. At Court, he was certain, he would encounter staggering new ways of capturing light, color, and perspective—innovations so extraordinary that he couldn't even imagine them.

Even before he left for Madrid, Velázquez had *enchufe*—connections. Pacheco had influential friends, so the requisite letters guaranteeing safe conduct were easy to acquire. And then there was the count-duke Olivares, who had promised to introduce him to the right people and look after him. Velázquez made his plans carefully, consulting travel books with routes and names of inns, and although many of the roads were terrible, he was ready for the challenge. The long days of plodding along on the back of a mule and the long nights in flea-ridden dormitories were a small price to pay, he thought, for the rewards that awaited him. He knew—or thought he knew—that as soon as he got to Court, he would be basking in elegance.

And so it was that on a warm spring day redolent with orange blossoms, the artist set out for El Escorial. He knew that even Pacheco's generosity wasn't enough to allow him to travel abroad to see world's greatest paintings, but El Escorial was the next best thing. Felipe II had built El Escorial as a royal hunting lodge near the monastery of San Lorenzo, in the outskirts of Madrid, and then expanded it into a vast complex that included a mausoleum, palace, retreat, and seminary. For weeks, Velázquez had thought of nothing but this place and its treasures, but when he saw the huge, forbidding compound, excitement turned to fear. This wasn't a hideaway, but a monastery-fortress with massive gray granite walls pierced at each corner by a huge tower—an elegant complex, perhaps even noble, yet far too austere to be called beautiful.

Of course Velázquez hadn't come to marvel at the building and its belfries, or the quadrangle with its crisscrossing passageways. He was here for the paintings—paintings by Spaniards, naturally, but also by Italians and Germans, by Flems and Venetians, by Lombards and Ligurians. This was his first foray into the world of art beyond Pacheco's school—the first step, he thought, in what would be his brilliant career. For a moment, he was too awestruck even to set foot inside. However, his anxiety was short-lived. He had come to see paintings, and see them he must.

What lay inside did not disappoint him. Felipe II had been a passionate collector, and he had decorated his complex with the works of Zuccaro, Tibaldi, Cambiaso, and Luca Giordano. Velázquez saw Titian's *Last Supper* in the sacristy and a Rubens in the gallery. He gazed upon magnificent frescoes and sculptures—brilliant pieces at every turn. Most remarkable of all was Bellini's Christ, which the artist had carved from a block of the purest white marble, naked and exposed to all the wickedness of mankind.

The toll of the campanile announced 14:00. Guests were gathering in the patio—Pacheco's academicians, their wives, local dignitaries, neighbors, and those of Pacheco's disciples who were from respectable families. The fresh winter air made it an ideal afternoon for an outside meal. Juana greeted each new arrival with a smile and a curtsy, but from time to time, she cast a furtive glance at her father. Velázquez still hadn't emerged from his rooms.

The guests chattered pleasantly. The ladies, their hair done up in fancy combs and their figures distorted by enormous farthingales, gossiped about the escapades of the handsome new king, whose chief counselor was reputedly also his chief procurer. Felipe IV had been married at ten to Doña Isabel de Borbón, but that didn't prevent him from prowling around shadowy corridors in search of fresh pleasures. The ladies flashed their golden rings and crucifixes and tossed their scented locks as they giggled and snickered. The men mostly wore black, with tight-fitting jackets, stiff white collars and lacy cuffs, short pantaloons, and velvet capes. They chatted about the recent controversies in the world of astronomy, most of them agreeing that the theories of those renegade foreigners, Copernicus and Galileo, were thoroughly harebrained. The Church had been absolutely right to forbid the notion of a sun-centered universe, said the majority, although a few thought that the Church should keep its nose out of science.

The opposing groups squabbled good-naturedly, while the ladies twittered over the young king's exploits.

"They say Olivares takes him to back-alley brothels! Imagine!"

"I heard that this Galileo once wanted to be a priest. Imagine!"

"The king of Spain! In public with a . . ."

"The earth spins around the sun, according to this clown."

"Don Diego will be able to tell us if Olivares . . ."

"The Holy Father did the right thing . . ."

"Well, Don Felipe is only nineteen . . ."

"I hear the palace is crawling with gorgeous young women of the kind that are, well, anxious to please . . ."

"He says the earth is just a planet like Mars or Venus . . ."

"Queen Margarita, his poor mother, would roll over in her grave . . ."

"False and contrary to scripture . . ."

"His poor wife, sweet little Queen Isabel."

" . . . what Father Mariana must think of heliocentrism . . ."

"Velázquez can tell us if . . ."

"And, by the way, where is Velázquez?"

Juana chewed her lip and fidgeted. She scanned the men's caucus, and when she finally caught her father's gaze, mouthed something imperceptible.

Pacheco slipped out of the patio and went to look for his son-in-law.

About fifteen minutes later he reappeared, followed by a man who looked nothing like what the company expected. Like his father-in-law, Velázquez usually dressed in black and carried himself with dignity in public. He wore his long, upturned mustache waxed and carefully groomed, as he had seen the count of Olivares wear his. He was not given to grandiose displays of emotion, but there was a playfulness in his eyes that revealed a mischievous, even rebellious streak. That day, though, Velázquez's shoulders slumped underneath his full-sleeved black coat. His eyes, usually bright and intense, were puffy and pink as though he had been drinking, although there was no wine on his breath. His hair wilted over his forehead and his mustache drooped shapelessly over his lip. He greeted the guests with a bowed head.

"Tell us about the Court!" urged the ladies. "Did you see the queen?" "Is she as clever as they say? Does she wear French lace?"

Velázquez remained taciturn while the callers whirled around him like dervishes, hurling questions whenever they spun to face him.

"Did you attend a banquet? The king is known for his sumptuous banquets!"

"Is it true he keeps dozens of dwarfs around the palace for his amusement?"

"Is it true . . ."

Velázquez felt his jaw tense. He knew that eventually someone would ask the dreaded question, and he could not sulk his way through the afternoon and allow people to suspect his trip was a failure. After all, Velázquez was a Sevillian through and through. He had a keen sense of self-worth and of family honor. To discredit himself in front of Pacheco's friends would be unpardonable. He lifted his chin and squinted slightly.

"Of course," he said. "It's all true."

The guests grilled him during the *comida*'s many courses. He deflected their questions by describing his journey across the Andalusian countryside. It was spring when he and Melgar set out, accompanied by two muleteers who carried saddle packs full of painting supplies. They passed through fragrant orchards of citrus, olive, and fig trees. The landscape was a patchwork of greens, lime upon olive, emerald upon jade. Greens dotted with yellow, orange, and tan. Music filled the air, as farmers sang as they planted. New shoots climbed trellises in the vineyards, and graceful cypresses reached upward, their tapering branches forming dark green flames against the blue sky. He drew out the narrative as long as he could, using words to draw pictures as vivid as those he created with paint. He reported that in Córdoba, after consulting his guidebooks, he had finally found decent lodgings. He sent Melgar to the marketplace to buy some meat and parsnips to give to the innkeeper's wife to prepare for them, and fortunately, she was a good cook. He dwelled on the beauty of the vegetables and the filth of the taverns. "One tavern keeper watered down the wine so much that . . ."

"But what happened when you got to Court?" demanded Father Pineda, Pacheco's persistent Jesuit friend. "Were you well received?"

Velázquez rambled on about the guide they had hired in Córdoba to lead them through the rugged passes to the north, where the land was sterile and sparsely populated.

"It was almost impossible find a place to spend the night. The few beds we found were flea-ridden and lumpy."

"But what happened at Court?" insisted Father Pineda. "Were you invited to the Alcázar?"

"Ah . . . the Alcázar . . . the royal palace," mused Velázquez.

"Let him tell his story in his own way," interrupted Pacheco.

Velázquez took a breath. It was clear he was not going to be able to put them off much longer.

"I *would* like to know, though," said Pacheco, in spite of his remark to Pineda, "if Juan de Fonseca was kind to you."

"Very kind," said Velázquez truthfully, grateful to be able to give an honest answer. "He introduced me to many influential men." Fonseca was an old friend of Pacheco's. He was Canon of Seville and now occupied an important post at Court. As the *sumiller de cortina*, he was responsible for supervising arrangements for the king's attendance at mass, seeing to his needs during religious services and opening or closing the curtain in front of him as needed to protect his privacy. Velázquez relaxed a bit. He even smiled as he recalled how the old priest had taken him under his wing and presented him to some of the officials—minor officials to be sure, but officials nonetheless—at the Alcázar.

"Did he introduce you to the king? Did you paint His Majesty's portrait?" The color drained from Velázquez's face.

Everyone had assumed Pacheco's son-in-law would take the Court by storm. They all thought it would be a matter of months before he received invitations to paint the king, the queen, and the king's sister María. After all, he was Pacheco's best pupil, and the king's chaplain himself had agreed to introduce him around. Fonseca was a Sevillian knowledgeable about art. It went without saying that he would secure a commission from the king for his countryman.

"The king is very busy now. Hostilities with the Protestants in the Low Countries have started up again. Besides, negotiations have begun for the marriage of Princess María and Charles, Prince of Wales."

"And what about Olivares?"

How could he tell them he hadn't even seen Olivares? He swallowed and tried to think of something to say. "They call him count-duke now," he murmured. "His Majesty made him the duke of Sanlúcar. He didn't want to give up his inherited title, count of Olivares, so he combined the two." As he spoke, he knew that he was telling the guests something they already knew, but he had nothing else to say.

There was an uncomfortable silence. Everyone was staring at him. Pacheco sized up the situation, took a gulp of iced wine, and spluttered triumphantly, "He painted Góngora!" He announced it as though it were a coup, as though painting a poet were as important as painting a king. "I myself arranged for it! I wrote to Fonseca and told him to make it happen! And it did! He painted the great bard Luis de Góngora, the pride of Andalusia!"

Velázquez froze. He expected the guests to snicker and scoff. Instead, they roared their approval. Góngora was, after all, Andalusia's greatest poet! Pineda burst into a recitation of Góngora's sonnet to Córdoba:

> ¡Oh excelso muro, oh torres coronadas
> De honor, de majestad, de gallardía!

> By honor, by majesty, by grace!
> Oh lofty ramparts, oh towers crowned

Somehow, Velázquez got through the meal, which dragged on until vespers. Some of the visitors stayed for the *merienda* and even for supper. It was after midnight before the last one left and Velázquez followed his wife upstairs.

His sullenness had returned. He mumbled something about having failed, about being ignored at Court, about never even seeing the king. Juana had no intention of allowing him to brood alone in his apartments that night. She was thrilled to have him back, and whether Velázquez had painted Don Felipe's portrait or not was of no concern to her. She took him by the hand and led him to her chamber, where Arabela had laid out her frilly night shift, immaculate and perfumed.

Juana stretched out beside her husband and ran her fingers along his spine, then over his buttocks, his hip, his groin . . . Velázquez allowed her to fondle his sex until at last he awakened to her touch. He sank down into her, and they rose and fell to the rhythm of their breathing, as though caught in an irresistible dance, cadenced and sweet. There was no more grumbling then, no mention of disappointment or exclusion, just tender whisperings of gratitude, fidelity, affection, love. The air was as serene as slumbering angels.

At about four in the morning, Juana awoke with a start. She was certain she had heard a scream.

It was Arabela. "It's the baby," she wailed. "Something is wrong with the baby!"

5

THE LADY ON THE ORB
1623

JUANA CLOSED HER EYES AND LISTENED. SHE HEARD THE BABY whimpering softly in the nursery. A bubbly gurgle. A ripple like the rush of a stream over pebbles. Juana sharpened her ears. She could hear Arabela cooing: "*Arrurrú, mi niña. Arrurrú.*" The baby giggled and clucked.

Arabela squeezed her hand. Juana jolted back to reality and choked back a sob. Arabela was not in the nursery. She was sitting on a cushion next to Juana in the *estrado*. The nursery was brutally silent.

Juana opened her eyes and peered at the plum-colored shadows flickering on the wall. The brazier sputtered and danced. Behind the beaded curtain of the *estrado* she perceived a silhouette: Venturo Almedina. She didn't want to see him. His very presence in her quarters made her feel violated, but her father had sent for him because he thought that if anyone could save baby Ignacia, it was the Moor. Almedina knew magic, medicinal magic of the East and the West, said Pacheco. But Juana feared the worst.

The strands of the curtain undulated in the dimness. Juana shivered.

Almedina stood before her with his head bowed. Juana focused on the hem of his cape, then on his doublet and the tip of his beard. Another frisson shot through her body. She dared not lift her gaze. She dared not look him in the eye.

Almedina stood in silence, shifting his weight from one foot to the other as if he had to urinate. Juana sensed the tension in his body.

She knew she had to say something, but words stuck in her throat. She felt as though she had swallowed cupfuls of sand. Finally she rose to her feet. Arabela slid an arm around her waist to steady her, and Juana forced out an utterance. "My . . . my little daughter . . ."

Almedina pursed his lips. He clasped his hands together with such force that his knuckles shone white under his olive skin. "I'm sorry," he whispered finally.

"You mean . . . there's no hope?" Tears dripped onto her collar. Arabela held out a hankie, and Juana stared at it as though it were an exotic insect.

"God had already taken her . . . when I got here." Almedina looked at the hankie as though he wanted it for himself.

Juana sank back down onto the cushion. "Oh, God," she sobbed. "Oh, God, my baby. My precious, precious baby."

Through her wet lashes Juana perceived the geometric patterns of the tiles. The rhomboids and stars seemed to float over the surface of the floor, swishing around Almedina's shoes, high-heeled and pointy, and his heavy woolen stockings. She struggled to stifle memories of the previous night, when instead of attending to little Ignacia, she had taken Velázquez by the hand and led him to her bed. Her cranium throbbed and her shoulders tightened into rope knots.

"I suspect a weakness of the lungs," Almedina said softly, "aggravated by a severe infection. Once it starts, there's no way to control it."

"She was delicate from the beginning," murmured Arabela. Her hands were trembling.

Juana waited for Venturo's indictment. "You insisted on nursing her yourself," she expected him to say, "instead of calling in a proper wet nurse." Instead he said, "There's nothing you could have done, *señora*. There's nothing anyone could have done. The mysteries of the Lord . . ."

Juana felt the room spinning around her. She suddenly felt too weak to hold up her own head, and she laid it in her nursemaid's lap, as she had so many times when she was a child. Arabela stroked Juana's hair, and Juana dozed. When she opened her eyes—perhaps a moment later, perhaps an hour— she supposed the Moor would be gone, but he was still standing there by the brazier, stooped and miserable looking.

"Don Venturo . . ."

"May God hold your darling child in His loving embrace," he murmured. Juana noticed that his voice cracked.

"Please give her some brandy and let her sleep," he instructed Arabela. "I'm sorry, *señora*," he sighed as he turned to leave. "I'm sorry I couldn't . . ."

Juana saw his shoulders trembling and knew he would collapse in a corner the moment he was out of the room. She knew that Venturo Almedina would weep for the baby he could not save.

"He's a good Christian," murmured Arabela when he was gone.

"Yes," said Juana, "he is. He really is."

If it hadn't been for the news the messenger brought from the Court only hours after Ignacia's death, Velázquez would have surely mourned as deeply as his wife. But as soon as he unrolled the letter marked with the royal seal, the artist's thoughts were fixed firmly in the future. Fortune, as everyone knows, is a lady. She stands on an orb that goes up and down as she walks. Lady Fortune had thrust Velázquez into the muck during his first visit to Madrid, but now, it seemed, she was about to pick him up and sluice him off.

In December, 1622, not long after Velázquez left the Court, Rodrigo de Villandrando, one of six royal painters, fell ill and died. Now there was an opening for a new Court painter. Pacheco's friend, Juan de Fonseca, lost no time reminding the count-duke that back in Seville there was a promising young man who would be perfect for the post. Fonseca knew that Olivares had fond memories of his stay in Seville and admired the city's writers and painters. It wasn't hard to convince him to give Velázquez a chance.

And so it was that on a cold day in January, 1623, a crowd of neighbors stood gawking in disbelief as the royal carriage rolled into the portal of Pacheco's home. The six white horses that pulled the vehicle were a far cry from the decrepit mules that had brought Velázquez back from Madrid. The carriage was a sleek number with an open body. It was covered in black leather decorated with geometrical designs formed by gilt tacks. The roof was a magnificent canopy supported by four pillars, and at the front was a huge chest for travel gear. Two coachmen rode on the front left and back right horses, maneuvering the coach with some difficulty through the narrow streets. Instead of curtains, window panes suspended by leather straps protected travelers from the elements. When the footmen opened the doors, you could see the plush red velvet interior, with four red seat pillows under each of which was—I hope you'll forgive me for mentioning it—a chamber pot.

No one was more surprised by this extraordinary interruption than Pacheco himself. As he stared out a window, he saw a servant in royal livery ring at his gate. Moments later, a messenger alighted. Pacheco gasped and clasped his hands when his own servant conveyed the news that the king's messenger had brought a communication for Don Diego Rodríguez de Silva y Velázquez from Fonseca, the *sumiller de cortina.*

The artist read and reread the letter in disbelief. He would have his chance after all! He had not yet fully unpacked from his last trip, and now a carriage was outside to take him back to Madrid. It would be easy enough to gather up pigments, brushes, canvases, resin, glue, dying materials, and his very best ruffs and stockings. He would pack the materials he had and obtain the rest there—eggs, cochineal, whatever else. As far as his wardrobe went, he had had a new *jubón* and cuffs made before the last trip. Velázquez, usually a measured man, could hardly contain his joy. He flung his arms wildly and let out a yelp.

Juana blinked at him, her eyelids tinged with salt, her eyes sunken in their sockets.

Velázquez reined in his flailing limbs and gulped air. "It's . . . it's an opportunity," he stammered. "It's what we've always wanted."

"Your baby girl hasn't been dead a day."

Velázquez stared at the floor. "I'll stay for the burial, but I . . . I have to go, Juana. I have to."

"Tell them no." Juana directed her words to the messenger, who stood at attention waiting for a response.

"Juana . . . This will change our lives . . . Everything will be better. We can have another—"

"Tell them no!" She shot him a look like a broad arrow. "How dare you," she hissed.

The following day, Juana and Arabela bathed the baby and dressed her in her baptismal gown. Juana counted and kissed each little finger, then cupped the child's hands in her own. Her tears fell on Ignacia's tender flesh—so perfect and yet so cold— and merged with the perfumed bathwater. How could this innocent little baby be dead? What had she done to make God yank her from her mother's breast so cruelly? And what had she, Juana, done to deserve this punishment? Nurse her child? Make love with her husband?

Although little Ignacia was destined straight for heaven, many things had to be done to expedite her journey. Early in the morning Pacheco had sent Ángeles to the market to buy victuals for a respectable spread, for the *velada* would be that very afternoon. It was the custom in Seville to bury the dead within forty-eight hours of their demise, sometimes even sooner. This meant that the house had to be readied for the vigil, and food had to be transported to the church for the funeral supper, which would take place after the burial. All present would attend, including the clergy. In addition, it was the custom to offer a feast to the poor—almsgiving would ensure the swift and safe flight of the soul to the Other World. A man of Pacheco's stature had the obligation to stage an elaborate funeral. The servants were still exhausted from preparing and cleaning up after Velázquez's homecoming, but now they had to clean and scrub all over again, then drape the windows in black, turn mirrors toward the wall, and buy candles for the funeral mass.

Neighbor women began to arrive at Pacheco's home around two. Then came Pacheco's students, the academicians and their wives, friends of the family, and the members of the painters' guild. Father Pineda led them all in prayer. After the vigil, neighbors helped Juana and Arabela shroud the tiny corpse in linen and place it in the miniature white coffin. Pineda grasped a cross and held it aloft, then stepped out into the rain-soaked street. One by one the parish priests fell in behind him in hierarchical order. The officers of the painters' guild took their places behind the clergy, followed by the dozens of laymen from different charitable confraternities who routinely attended funerals, and the children Pacheco had paid to walk in the cortège and wail loudly for the deceased. In order for Pacheco to make a proper statement, the mourners had to be numerous and noisy, and so he promised as many children as his servants could round up a couple of coins and a hearty meal for their services.

At the end of the cortège came Velázquez and Pacheco carrying the coffin, followed by Juana, Julia, the household servants, and, finally, Arabela with Paquita in her arms. As the cortège wound its way through Seville's twisted alleys the rain, which had stopped momentarily, started up again. Velázquez was ashen under his wide felt hat. Droplets dribbled from the brim, saturating the shoulders of his cape. He seemed not to notice the downpour, but stared ahead with deadened eyes. Pacheco stooped over the casket, his expression stoic. He walked mechanically, one foot in front of the other, praying in a whisper. Juana trailed behind them, weeping softly. Tears, snot, and raindrops bathed her chin. Periodically she teetered on the slippery cobblestones, then flailed and grabbed Julia's hand. The servants of the wealthier mourners carried a canopy that they held over their masters' heads to protect them from the rain. Those with no servants carried their own canopies or trudged over the muddy cobblestones clutching wool wraps to their heads. Their grubby hems clung around their ankles or trailed out behind them like dripping fishermen's nets dragged over sludge. Juana carried no canopy, and soon she was drenched. In spite of the storm, the cortège swelled as standers by joined in the marching and moaning.

When the mourners at last reached the parish church, men and women divided into their respective sections. The tabernacle was ablaze with tapers that gleamed and glittered like a million sparkling stars. Wax was dear, but Pacheco spared no expense to show the depth of his love for his grandchild. (Of course, he was just as concerned with impressing his neighbors and his relatives. After all, how better to flaunt your wealth than to squander money on five hundred candles for a deceased infant?) After the mass, little Ignacia was laid to rest inside the crypt next to her grandmother, Doña Leonor de Miranda. Then Pacheco invited the entire crowd for refreshments. People sniffed and sighed and fell into clichés.

"Poor little angel."

"She's with God now."

"Better to die without sin and soar straight to heaven."

Eventually they dried their tears and dug into the food. Soon everyone was gossiping and even laughing—the gloomy ceremony had become just another social event. The mourners had forgotten about little Ignacia—all, of course, except for Juana, whose eyes were set in a blank stare.

Velázquez had consented to Juana's demand that he remain in Seville, and so the king's coach returned to Madrid without him. Now the artist stayed in his studio. He rose early and worked all morning. He took his meals in his room. Although they lived in the same house, Juana hardly saw him. He was like a ghost who slipped through door cracks, appearing and disappearing mysteriously—silent and stealthy.

Soon enough, Juana began to suspect what he was up to. It had been raining since March, but once the precipitation began to let up in mid-May, she saw the slave Melgar coming and going, carrying canvases and pigments and compounds. She caught sight of the tailor, who had come to measure Velázquez for a new suit of clothes. She heard the academicians in the *sala* murmuring about his chances at Court on a second try.

"This time there's a definite position for him."

"He should paint Olivares and circulate the portrait."

"If only the king could see his work . . ."

Every few days, Juana would stand in the hallway and try to eavesdrop, but most of the time she wandered through the

house like a somnambulist or stood for hours peering into Ignacia's empty cradle. Sometimes she wept into her sheets, her tears
falling like rain on a barren, snow-covered field. Other times,
she grabbed Paquita and smothered her with kisses, holding her
so tightly that the child shrieked.

Velázquez set off for Madrid in July, but this time, no royal
coach came to ferry him over the difficult terrain. He had the
stable boy saddle the mules, kissed his wife and daughter good-
bye, embraced his father-in-law, and set off toward Córdoba with
Melgar, just as he had the year before. Juana turned away dry-
eyed. She knew his departure was inevitable. After all, Fonseca
had called for him. But it was also necessary. Velázquez had to
realize his dream and succeed at Court. Otherwise, he would
dissolve into melancholy.

As they rode through the lush Andalusian fields, Velázquez
dreamed of elegant state dinners, fur-trimmed capes, and maybe
even acceptance into a prestigious society such as the Order of
Santiago, reserved for the most prominent men in the land.
Never mind that he hadn't even been appointed to the post of
royal painter. He was already convinced that once at Court he
could achieve anything. Wasn't Fonseca a cleric-courtier? Then
why couldn't he, Velázquez, be a painter-courtier? Painting
would be his entrée to a world of power, influence, glamour,
and excitement—not an end, but a means. Velázquez once told
me that even before he reached Ciudad Real, he was convinced
that this time, he would triumph. I can imagine him prodding
his little mule along the rocky roads from Ciudad Real to
Toledo, shoulders back and chin thrust out, his breathing exud-
ing self-confidence, as though the very air should have been
honored to fill his lungs.

When he arrived in Madrid early in August, he was not surprised to find Fonseca ready for him. The gritty old chaplain had promised Pacheco that the previous year's fiasco would not be repeated, and to that end, he devised a strategy. Fonseca wasted no time putting Velázquez to work. He lodged him in his own apartments and set up an easel for him in a well-lit loft that had been used for storage.

"Paint my portrait," ordered Fonseca. "Right here and now."

Velázquez was exhausted from the road. He thought he would rest a while and then take a leisurely stroll along the Prado before setting up his workplace. Besides, he had not come to Madrid to paint the *sumiller de cortina*. He had in mind to start with a portrait of Olivares, or maybe the king's younger brother, the *infante* Fernando. The priest-courtier studied the crestfallen young painter and sized up the situation. Fonseca was a kindly man, loyal to his Sevillian friends and ambitious for his protégé. He was also shrewd and savvy.

Velázquez thought to stand his ground, but upon examining the face of the man before him, he felt suddenly disarmed. His host, Velázquez realized, bore an astounding resemblance to a ferret. He had rounded ears; a bulbous, pink, upturned nose; and black, inquisitive, globular eyes. His mustache and beard were white and smooth. Yes, there could be no doubt at all: for all his elegance, Fonseca looked charmingly like a ferret. In spite of himself, Velázquez smiled. Fonseca peered at him over his long ferret muzzle, out of his tiny ferret eyes.

"I know I'm not Apollo the Beautiful," he chuckled, "and I know I'm not the grand Olivares. But for our purposes, my likeness will do. Paint my portrait. You have one day."

Velázquez positioned Fonseca and assessed his features. Velázquez was beginning to suspect that Fonseca not only looked like a ferret, but also had the sneaky animal's ability to wiggle into clandestine spaces and observe what no one else could see. The artist pondered whether to paint a perfect likeness or to camouflage Fonseca's ferretness in order to create a more pleasing image. It occurred to him that by placing his model at an angle, he could disguise the length of his long, muzzle-like face. He repositioned the priest, then stood back and took measure.

"You only have one day," Fonseca reminded him.

"I need only a few hours," countered Velázquez.

"Arrogant young pup," mumbled Fonseca under his breath.

By mid-afternoon, the work was ready. The chaplain ordered a messenger to take it immediately to the palace of Gaspar de Bracamonte, fifth son of the Count of Peñaranda, who was an assistant to the *infante* Fernando. By evening Don Fernando had shown it to his brother the king, and Don Felipe had made his decision.

6

Venus speaks
1660

INGERS LIKE KNOBBY TWIGS LIE USELESSLY IN A HEAP. HANDS like rough bark fouled by wormy veins that weave among patches of fungus. Time is a villain. My face—I imagine it furrowed and crinkly, eyelids drooping, lips thin as ink lines. I think I have a wart above my eyebrow, but I cannot be sure because we're not allowed to have mirrors. Books are forbidden, as well—even bibles. Scripture in the vernacular was banned decades ago, as were most inspirational books of the kind they read in the days of Saint Teresa. I have my poem, though—the one written by Rioja that I once copied down. From time to time I pull it out from the lining of my shift and read it: "leaves and thorns surround you, / and rob you of the pure radiance and dazzling / purple I saw beginning to tinge your petals, / and at the same time, of the sweet vitality of / the verdure, through which peeks an ardent rose." I, Venus, am that rose—once pure radiance and sweet vitality. Once, a long time ago.

Tears dribble over my quivering lips, onto my chin and

then into my wimple. I sniffle and wipe the sleeve of my habit over damp lids that sheathe ailing eyes. "¡*Mal haya el tiempo!*" I say aloud. "Damn time!"

But I'm not going to snivel. What's the use of crying over the inevitable? I have work to do. I have this history to finish, and I can only write during the hour of recreation, right before vespers. When the bells call us to prayer, I will have to hide my writing materials in the little chest I keep locked under my cot and take my place in line with the other gray veils. My friend the convent chronicler—her name is Sister Tomasina—sneaks paper to me. Paper is dear, of course, but she can get it, since she keeps the house records. You have to be wily to accomplish anything, not just here, but everywhere. Anyhow, I couldn't work for longer, even if I had the whole day free. My hands ache and my eyes are going bad. I see everything through a milky lens, and writing makes my head throb. It's just as well that the chapel bells call me away.

I should be clear: I'm not a nun. I'm just a boarder at Santa María de los Ángeles. Where else but the cloister can an old woman with no family go? This convent is full of stray cats— orphans, deflowered girls, widows and spinsters—homeless females who dwell here at the mercy of the mother superior. We wear habits like the sisters, but ours are gray, not black like the aristo-cratic choir nuns' or white like the scullery nuns'. Naturally, we keep the same schedule as everyone else: up at four, before sun-rise; morning prayers; chores, then breakfast; more prayers. I could go on and on about these routines, which, no matter how familiar, never fail to depress me. But it's far more exciting— and wonderfully distracting—to remember everything that hap-pened when Velázquez got to Court . . .

His Royal Highness Felipe IV, King of Spain, Portugal, and the Netherlands, stood before Velázquez's quickly crafted portrait of Juan de Fonseca, a brother on either side.

"Hmm . . ." says Don Fernando a bit uncertainly. "It looks like . . ."

"It looks just like him," says the king.

"Yes, yes it does. It looks just like him. But doesn't it look like . . . look strangely like . . . What I mean is, doesn't it remind you of . . . some sort of animal?"

"Hmm . . ." says Don Carlos. "I see what you mean. Perhaps a . . . let's see . . ."

"Maybe a ferret?" says Don Fernando.

"Exactly," says the king, "a ferret. But in truth, Fonseca does look rather like a ferret."

"Yes," whispers Don Fernando, "indeed he does."

"I agree," says Don Carlos. "He looks like a ferret."

I wonder sometimes if it occurred to the three of them that if Velázquez painted such a realistic, unflattering portrait of Fonseca, he would one day do them the same favor. The Habsburgs, after all, are all notoriously ugly, with overgrown jaws that protrude so much that they prevent some of them from eating properly. Add to that noses so long they can wipe them with their tongues. I suppose that Don Felipe figured that a Court painter would never dare to portray a monarch with all his defects and impurities, and he was right. Velázquez knew what he had to do to survive. By day's end the king had commissioned him to paint the royal portrait—but not right away. Velázquez would have to wait until after the festivities in honor of the Prince of Wales. Anxious though he was to begin the portrait, Velázquez was so thrilled over the possibility of seeing the prince that he joyfully postponed beginning work.

And what does Charles, Prince of Wales, have to do with any of this? Well, Prince Charles's sister Elizabeth was married to the Protestant German Frederick V, King of Bohemia, whose people had just replaced him with a Catholic ruler. King James, Charles's father, wanted to help his daughter and son-in-law reclaim power, but he was afraid that would mean an expensive war with Catholic Spain. That's why he decided to marry his son Charles to Princess María Ana, King Felipe's sister. Not only would the princess bring a hefty dowry, but the union would secure an alliance between our two countries, thereby avoiding yet another war.

Prince Charles was all for it, but when he saw that the marriage negotiators were dragging their heels, he decided to take matters into his own hands. Twenty-three years old and full of himself, he set off incognito for Spain with his pal the duke of Buckingham. I can imagine the two of them crossing the border in the dead of night, capes drawn over their eyes like characters in a play by Calderón. The night is dark and starless. Their carriage rolls over the bumpy cobblestones of the Calle de las Infantas, curtains drawn, Buckingham shuddering at the noise, the prince giddy with excitement. They send a servant to awaken the English ambassador and plead for lodgings. The poor man, kneeling at his prayers in his nightshirt, is alarmed by the thumping at his door and astonished to learn that he has visitors at such an ungodly hour. Sleepily, he patters behind a servant carrying a candle, forgetting to don his dressing gown. In the vestibule, two men wait in silence, their faces concealed. Suddenly, the prince throws off his cloak and bursts into giggles.

"Your Royal Highness," hiccups the duke of Bristol, Ambassador from the Court of King James to the Court of King Felipe IV. He bows until his nose is parallel to the floor.

Charles nods carelessly. "A b . . . b . . . bolt from the blue, eh, duke?" If he is self-conscious about his stuttering, he doesn't show it.

"Your Grace," whispers Buckingham conspiratorially, "we have come to get a look at the princess before the official presentation. His Royal Highness is hoping to woo her on his own rather than leaving it all to . . . you know . . ."

"Diplomats, Your Grace?" Bristol, still stunned, stands there before the royal party in his nightshirt, which is embarrassingly transparent in the candlelight.

"Gaston," he whispers to the servant, "run and get my dressing gown for me, will you?"

"His Royal Highness wishes for a more spontaneous, sincere relationship with his bride, you see. One that isn't, uh, pure business." Buckingham winks. "The representatives of both governments are dawdling. His Royal Highness prefers to see the negotiations concluded *post haste* and believes our presence here can hurry things along."

The next day, Bristol reported to the Spanish monarch that the illustrious trickster, Prince Charles of England, was on Spanish soil. The count-duke ordered that the *cuarto viejo* of the Monastery of San Jerónimo, which was reserved for royal visitors, be sumptuously appointed for the guests. Soon afterward, the prince's entourage arrived and the galas began.

The moment King Felipe was informed of Charles's presence on Spanish soil, he suspended the sumptuary laws so that Madrileños could dazzle his guest with the opulence of their palaces, their carriages, and their costumes. In fact, he was so anxious to impress his future brother-in-law that that he lent thousands of ducats to his noblemen so that they could put on the best show possible. In order to convince the Prince of England that he had Spain's support, Felipe let scores of prisoners out of jail and paid them to cheer and scream with enthusiasm as Charles rode through the streets.

As soon as Charles had settled into San Jerónimo, every commission, council, and committee in the realm processed to the monastery to show its respects. The Englishman sat upon a dais in the courtyard as bailiffs, constables, scribes, secretaries, lawyers, accountants, magistrates, advisers, and guards paraded before him, each one on horseback and bedecked in his very best clothes. Next came German and Spanish military ranks preceded by flutists and drummers; then officers of the municipality of Madrid marching to the rhythm of clanging cymbals; followed by countless nobles and their escorts in velvet, gold, and jewels. Finally, servants accompanied Charles to an intimate salon, where His Majesty and Olivares, who had entered through a secret door, regaled him with delicacies and conversation the rest of the afternoon.

Charles spent spring and summer bowing and smiling and wooing the princess at parades, receptions, banquets, masked balls, bullfights, *cañas*, hunting parties, tournaments, and religious festivals. He was reputedly charming, witty, gallant, and a bit childish. I imagine him smirking and winking at Doña María, in that impudent way Englishmen have, while she, with customary Spanish hauteur, turns away, chin raised, eyes narrowed. And Velázquez? Velázquez was just an aspiring Court painter, more or less forgotten amid the parties and parley. But then, one day as he was finishing up a sketch of a palace cook to be used someday—the painter wasn't sure when—as a character in some religious painting, a page appeared in the atelier.

"Don Diego," the boy said deferentially, "the count-duke requests that your mercy follow me."

A painter cannot simply drop everything in the middle of a session, yet a summons from the count-duke of Olivares was not to be ignored. Velázquez straightened up as best he could, dismissed his model, doused his smudged hands in a basin of water, and followed the page through labyrinthine corridors to an antechamber. The wide double doors were open. A lesser courtier appeared and escorted Velázquez into another room, where he was met by one of Olivares's personal servants, who in turn led him to an office where a secretary sat writing at a heavy wooden desk ornately carved with vines and grapes.

"Please be kind enough to wait here," said the secretary coldly. "His Lordship will be with you shortly."

Velázquez remained standing. He had not been invited to sit down. He fidgeted with a silver chain in his pocket, a good-luck gift from his father-in-law. Was the count-duke going to dismiss him? Had the king changed his mind about his portrait? Had the Committee of Works decided that there was simply not enough money to replace Rodrigo de Villandrando, the Court portraitist who had died? Everyone said that cash was tight. Eugenio Cajés, one of the senior painters, hadn't been paid in months. Suddenly, an interior door opened and a servant in royal livery swept in.

"Don Diego Rodríguez de Silva y Velázquez? Please follow me." Another series of hallways, and then a massive, ornately carved door. The servant introduced Velázquez into an exquisite salon with furniture upholstered in velvet. The wall hangings were breathtaking—finely stitched Belgian tapestries depicting knights and ladies romping in a field. Olivares was standing next to one of them.

"A fifteenth-century Flemish piece," he was explaining to a guest. "A gift from Archduke Albert of the Netherlands."

Velázquez took in the scene and bowed low, as much to give his stomach time to settle as out of courtesy. He stood, he realized, before two of the most powerful men in the world. His mouth felt dry, and he felt a strong urge to urinate. Olivares turned to the painter and greeted him as breezily as if he had been talking to an equal. "His Royal Highness, Prince Charles Stuart of England," he announced by way of introduction.

Velázquez tried to swallow, but his throat tightened, leaving him momentarily mute. "Your Highness," he breathed finally. He bowed once more. *Three* of the most powerful men in the world! King Felipe IV of Spain, the count-duke of Olivares, and Prince Charles.

"Don Diego Rodríguez de Silva y Velázquez," Olivares continued, "one of the finest young painters in Spain."

Velázquez didn't blush. He knew it was true.

The prince let out a playful snort. "Get to see a lot of nice t . . . t . . . titties in your line of work, eh, V . . . Ve . . . Velázquez?"

Velázquez stared at the floor, at once stunned and amused, unsure of whether to be offended or flattered by the intimacy.

"I don't know whether it was his stammer or his impudence," Velázquez later told me, "but it was hard to take the man seriously."

"You'll have to t . . . t . . . take him with you when you m . . . m . . . ma . . . make the rounds," chortled Charles, looking at the king, whose facial muscles seemed fixed in wax. "He seems a little g . . . green."

A tallish young man with a narrow face and a high fore-head, the prince wore a permanent smirk between his upturned mustache and his short, pointed beard. He was just Velázquez's age, but looked older. He wore a tight-fitting doublet of gold and black horizontal stripes and calf-length britches of the same pattern. Instead of a ruff, a wide collar decorated with saffron-colored lace graced his neck—that was the English style—and a floor-length white cloak embroidered with gold threads lay across his shoulders. He oozed wealth and power, even though he had the voice of a dwarf.

"I am escorting the prince to the king's private art collection," said Olivares. "I thought you'd enjoy seeing it, too."

Nothing Velázquez had ever seen before could compare to this assemblage of paintings, not even the collection at El Escorial. There were many beautiful Titians, and none more impressive than the "Venus of El Pardo." Velázquez stood before it awestruck.

I should say that I could never have posed for a painting like that one, not in a thousand years. Even if I didn't get caught, I would surely roast in hell for all eternity, and so would Velázquez. But those Venetians have no morals . . . and no fear of God. Titian's painting is so sexually charged—a reclining female nude in a landscape full of figures. As she sleeps—fully exposed—a satyr approaches, ready to pounce. I wonder who posed for that painting. Whoever she is, I'm telling you she has no shame and no fear of God because you can see *everything*.

She's enticing, all right, luscious and enticing. My Venus is discreet. I'm facing the back wall, rather than the spectator, and I invite him to admire me from a distance, nothing more. But *that* Venus . . .

There were other beautiful Titians in the collection as well—a whole series of mythological paintings created for Felipe II called *Poésie,* many of which featured magnificent nudes. Charles wanted them all, and in fact got a lot of them. He played that old trick, complimenting the host until he feels compelled to give you what you want out of courtesy. Felipe not only gave him some of the nudes but also Titian's portrait of Carlos V with a hound as a token of imperial power. Charles grabbed as much as he could.

Of course, I only know these things because Velázquez told me. And another thing I know: Charles's enthusiasm for Felipe's collection galvanized Velázquez. He began to realize just how much art was valued by great men. He began to understand what a treasure he possessed in his ability to create beautiful images. He also grasped, as he never had before, the power of this new kind of art, which men like Titian were producing. These weren't the staid and static paintings of Pacheco's workshop—this was fluid, dynamic, energetic art. Art that could offend, art that could inspire.

I realized something, too. I realized that the men in power, even our revered Felipe who ruled by divine mandate, were phonies, absolute hypocrites. I hope I die before anyone reads these pages because I'd surely burn at the stake for saying this. And yet, I just have to write it down and get this rage out of my heart. The powerful men at the palace that day—and their successors and all of the successors that will follow—they're all frauds. They make a public spectacle of their devotion to Catholic moral principles, even breaking the penises off of Roman statues and placing aprons over the loins of poor Jesus, naked and suffering on the cross. And then, in their private quarters, they pant over fleshy Venuses and Daphnes.

On August 18, all of Madrid celebrated the birthday of the infanta and future queen of England at an enormous party the king held on the palace grounds. The heat was so oppressive that your sweat boiled as it emerged from your pores. The Devil would have stayed away, preferring the cooler climes of hell, if his presence weren't required at the event.

But Velázquez was indifferent to the temperature. Some of the most important men in Europe were at this fete, and some of the most elegant women. Velázquez watched the goings-on with greedy eyes. Everywhere men in elaborately embroidered jerkins discussed the invasion of Lombardy by papal troops and the afternoon's bullfight in the same animated tones. The Spaniards wore mostly black or navy, although some of the younger men preferred a continental palette. The foreigners sported an array of hues, especially the Frenchmen, whose frilly shirts and pink, lilac, and baby blue suits elicited snickers from their Spanish cousins. Gorgeous young girls moved like inverted umbrellas over the grass or sat in groups, fanning themselves and giggling. Among the merrymakers wandered dwarfs, midgets, jesters, and clowns who somersaulted, juggled, gestured, and sang songs in high-pitched voices. His Majesty was particularly fond of monsters and kept scores of them for the amusement of his friends and children.

Velázquez fiddled with his mustache as his eyes darted from one spectacle to the other.

"It's so hot the eggs popped out of the hen hard-boiled."

The painter glanced around. A girl who looked to be about fifteen or sixteen, but had the bearing of a mature woman, was looking right at him.

"Are you speaking to me?"

"Who else would I be speaking to?"

Velázquez was not accustomed to such audaciousness in women. At home in Seville, girls were spirited, but no decent young lady would ever address a man in such a forward manner.

"Who are you?" she asked. "You don't look like a count or a duke."

Velázquez felt ashamed—was it so obvious from his attire and his conduct that he was a nobody? "I am Don Diego Rodríguez de Silva y Velázquez," said the painter as haughtily as possible. "Who are *you*?"

She ignored his question. "What is your position at Court?"

"I am a painter." He began to fidget. It was bad enough that "painter" conferred practically no status at all, but worse still that he didn't even know if he *had* a position at Court. He had not yet received an appointment. "I hope to be named to the royal corps very soon."

"I see. You hope to be, but you're not sure you will be."

Velázquez pursed his lips and didn't answer.

"And if you were appointed Court painter, would you paint me?" Velázquez gazed at his tormentor. She was a delicate-looking girl, with porcelain skin and flirtatious eyes. She wore her soft brown hair twisted into a high knot, elegantly fixed with wires and adorned with a jeweled coif. She wore a cream-colored dress with mutton sleeves, puffed at the top and tight from elbow to wrist, and a wide farthingale covered by a cream-colored skirt and a black overskirt scalloped at the hem. At her throat, smooth and white as alabaster, hung a heavy rope of pearls fastened by a diamond clasp and garnished by a medallion inset with rubies and sapphires that sparkled in the sunlight. Her waist was so slender that Velázquez thought he could encircle it with his two hands. She was sassy and bold, but she looked like an angel. The painter caught his breath.

"No," he said coldly.

"I am Doña Constanza Enríquez y Castro, and you would be wise to be nice to me. I am in the service of the queen." A French courtier in a pastel blue jacket and a billowing ruff strolled by. She paused. "I must go, but you will see me again."

She is fixed in my mind, this beautiful child. I see her soft white hands, two fluttering doves. I see her firm chin, her flushed cheeks, her smooth chestnut hair. I look down at my own withered fingers, gnarls like walnuts, splotches like mildew. I run my fingers under my own chin and feel the slack flesh of my jowl.

A moment later Velázquez felt the hot breath of Fonseca on his neck.

"I see that you are quickly mastering the art of the *galanteo*," murmured the chaplain.

Again, Velázquez was caught off guard. There was an uncomfortable pause. "I'm not . . . I'm not trying to woo anyone. I'm a married man."

"They're all married men. They're here at Court all alone, without their wives, so what's to keep them from seeking a bit of company to fill the lonely nights?"

Velázquez stared at the king's spiritual guide in disbelief.

"Besides," Fonseca went on, "it's expected. The Court is full of damsels and widows as well as married ladies who are only too happy to be 'served' by a gentleman. For example, Doña Constanza will desire you to follow behind on horseback when she accompanies the queen in her carriage to the Church of Nuestra Señora de Antocha. She will expect you to send her gifts—flowers, a tasty delicacy, a bauble, that sort of thing."

"But people will talk."

"At Court no one thinks anything of such trifles. People will be more apt to talk if you refrain."

"Are you advising me to . . ."

"I'm not advising you to woo anyone. After all, I'm a priest."

Three days later, on August 21, King Felipe IV hosted another party—this one in honor of the betrothal of Prince Charles Stuart and the Infanta María Ana. It was the most sumptuous celebration most Madrileños had ever seen. In the late afternoon, more than twelve thousand persons gathered in the Plaza Mayor to witness a *juego de cañas,* in which the participants—Christians all, but dressed as Moors—attack each other on horseback with light reeds. Each quadrille sported its own livery, which consisted of cloaks and hoods of dazzling colors, silk upon silk, sequins upon sequins, jewels upon jewels. They wore no armor, only brocade doublets and short wide pants, their arms and legs bare. Scimitars hung from their shoulders in gorgeously tooled casings. It was a windstorm of colors—reds and greens, turquoises and magentas, yellows and azures.

Velázquez was captivated by the brilliance of the spectacle. I can imagine him drinking in the luscious colors, the luminosity of sweat-drenched arms, the muscular gallop of the horses, the shifting forms of quadrilles that, like the specks in a kaleidoscope, gather, transform, and disengage. And perhaps he was also scanning the crowd for the brown-haired Constanza.

During the weeks following the betrothal party, Velázquez worked at a frenzied pace, and on August 30 he rapidly executed a small portrait of the king. To Don Felipe's delight, he reduced the royal head in length, thereby minimizing the obtrusive jaw. He also made portraits of Charles Stuart and the infante Fernando's favorite dwarf, Calabazas, as well as three or four sketches of minor courtiers and another of the infante Carlos's dog.

But more important, he learned the ways of the Court, for Court etiquette was no laughing matter. Any gaffe could be fatal. You had to know when to don your hat and when to remove it, how low to bow to a duke and how to address a count, the role of the *mayordomo mayor* and that of the *camarero mayor*. The king and queen kept separate households with parallel structures and staffs, and you had to learn who was who. You also had to know the order of things—who ate when, who preceded whom. Which dishes, which glasses, which knives. Which ruffs, which gloves, which feathers. You had to remember to yell and cheer at the Court theater as though it were a *corral*. And you had to perfect the *galanteo*, a practice the pleasure-seeking young king held in high regard.

With all these demands on him, Velázquez found no time to write to his wife and father-in-law. However, at the end of October Fonseca took pen to paper. I saw his letter myself—

Pacheco kept it for years folded between two pages of the man-
uscript of his book, *El arte de la pintura*. It was found among
his papers when he died.

My dear and esteemed friend,

*May Christ be with you and give you strength. I was deeply
saddened to learn of the passing of your little granddaughter.
Know that she rests with God and with the Holy Virgin, our
beloved mother, who will hold the child in her loving bosom for
all eternity.*

*Since I know you are anxious to learn news of Don Diego,
I hasten to inform you that your son-in-law has indeed acquitted
himself nicely at Court. On the 6th day of October of this year of
our Lord 1623, he was named royal painter with a stipend of
twenty ducats a month. He will be paid an additional sum for
any painting he produces. This last entitlement is a sign of His
Majesty's favor, for it has not been granted to other Court
painters. More significant still, Don Diego has been given the ex-
clusive right to paint His Majesty. Furthermore, he has been provided with comfortable lodgings on the Calle de Convalecientes,
which are probably worth some two hundred ducats a year. The
house is ample enough for the whole family and is located near
the Plaza Mayor and the Alcázar, in the vicinity of the count-
duke's own palace, so you can imagine how well-positioned it is.*

*Regarding the longed-for union between the Prince of England
and our own Infanta María Ana, I must apprise you of the failure
of the negotiations. His Majesty's sister quite rightly refuses to compromise her faith and marry a Protestant, even to avoid war. His
Majesty and the count-duke had entertained the illusion that Prince
Charles would embrace Catholicism upon his marriage to the*

infanta, but that was never his intention. When one thinks of His Majesty's extravagant expenditures, Prince Charles's rejection of the one true faith seems all the more treacherous. The greatest scandal of all is that the prince intended to make off with the entire collection of Titian's "Poésie" and had the canvasses all packed and ready to be shipped to England. It took considerable diplomatic intervention to get them returned.

In spite of this diplomatic setback, the mood at Court is optimistic. Olivares is so devoted to the king, rumor has it that he once kissed the prince's chamber pot as a sign of submission. Although we are still feeling the collective melancholia produced by the loss of our armada to the English more than three decades ago, the count-duke is determined to rebuild both national morale and the military. In the Low Countries, our troops continue to struggle to reclaim our hold on the Northern Netherlands. Last year the Dutch repelled our attack on the important fortress town of Bergen op Zoom, but the tide is certain to turn in our favor very soon, for Spain has always been the Almighty's most beloved nation. Money remains a problem, as the colonies are producing diminishing quantities of silver and the outlying provinces of the realm are beginning to rebel against the high taxes required of them.

There is also growing alarm here over Richelieu's recent rise to the rank of Cardinal. His influence in affairs of both Church and State makes him a formidable adversary for Olivares. His premier objective is clearly to challenge the supremacy of the Austro-Spanish Habsburg dynasty, and, although a Prince of the Church, he does not hesitate to forge alliances with Protestant states in order to achieve that end.

So you can see, my dear Don Francisco, that life here is full of challenges. I can assure you, nevertheless, that your precious son-in-law is advancing nicely in the favor of His Majesty.

I pray you remember me to your daughter Juana and grand-daughter Francisca. May God make you holy and protect you and your family from the Enemy, who lurks everywhere.

I humbly kiss your hands and feet,

Juan de Fonseca,

Sumiller de Cortina

Of His Majesty, our Most Holy Catholic King, Felipe IV de Habsburgo

There were a number of things Fonseca had refrained from mentioning to Don Francisco. One was the jealousy of Velázquez that was already brewing among the older Court painters. Another was a scene he had observed from his window the evening before: a chestnut-haired *doncella* had stepped into an elegant carriage and rode away, followed a few moments later by a young man on horseback in a dark suit, a black cape, and a wide-brimmed, feathered hat—a young man who looked very much like Velázquez.

7
Alterations
1623 – 1624

JULIA HELD UP A BURGUNDY DRESS WITH WHITE LACE AROUND the décolletage. "This one, *señora*?"

"Hmm, perhaps." The maid folded the frilly pink shawl she was holding and laid it on the dresser. "No, I've changed my mind . . . You can have that one, Julia. You love flounces more than I do."

"Thank you, *señora*. What about this one?" The blue gown in Julia's hands had a generous collar that billowed over the breast and wide sleeves trimmed with yellow braid.

"That trim . . ."

"I know, *señora*, but it's impossible to find good embroidery since the Moriscos left. We used to be able to get such beautiful handwork, but now we have to settle for braid."

Juana draped the dress over her left arm and squinted at the sleeve.

"Maybe once you get to Court, you can have a dress made in the French style," said Julia. "Oh, but this one is lovely, *señora.* You should certainly take it with you." She placed a gold silk gown with a long, pointed bodice and wrist-length puffed sleeves on the divan. The wide skirt billowed gracefully as it settled. "It hangs so nicely over a farthingale, and the rose-colored inner panel contrasts beautifully with the rest."

Juana took a deep breath and closed her eyes. "Yes," she said with a sigh. "I suppose you're right."

The maid was delighted that Doña Juana was showing some interest in packing her trunks. In the months that followed little Ignacia's death, she had lain in bed shrouded in melancholy during the day and floated through the hallways like a specter at night. When Fonseca's letter arrived shortly before All Souls' Day, 1623, Juana sank into a well of moroseness so black that Pacheco feared she would die. Almedina came by daily with exotic herbs from faraway places—*myristica fragans, aquilaria agallocha*—but nothing helped. Then, as Seville began preparations for Holy Week, Juana ventured out occasionally to visit Sister Inmaculada, sometimes hearing mass and taking her midday meal with the nuns.

"God bless the Carmelites," murmured Pacheco. "They're helping my poor child through this Calvary. And God bless Don Venturo Almedina and his magical herbs."

Holy Week in Seville is a paradox—a simultaneous explosion of contrition and color. Each guild parades through the streets in penitential garb of a distinctive hue—carpenters in blue, masons in gray, cobblers in green, painters in magenta. Men wail in remorse for their sins as they carry figures called *pasos* set atop richly carved wooden floats. In their long robes and pointed hats they wind their way through the streets from their local churches toward the cathedral, a trek that can take four hours or fourteen. Most guilds carry three *pasos*. The first is a scene that depicts either Christ's Passion or an aspect of His greatness, for example, the miracle of the loaves. The second consists of an image of Jesus himself, usually life-sized, with porcelain skin, blue-marble eyes, and human hair crowned with thorn branches. Last comes a figure of the Virgin, *la Dolorosa*, sorrowful but restrained, wearing the best dress the brotherhood can provide and adorned with garlands of flowers. After sundown, the three *pasos* are surrounded by candles that flicker and dance, casting an eerie glow on the figures as they move through the shadows.

As the painted sculptures float above the people lining the streets, they stare out with their glassy eyes and bless the crowd with their outstretched plaster hands. They sway to the rhythms of drums and trumpets beating out a joyous dirge, the sweet lamentation of communal suffering. I am a sinner, yes, but even so, I never fail to be moved, deeply moved, by the agony of Our Savior, and horrified by the wickedness of the men who nailed Him to the Cross.

During that Holy Week, Juana did not follow the procession on foot as she had in happier times, but instead sat by her window to watch it pass. "Oh, holy Mother," she whispered as Mary glided by. "Hold my beloved baby close to your heart." She wept silently into her handkerchief.

A few weeks after the pretty statues had been safely returned to their churches, Juana opened her eyes and blinked hard. Who was this little girl, this child of six with mutinous chestnut curls and heartbreaking eyes? Juana hardly recognized her. She remembered Francisca as a pudgy-cheeked toddler. But that had been half a year earlier, when her older daughter played by her side with a kitten and a ball of string while she, Juana, nursed Ignacia. The wise-looking child who stood before her now had a steady, unforgiving gaze. Her lips were pursed, as if holding back an accusation. Juana looked away.

She felt as if she should apologize, but how do you apologize to a six-year-old? And why should she, a woman who had suffered a terrible loss, have to beg forgiveness from anyone? Juana felt the floorboards go wobbly under her feet.

"Paquita . . ." she began. "Paquita, I've been . . ."

In the days preceding her rediscovery of the existence of her first-born child, Juana would often press one of Ignacia's soft blankets to her cheek. She would stroke a carefully hemmed diaper as though she were caressing the supple skin of the babe herself. She'd curl her fingers over its folds or hold the cloth to her nose as if searching for the pungent scent of baby pee.

But now, Juana realized, all that would have to stop. She had neglected Paquita. She had been looking to the Holy Mother for guidance, but she hadn't been listening to the Holy Mother at all. With her joyful music and outstretched arms, the Virgin had been trying to tell her to stop sniveling and get on with her life. "Be grateful for what you have," growled the Virgin in no uncertain terms. "I lost a child, too, and *He* was the son of *God*! Pull yourself together, woman!"

Juana resolved that from then on, she would rise early every day and head off to the Discalced convent, bringing Julia, Arabela, and Paquita with her. In the past, the sisters always cooed over the little girl, offering her sweets and lemonade. Now they would coddle her again. Francisca deserved to be coddled, thought Juana, and she deserved to be loved. Most of all, she deserved to be raised by a mother who did not ignore her.

Little by little Juana grew steady on her feet. She went to the kitchen and gave Ángeles instructions for dinner. She complimented Zoraída on her singing. She noticed a cobweb in a corner of the *sala* and ordered Lidia to dust the entire room. She inquired about Paquita's reading lessons and taught the child to use an embroidery hoop. She learned to put one foot in front of the next and get through the day.

Temperatures were rising, and Seville was preparing for another hellish summer. Venturo Almedina approached Pacheco one day in his study. "Perhaps," the doctor suggested cautiously, "a change of scenery would be good for Doña Juana."

Pacheco thought about it a while. "Madrid, maybe. I think it would do her good to join her husband at Court."

"What I had in mind was a trip to the country," said the doctor. "I'd be cautious about making any radical change right now. It's too soon after her loss."

But Pacheco insisted. "They've been apart too long. It's not healthy for either one of them."

"Well," said Almedina thoughtfully, "as she grows stronger, you could start sowing the seeds. What I mean is, you could mention the possibility of travel to see how she reacts. But please, Don Francisco, proceed slowly." It occurred to Almedina that Pacheco's motives weren't wholly altruistic—as royal painter, Don Diego would be in a position to recommend his father-in-law for a position at Court. On this subject, however, the doctor kept silent. "Any abrupt alteration in Doña Juana's routine could set her back," he added. "Her health is still fragile."

Pacheco rested his chin on his fist. "I understand, but a move to Madrid would require months of preparation. She'd have time to get used to the idea. Besides, the simple task of deciding what to take and what to leave behind would fill her time and distract her from her grief.

Almedina smiled. "Of course, Don Francisco."

"And she looks much better. She seems more alert. I think she could handle it."

To Pacheco's delight, Juana did not brush off the possibility of relocating to Madrid. On the contrary, the idea sparked a flicker of enthusiasm in her eyes.

"You will have a big responsibility," Pacheco explained, as though speaking to a four-year-old. "You will have to go through your wardrobe and decide which dresses to take. You should only take the essentials—we can have the rest sent later."

While Julia fretted over her frocks, Pacheco pondered the big issues: what to do about the school, for example. Should he close it down temporarily or entrust it to one of the advanced students? There was still much to decide, but Pacheco went ahead and wrote to his son-in-law to inform him of the arrival— not imminent, but absolutely certain—of his family.

Packing would be complicated, since Juana and Francisca would be staying in Madrid permanently while Pacheco would return to Seville.

In Madrid, the winter moon hung low in the sky, a frosty disk suspended like a hovering ice fairy. Under a shimmering firmament, three shadowy figures made their way down a nameless alley, hugging the walls and cloaking their faces. They were shabby-looking creatures. One wore a patched servant's cape and a wide, featherless hat with a droopy brim. Another had boots so scuffed they were nearly worn through. The third revealed moth-eaten britches as he tiptoed along the façades of crumbling buildings. When they reached an unmarked wooden door at the center of a row of decrepit houses, the most portly of the three lifted his hand to rap softly.

"*Ah de la casa*," he called in a gruff whisper. "Is anybody home? Cintia?"

In a moment the door opened and the face of a woman became visible behind a flickering candle. She looked to be in her forties and wore a flannel gown cut low on her ample breasts.

"Ah, count-duke," she said. "We were waiting for you."

"Shh!" whispered the man who had knocked. "Someone might hear you."

"Forgive me," whispered Cintia. "Come in!"

The three men slipped in through the door. Olivares threw off his cape to reveal an elegant suit of black velvet. He did not wear his customary symbols of power—the golden key and the golden spur that identified him as the *sumiller de corps* and the *caballerizo mayor*—but his bulk alone was enough to create an imposing figure. He had put on weight since Velázquez had met him in Seville, and his bloated trunk gave him an air of authority.

Cintia burst out laughing. "Quite a get-up, Don Gaspar! Your disguises get better every time!" The mole on her chin looked like a large tick.

"We left the carriage near the Plaza Mayor and came on foot to avoid being recognized, as usual," said the man in the worn boots. "Aside from a few straggly beggars sleeping in the street, no one was around."

Cintia sank into a low curtsy. "Your Majesty," she murmured, "it is always a pleasure to receive you in my humble abode. May I offer you some refreshment? Of course, I have nothing comparable to what you're used to, but I do have some fine Belgian beer."

"It's not your beer His Majesty is interested in, but yes, thank you, we'll have some," said Olivares with a snort.

"And this fine gentleman?" Cintia asked, gesturing toward the visitor with the threadbare britches.

"Don Diego Rodríguez de Silva y Velázquez, the royal painter," said Olivares, as though announcing a luminary at a state dinner. "Give him a frisky whore. His wife is coming to join him in a month or two. We expect him to settle into domesticity then."

"Marriage never stopped Don Felipe!" laughed the madam. "He's been a regular here since he was a mere pup—all thanks to your expert guidance, Don Gaspar!"

Velázquez was astonished at the familiarity with which Cintia treated the king. It's true, of course, that they were in a brothel in a seedy street in Madrid, but still, she knew that a monarch was no ordinary mortal. He was the presence of God on Earth. And this particular monarch was Felipe IV, King of Spain, the Low Countries, and the Spanish colonies, great grandson of the exalted Carlos I, on whose realm the sun never set.

"The venerable Doña Isabel de Borbón is quite aware of His Majesty's recreational activities, but she knows a man is a man," responded the count-duke easily. "Who do you have for His Majesty tonight?"

Velázquez noted that the king remained silent.

"Anyone His Majesty wants. We reserved the house for His Majesty, since the count-duke was kind enough to send word in advance that His Majesty was coming. We have a few exotic dishes on the menu tonight—a beautiful Brazilian with breasts like porcelain teacups, for example. There is also a baptized African girl of about fourteen and a blond German of monumental proportions. And, of course, our usual assortment of Portuguese standbys—not particularly gorgeous, but well seasoned. Oh, and a Morisca . . ."

Don Felipe's eyebrows contracted subtly.

"Oh, she's not really a Morisca, of course. Don't worry. What I mean is, she's as swarthy as an Arab, but she's actually Italian. Her family left her here when . . . because they couldn't support her. To be honest, I can't remember the details . . . I took her in out of Christian charity." Cintia paused a moment, realizing she had taken a false turn down a dangerous road. But Cintia was a consummate businesswoman with a cool head. She paused, took a swig of beer, and collected herself. "Or would you prefer your usual girl, Fabia?" she added as if as an afterthought.

The king chortled and left it to his counselor to respond.

"Hmm," laughed Olivares, "I think His Majesty will want to sample them all."

Don Felipe's appetite was legendary. Virgins, widows, matrons all fell prey to his desires. He didn't care if a woman was a duchess or a serving girl, a burgher or an artisan, an actress or a shepherdess, a water-seller or a nun, a princess or a prostitute. He didn't even care if his quarry was the child of one of his most illustrious courtiers. It was an open secret that he had seduced the nubile daughter of the Count of Chirel, giving her father command of the galleys in Italy to get him out of the way.

"Of course! As His Majesty wishes. And what about the young painter?"

Naturally, Velázquez wasn't the one who told me about this escapade. My informant was Cintia herself. I came to know her when she was an old woman. Gendarmes had closed down her house in the early 1630s acting on the official prohibition of prostitution, decreed in 1623, with the support of none other than the royal hypocrite himself, King Felipe IV.

Poor old Cintia had nowhere to go, but she did have plenty of money for a dowry, so she made her way to this convent and professed as a nun. "It's no thanks to the king that I have a few ducats saved up," she told me. "He was a stingy bastard, didn't even leave a tip." She didn't tell me much about Velázquez—not so much out of discretion, but because he wasn't high nobility. Her service to the king and his counselor was the real source of pride for her. She talked about it endlessly.

No wonder that later in life, Velázquez became obsessed with mirrors, reflections, and images within images. He must already have begun to grasp that Court was nothing but a game of doubles. The tatters the king wore to Cintia's house that night were no more the king himself than the splendorous velvets and brocades he wore in public. The beggar-king and the jewel-bedecked king were both fantasies that masked a hungry boy who was perhaps more real, more authentic, when he tumbled Fabia than when he played the omniscient, omnipotent, semi-divine ruler at Court. At least at Cintia's he could really assert power. In the palace, he was the pawn of Olivares, and of political circumstances not of his making. That night, Velázquez must have perceived the humanity beneath the image of the divine monarch.

Pacheco, Juana, and Paquita left for the Court early in April, after the worst of the winter snows. In December and January the mountain roads are nearly impassable, and blizzards turn the atmosphere into a frenzy of white and wetness. Drifts the size of men form and scatter like ghostly soldiers; they amass and then vanish into nothingness. The snow veils precipices over which intrepid riders tumble. They swathe fissures in the earth with a delicate white covering, which gives way to a void under pressure from a hoof. But by early spring, the treacherous weather has subsided. Most of the ice has melted, and a caravan of coaches, wagons, and mules can make its way northward through the narrow, rocky passages.

The first time Juana Pacheco de Velázquez talked back—really talked back—to her father was on February 3, 1624. Until that morning, preparations for the trip had gone smoothly. But it was time to make the final decision about who among the household staff would go and who would stay, and on this issue father and daughter did not see eye to eye.

Both agreed that Arabela would go, as she was needed to take care of little Francisca. Julia was Doña Juana's personal maid, and so likewise was indispensible. Neither of the women resisted—Arabela wanted only to be with her darling Paquita, and Julia was anxious to see the Court. Juana argued for including Ángeles, but Pacheco thought she was too old. She should stay behind, he said, along with the two slave girls, in order to prepare meals for the students. Juana was disappointed, but gave in without a fight. On the subject of Lidia, however, she was adamant.

"She's just a common housemaid!" she shouted, trembling with rage. "She can be easily replaced in Madrid."

Pacheco was not used to being contradicted, especially by his daughter. Nevertheless, in view of her delicate health, he thought it best to take an enlightened approach.

"As you say, Juanita, she's just a girl of no consequence, but she knows the household and she'd be useful." Pacheco was proud of his self-restraint. He sounded calm and paternal, he thought. But to Juana, he sounded patronizing.

"I don't like having her around," she said. "She's . . . sly."

"Sly?" laughed Pacheco. "Whatever can you mean? She's been with us for years and Don Diego is fond of her. I'm sure he'll feel more comfortable handing his household over to Lidia than to some unknown Madrileña."

Juana remembered the smirk on Lidia's face the day she'd interrupted Velázquez painting her as the Virgin.

"She's crafty and ambitious," hissed Juana. She was certain the girl would turn the lax atmosphere that reputedly reigned in Madrid to her advantage. "And she's a troublemaker! Besides, Diego already has a staff. We don't need her."

It was a gamble. Juana didn't actually know if Diego had need of a housemaid or not.

"Don't be silly, child," tutted Pacheco.

"I'm not a child!" exploded Juana. "I'm the woman of the house and I'm telling you that we don't require her services!"

Pacheco looked at his daughter long and hard, and then took a step toward her. He had never struck her, but his stance was menacing. They stood there staring at each other a moment, she with her lips pursed, he with his jaw set. Then he softened his gaze and smiled.

Two months later, when they set off for Madrid, Lidia, along with Arabela and Julia, rode in Pacheco's carriage with the family.

Madrid was nothing like Juana had imagined. She had expected wide, tree-lined avenues, palatial buildings, elegant coaches, stylish gentlemen, and fashionable ladies. But as the coach rolled into the city that morning, the odor of chamber pots still fouled the air, and the streets that radiated from the plaza were strewn with drunken soldiers sleeping off their hangovers. Clusters of poor wretches swarmed around alleys begging or scavenging for food. A ragged mother dragging a ragged child flashed a toothless smile at Juana through the window of the carriage. Her skin was pocked and furrowed, yet she had the firm, slight figure of a young girl. She could have been eighteen or eighty. Juana couldn't tell for sure. The woman thrust an open palm toward the curtain and Juana could see that her fingernails were broken and grimy.

"Oh, God," she whispered. "Why do You permit such suffering?"

"You know why God puts these creatures on Earth, Juana," said Pacheco matter-of-factly. "It's to permit the rest of us to earn salvation through acts of charity."

"Then why didn't you give that poor woman something?" snapped Juana. But by then the carriage had left the pitiful being and her ragamuffin little girl far behind.

"Don't be sanctimonious, Juana. Who knows if she's even a true beggar." Throughout Spain municipalities granted permits to certain poor souls, usually the blind, to beg in the streets and join the beggars' guild, but hundreds of uncertified wretches roamed the city with their hands out.

"Whether she is or not, she needs help."

Juana closed her eyes and clutched Francisca to her. In her mind she held the memory of the desperate woman stretching out her hand for a miserable coin, her shabby little daughter by her side. Had they eaten that morning? Had they foraged in the gutter for a piece of rotting fruit or a crust of bread? Would that poor mother ever abandon her daughter as she, Juana, had nearly abandoned Paquita? Juana pressed Paquita's little hand to her breast with such force that the child squirmed and pulled away.

Juana had seen poverty before. In the recent past, droughts had forced thousands of peasants off the land and into the cities. In Seville, countless beggars, impelled by starvation and plague, dragged their sore-infested bodies onto the cathedral steps to importune good Christians with cries of "*¡Por Dios, señora! ¡Por el amor a Dios, señor!* A penny for my starving baby!" But in Madrid, it was worse. In front of every church, stinking, festering throngs crowded around parishioners on their way to Mass. In the side streets, gangs of thugs congregated around pillars, ready to knock passersby to the ground and steal their bundles. Juana peered out of the carriage window at the shady-looking characters and shuddered. By the time they reached Velázquez's quarters on Calle de Convalecientes, she had decided that she didn't like the capital.

Juana entered her new house with her head bowed, then looked around with the startled eyes of a trapped fox. Velázquez smiled at her politely, as though she were a stranger, and perhaps she was. She had grown thin and wan since the loss of her baby.

"Doña Juana," he murmured. He held out his hand with what seemed like contrived gallantry, as though he were asking her to dance.

"Don Diego," she said, taking it. She curtsied awkwardly. "Paquita, greet your *papá*."

The child peered out from behind Arabela's skirts.

Julia unpacked Juana's trunks and aired out her dresses. Arabela transformed a room near Juana's suite into a nursery with two low beds, one with a feather mattress for Paquita and one with a straw mattress for herself.

Thanks to the demands of his position, Velázquez was away from home most of the time, so Juana had time to explore her husband's latest acquisitions—the Murano goblets and dishes with gold leaf and blue enamel, the Venetian beaker with applied decorations of pink and yellow, the brownish-red footed bowl of chalcedony glass, and the double-handled filigree vase. She wondered whether the man had come into a fortune, or if these treasures were gifts from the count-duke. She took charge of the staff and gave orders to her new cook. She hired a washerwoman and had her boil all the sheets. She kept Lidia so busy that the girl complained to the other servants that the *señora* was trying to work her into an early grave.

Velázquez was too busy to pay attention to the cleanliness of the sheets because the king required one portrait after the other. He had himself painted bedecked in armor, clothed in black and gold, standing, seated, on horseback. He sent paintings to friends and foes to make sure they knew who he was— the most powerful man on Earth. He had them hung in municipal buildings to inspire awe and respect in his subjects, and in private palaces to cement alliances. I saw some of these

paintings when I was at Court. I especially remember one equestrian that I really liked. It showed Felipe on an elegant black
horse with its forelegs raised. It was as if Velázquez had caught
the animal in motion, in mid-gallop, just before its hooves hit
the ground. It was not an unusual pose for a royal portrait, but
Velázquez gave it such life, such drama.

In Velázquez's portraits, the king was always regal, serious,
and aloof in his elaborate robes. These paintings were not meant
to capture the essence of the king's personality, but instead to
show him as a great monarch. He was the master, and the horse
was the unruly masses, which the king controlled with a loving
but firm hand. Portraits of the king are supposed to communi-
cate power, superiority, heroism, and authority, not tell you what
the king actually looks like.

But it wasn't only the king who took up Velázquez's time.
Olivares also required portraits. The count-duke had acquired a
mountainous figure, made even bulkier by his brocades and
enormous capes. His face had grown squarish, and his upturned
mustache resembled an angry, somber, inverted crescent moon,
or else the horns of a mad bull. Even though Velázquez posed
his subject at an angle to reduce his bulk, Olivares no longer
cut the dashing figure of his youth, and there was no way to disguise it. He looked supercilious and *antipático*.

During all this time, Velázquez never painted a portrait of
me. Even though I was right there at Court, he hardly noticed
me. Perhaps he was just too busy to pay attention to the young
brunette with the silky hair—the woman who worshipped him.
When he wasn't painting, Velázquez attended Court functions—hunting parties, banquets, that sort of thing. And when
he did have a free moment, he made his way to the *mentidero*,

or gossip corner, on the steps of the Church of San Felipe, at the intersection of Esparteros, Correo, and Calle Mayor.

As an aspiring courtier, Velázquez had to know what was going on both in and outside of Court. From the top of the steps of San Felipe, there was an excellent view of the surrounding districts, and thus the day's scandals. Without too much squinting, anyone who had time to kill—dukes and pickpockets alike—could see who was sneaking out of his house, and who was meeting whom. The local gossips knew what was going on abroad, as well. Velázquez learned, for example, about Charles Stuart, now king of England, and his constant fights with his new wife, the Frenchwoman Henrietta Maria of France, whom he'd married after the fiasco of his courtship to Princess María Ana here in Spain. The artist needed to hear such tidbits, so that he could bring them up at Court. Knowing the latest gossip cemented his position as an insider--but it was also beginning to produce resentment among the other Court painters, who weren't paid nearly as well—or as regularly—as Velázquez and who, unlike their rival, weren't at the center of things.

By fall Juana had settled into her routine in the house on Calle de Convalescientes. One day in the early winter, as Velázquez was painting the final flourishes on the ruff of one of the Court secretaries, threads of paint began to undulate before his eyes. He took a deep breath and blinked hard, but the lace wouldn't lie still. Velázquez wiped his forehead with the back of his hand. His brow felt clammy.

"Do you feel ill, Maestro?" Melgar asked nervously, approaching Velázquez as if to steady him.

"I'm not sure . . . do I look ill?"

"You look feverish. Would you like me to bring you some water?"

Velázquez swallowed saliva and realized that this throat was burning. "Yes," he said hoarsely. "Bring me some water."

The slave poured him a cup from a pitcher. As Velázquez brought the water to his lips, his hand trembled and his fingers shot outward. The cup crashed against the floor tiles, exploding like a fire grenade. Velázquez watched the spectacle as though it were happening elsewhere.

"The floor is dirty," he said finally.

"Maestro," murmured Melgar, "you're shivering. I'll take you home."

"I don't want to go home. I have to finish this while the light is good."

When Velázquez opened his eyes, he was lying in his own bed, bathed in sweat and smelling fetid. As if at a great distance he heard voices and recognized one of them as Juana's.

"Don't go in there again! You're disturbing him with your constant running in and out."

"I'm not disturbing him, *señora*. He's sound asleep."

"I order you to stay out of that room!"

"I just wanted to bring in this holly, *señora*, so that when Don Diego wakes up the room will look cheerful, not gloomy."

Juana glared at the maid as if trying to obliterate her with her gaze. "The vases are already bursting with holly, Lidia."

"It's just that I'm so worried, *señora*. He has been asleep for nearly three days. I pray and pray to the holy Virgin Mother, but . . ." Lidia gulped and opened her eyes imploringly, as if expecting sympathy for all her suffering.

Juana took a step backward and appraised the situation. She took a long, hard look at the maid: her alabaster complexion, her perfect brow, the mischievous wisps of chestnut hair peeking out from under her toque, her slim waist unthickened by childbearing, her dainty feet. She knew then what she had to do.

"Lidia," she said softly. "I appreciate your prayers. But I forbid you to enter Don Diego's room again."

Then, without waiting for a response or a curtsy, she turned and left the room.

8
Rivals and Plots
1626 – 1627

JUANA STOOD IN THE LIBRARY, FEET PLANTED FIRMLY, ARMS crossed, eyes hurling lightning bolts. "I insist! It's time! You have to attend to this!"

"I'm busy, Doña Juana! I'm writing a letter to Venturo Almedina to ask him to come take care of your dear husband."

"The count-duke sent his private physician to attend to my dear husband this very afternoon. Velázquez doesn't need Don Venturo."

Pacheco pretended to be very interested in sharpening his quill. He ran his knife smoothly down the nib. "I see . . ." he said after a long pause. "Why wasn't I told?"

"You were locked up in your apartments, father, perhaps reading Plato or doing something else similarly useful. You must take care of this. It's irresponsible to keep putting it off, and it's unfair to *her*!"

Francisco Pacheco was a mild-mannered man, but his daughter Juana was pushing him over the edge. She had always been somewhat strong-willed, and during her illness, she had gotten used to always getting her own way. Now she wouldn't take no for an answer.

"I'm sorry. This is not a good time. I have many things on my mind, what with Velázquez trying to get me an appointment as a Court painter . . ."

"Velázquez can't do anything for you now. He's lying on his bed with his back covered with leeches, under the supervision of the royal physician."

Pacheco grimaced. When had his homely, meek little daughter become such an imposing woman? She was still plain, but in Madrid she'd begun to treat her hair with a combination of black sulphur, alum, and honey to give it a soft, textured look. Back in Seville, Pacheco had forbidden the practice because Church moralists constantly inveighed against the evils of artificial hair color (so fashionable among the aristocracy), but he had to admit it looked quite pretty, really. Anyway, no matter how many times he forbade it, she ignored him. And now her maid Julia was coloring her hair, too. Juana had also taken to rubbing her hands with grease to soften them and lightening her skin with a powder made of egg whites, carbonate, and he couldn't imagine what else. Pacheco knew that all the Court ladies used makeup, but Juana? It was bad enough she'd become opinionated, but now she wanted to be stylish, too!

Pacheco sighed and rested his head in his hands. "All right," he grumbled, "I'll try."

"Someone of her own class."

"Of course. Lidia's a pretty little thing, and I can give her a small dowry. It shouldn't be that hard to find her a husband."

"Well, please make sure you don't forget, father."

Every day for weeks, Don Antonio Benazar, private physician to the count-duke of Olivares, visited Velázquez with compounds and elixirs. He made compresses of camphor and eucalyptus to open the chest. He prescribed teas of dandelion leaves to clean the blood. Lidia and the other maids wailed and prayed the rosary. How could God allow this to happen to their dear Velázquez? But not everyone was wailing. Rumor had it that the count-duke had petitioned Pope Urban VIII for an ecclesiastical benefice of three hundred ducats a year for the painter, and the pope had granted it. When the other Court painters heard, they were furious. Vicente Carducho and Eugenio Cajés hadn't been paid for months, and Angelo Nardi had been appointed without any salary at all. To Velázquez's rivals, it seemed only fair that a serious affliction should befall an artist who was paid far more than they for doing the same work.

Fonseca, who made it his business to know everything that went on at Court, especially as concerned his compatriot Velázquez, kept his ears open. Snippets of conversations floated through the royal atelier and over the din at Court functions. You could gather essential tidbits during a supper, before the theater, after the bullfights, or even during a hunt. Everywhere, Velázquez's name was spoken in whispers, the "th" of the second and third syllables sounding like a breeze through leaves: *Veláthqueth, Veláthqueth, Veláthqueth.*

"He paints directly from nature like that Italian barbarian Caravaggio!"

"He shuns the copybooks for real life!"

"He's nothing but a portraitist, a painter of heads! He can't paint a story."

"He's godless! He hardly finds inspiration in the bible . . ."

"Or in Our Holy Mother Mary!"

"And he's the king's pet, with those stipends and benefices! And his big house on Calle de Convalescientes!"

"They say there's no money in the royal treasury, but they always find money for *him*, for *Veláthqueth*!"

"Now that he's good and sick, let the Devil take him!"

"The Devil take him!"

Fonseca knew he had to act. Petty gossip would not only destroy the king's favorite, it would sap the energy of the other royal painters and diminish the quality of the art produced at Court. The honor of the Crown depended on Spain's ability to produce great artwork, not just her ability to combat Protestants in the north and subdue Indians in the colonies. He had to devise a plan to establish an absolute, unassailable hierarchy among the Court painters. It was the only way to put an end to this jealousy, this backbiting and squabbling. If everything went right, Velázquez would come out on top, and that would be the end of it. But he couldn't do it alone—he needed help.

Lidia was sweeping leaves off the walkway when Arabela signaled to her to come into the house. "I'm busy!" snapped Lidia. "If I don't finish this, by tomorrow you won't be able to find a path across the garden!"

The maid had been ill-tempered of late, observed Arabela. She must suspect that something was brewing. Everyone had heard Doña Juana's muffled voice through the thick library doors. "Lidia . . . see to it . . . attend to it . . . someone of her own social class . . ." Like Lidia herself, Arabela assumed that Doña Juana wanted to marry the girl off to some stable boy. But Lidia was going to fight it tooth and nail and not give in. She had no wish to leave the service of Don Francisco.

"You're wanted in the library."

Lidia didn't budge. "I'm too sweaty and messy to go into the library. I've been sweeping and cleaning all morning."

Arabela was a small woman, but she was old enough to be Lidia's mother. Her son was older than Lidia and she'd nursed the lady of the house with her own breasts. She was not about to take any guff from a cheeky housemaid, a nobody. She marched over to the girl and stood in front of her.

"When the master calls, you obey," she growled.

"I'll go in a minute."

Arabela kicked over the pile of leaves and debris. "You'll go now!" She grabbed the broom from Lidia's hands.

The color was rising in the girl's cheeks. She clutched the edge of her apron. Her knuckles were white. Her jaw was quivering.

"Go!" hissed Arabela.

Lidia grabbed back the broom, then threw it down and marched into the kitchen. She leaned over a basin and splashed water on her face and wiped it with a rag. Finally, she trudged back through the courtyard and into the house. She stood in front of the library door a while, as if trying to muster the courage to knock.

Arabela waited out of sight in an alcove until Lidia entered, then tiptoed into the hallway and strained to hear what was taking place behind the library door. But she could hear nothing.

She expected a shriek or a sob. She expected Lidia to emerge wailing and pawing the ground. Instead, she came out of the library with a confident smile. Chin raised, eyes front, she sashayed past Arabela and disappeared into the yard.

That night, Fonseca was relaxing in front of the fireplace, a glass of brandy in his hand. He sniffed the liquor with his pointy nose, then slouched back in his chair. He smiled. Things were going according to plan. The count-duke had endorsed his idea of an artistic competition, and they had selected February of the following year as the date. The king himself had chosen the subject: Felipe III's expulsion of the Moriscos. It was a glorious theme intended to celebrate the Habsburgs as champions of the faith, and Fonseca couldn't be happier. Now Velázquez would be able to demonstrate that he was perfectly capable of producing a narrative painting, that he wasn't a mere portraitist. The winning canvas would be hung in the *salón nuevo* of the Alcázar, a place of honor that would give the young man constant exposure.

Of course, Velázquez still had to win, and there could be no slipups. Because the whole purpose of the competition was to enable his fellow Sevillano to crush his rivals, Fonseca couldn't take any chances. With impartial judges, Velázquez's victory was not assured. Only a few months earlier Cardinal Francesco Barberini, a highly respected connoisseur of art who was visiting the Court, had called Velázquez's work melancholy and severe. Well, thought Fonseca, what could you expect from an Italian? They were all daft from the intense sunlight. Overfed and oversexed. Barberini wanted rich colors. He wanted bright reds and oranges! No, thought Fonseca, the competition couldn't be left in the hands of the likes of Barberini.

Fonseca picked up a quill and scribbled a note to Olivares, then rang for a servant. The next afternoon he and the count-duke sat down without secretaries or assistants to work out a secret strategy.

The count-duke puffed on his pipe and took a sip of chocolate, the favorite drink of aristocrats. "We need friendly judges," he mused.

"My thoughts exactly," murmured the royal chaplain. "Not de Fabrizzi. He's too honest."

"And not Severino, either. He's too old-fashioned."

"You're right. We need someone who appreciates the modern style, someone who isn't mired in the old copybooks."

"Someone who values strong characters drawn from life."

"Friar Maino?"

"Yes, Maino—of course!"

"And what about Crescenzi?"

"Perfect!"

Both Maino and Giovanni Battista Crescenzi were admirers of Caravaggio. Maino respected Caravaggio's close imitation of nature, as well as his sense of the dramatic, which he achieved through radical shifts from light to dark. Maino's use of chiaroscuro and vibrant color showed him to be a true disciple of the master. He had lived in Italy and was up on the latest trends. Of late he painted little, which was an advantage. He wasn't in competition with Velázquez and so could probably be persuaded to advance the Sevillano's career.

Crescenzi was even more reliable. He was an Italian who liked the modern style, but he painted mostly flowers, not Madonnas or portraits. In reality, he was more an architect or a designer than a painter. He had adorned many papal buildings, and in Madrid he had helped decorate the Pantheon of the Kings in El Escorial. The king loved him, and Crecenzi was eager to stay in his good graces. If that meant tipping the scales in favor of Don Felipe's favorite portraitist, Fonseca was confident that Crescenzi would make the right choice.

Within a week, both artists had agreed to serve as judges for the royal painting competition. With this accomplished, Fonseca turned to Velázquez, whose health was slowly improving. He visited him daily, insisting with great urgency that to win this competition, the artist needed accomplish something spectacular. If he didn't, everyone would suspect the worst, and instead of silencing Velázquez's rivals, the competition would only provide them with ammunition against him.

I only saw Velázquez's painting once, and very briefly, so my memory of it is vague. I recall a regal figure with an outstretched arm, and hordes of Moriscos in turbans and *marlotas* trudging out of Spain toward the golden picture frame. Velázquez told me that the night before the judging, he couldn't sleep, couldn't even close his eyes. Fonseca slept like a dead man, certain that his protégé would take home the prize, but Velázquez paced the floor until the first hints of sunrise.

"Things are never as they seem," he told me years later, when I asked him why he had been so nervous. "You think people are one way, and they turn out to be another. You think they'll do one thing, and they do something completely different. You see masks. You see mirrors. You never see the truth."

By the time he told me this, he was an old man. He knew that behind the veneer of propriety and decorum that reigned at Court, everything was rotten to the core—rotten, putrid, and decomposing.

I can remember one other detail about Velázquez's painting. Among the masses of Moriscos exiting Spain, there were two familiar faces. Faces I never expected to see in *The Expulsion of the Moriscos*—women's faces. One belonged to Lidia. The other belonged to a woman whom I had often seen in Court, although I didn't find out her name until much later. It was Constanza.

If Juana had been a cat, her tail would have been twitching.

"How *could* you? What were you thinking?" She emitted a low growl, distinctly feline.

"He's the perfect match, Juana. A carpenter, like Our Lord Jesus Christ." The tone of Pacheco's voice made it clear he had no intention of discussing the matter further.

"That's not the point and you know it!"

"Juana! What's gotten into you? In God's name, how dare you speak to me in that tone of voice? I am your father!"

Juana crossed her arms and stared right into his eyes. "You know what I'm talking about. The Gómez boy is an apprentice to Emilio Fuentes Toledo."

"Exactly. The master carpenter at the Alcázar."

"And you thought I would approve of Lidia marrying a member of the palace staff?"

"A member of the palace staff? He's an apprentice carpenter, Juana, not the *sumiller mayor!*"

"An apprentice carpenter at the palace, father. At the palace!"

"What difference does it make?" Pacheco lowered his gaze. "Oh, Juana, don't tell me you're afraid that Lidia . . ."

"Now Lidia is at the Alcázar night and day . . . washing laundry, emptying chamber pots, dusting furniture . . . I don't know . . . whatever they give her to do . . ."

"And you think she'll find her way into Velázquez's studio."

"I'm sure she already has! Maybe they've assigned her to some paramour of the king who thinks it's amusing to help chambermaids wriggle their way into the beds of married men. Everyone knows Don Felipe's Court is a crucifix-adorned brothel."

"Juana! Control yourself. You're speaking about our king, God's instrument on Earth."

"Our most Catholic king, who weeps like a magdalene during mass and then screws himself blind in a different bed every night! Don't play dumb, father. Everyone in Madrid knows about the king's escapades."

This was true, of course. Pacheco had to have known what every scullery maid and chandler in Madrid knew: that our most Catholic King Felipe IV had watered more flowers than any gardener. Pacheco pretended to study some sketches on his desk while he tried to decide what to say. He could have ordered Juana out of his office. He could have bared his teeth and lunged. Instead he said calmly, "I wouldn't worry about it, daughter. Lidia has been married for a month already. I imagine she'll be with child before long."

Juana felt hot tears on her lids. Her nose quivered and went runny, and her temples throbbed as though a horse had kicked her in the head. She squinted and turned away so that her father wouldn't see her cry. Back in her *estrado* she thought long and hard. In order to protect what was hers—her honor, her self-esteem, her family—she would have to take risks. She would have to work her way into the inner recesses of the Alcázar. The price of failure would be terrible, but Juana was willing to take a chance.

The king himself announced the winner of the competition on February 18, 1627. No one was surprised. All the contestants knew the cards were stacked in favor of Velázquez. Carducho, Cajés, and Nardi had all created respectable paintings, but they had no illusions. Only Velázquez thought the judges might actually render a fair verdict, but in the end, whether they did or not remains their secret. At any rate, everything worked out just as Fonseca had planned. Velázquez was declared winner and crowned with laurels, while the others were fed myrrh. The king was ecstatic because his favorite had proven himself. By then, Barberini had long since left Madrid, so there was no one to contradict the judges.

Rewards soon followed. Less than a month later, Velázquez was named usher of the privy chamber, his first appointment to the royal household. It was a minor assignment, but for a man who wanted desperately to advance in the royal hierarchy, it was a crucial first step. As a mere painter, Velázquez was barred from advancement, but as an usher he could aspire to more grandiose titles in the future. And he could now draw a salary from the budget of the royal household, more substantial and secure than that of the Committee of Works, which was normally tasked with paying artisans. Given his brilliant horizons, Juana knew it was the wrong time to bring up Lidia, so instead, she cooed and smiled and fawned over her husband.

But Velázquez hardly noticed his wife's hyperbolic displays of affection, her extravagant praise, her brandied flan (prepared by the cook, but ordered by the lady of the house), or her availability in bed. His attention was elsewhere—on the fascinating newcomer to the Court: Peter Paul Rubens.

Velázquez had been writing to Rubens for some time about an engraved portrait of Olivares the great Flemish painter was preparing. Velázquez had supplied the model, but Rubens didn't care for it and changed it radically. Velázquez bit the bullet and took the great master's criticisms in stride. Criticism, after all, was a thousand times better than indifference. The fact that Rubens paid any attention to him at all was a compliment.

Anyway, Velázquez liked Rubens and knew that he could learn from him, for the old Flem was exactly the kind of courtier-artist he aspired to be. Rubens was the epitome of sophistication—diplomat, statesman, intellectual. He had come to Madrid to complete the groundwork for a peace treaty with England, but he had not forgotten that the Spanish king was an art lover and had brought many of his paintings with him. A few months later a series of exuberant tapestries for the royal Convent of the Descalzas Reales arrived. Velázquez studied the new works. In his style, Rubens was more Italian than Flemish. His biblical and mythological paintings were replete with luxurious bosoms and cheerfully displayed buttocks. Studying the Flemish painter's richly sensual work, Velázquez recalled Barberini's criticisms of his own art: melancholy, drab, lacking in color.

King Felipe was, of course, enthralled with Rubens. Violating the monopoly he had conceded to Velázquez, he commissioned the visitor to create a number of royal portraits, including a sculpted bust. If Velázquez felt slighted, he never said as much to me. And anyway, he was astute enough not to come between the king and his honored guest and, more important, to recognize Rubens as a teacher, not a rival.

In comparison with his own austere portraits, Rubens' were vibrant and plastic. The Flemish master placed the monarch in luxurious architectural settings and lush landscapes. Velázquez saw that next to the master's, his own portraits were drearily unsophisticated. King Felipe noticed it, too, and replaced Velázquez's equestrian portrait in the new gallery of the Alcázar with one by Rubens.

One day the Flem invited Velázquez to spend a few days with him at the Escorial. "*Hijo*," he said, as they wandered around one of the upstairs galleries, "you are a young man of great potential."

Velázquez smiled at Rubens's efforts to speak Spanish. "Thank you, Maestro."

"I think we can both learn important lessons from the great Titian, don't you?"

Velázquez knew what Rubens was doing. The old master didn't want to embarrass or lecture the younger man, so instead, he pretended they were both taking lessons from Titian. They walked around the gallery, commenting on the paintings—on the sense of movement produced by a twist of the hand or a creeping shadow, on the element of surprise created by an unexpected grouping.

Over the next few weeks Rubens did a series of copies of works by Titian and as he painted, he commented on the originals. Velázquez came to better understand Titian's use of light and color and his manipulation of body position. As he walked through the galleries with Rubens at his side, he was overcome by a sense of exuberance, but also by a familiar disquiet. The moon came to mind, the intense white moon that one night in Seville had threatened to fall out of the sky and come crashing down on his head. He was suffocating in Madrid. There was nothing more for him to learn here. In order to grow as an artist, he had to go to Italy. But how could he walk away from his position at Court and cross the Mediterranean? And yet he knew he had to find a way because when he closed his eyes and dreamed, the embrace that beckoned to him was not a woman's —not Lidia's or Constanza's or even Juana's—but the sumptuous, sensuous embrace of the Italy of his imagination.

9

New directions
1628 − 1629

HER SCREAMS CURDLED YOUR BLOOD. THEN CAME THE POUND-
ing—the explosive racket of someone banging at the door.
"Let me in!"

More pounding. Thunderous pounding that made your
head throb.

She charged into the room with the fury of a tornado, her
dress in tatters, her disheveled hair falling across her eyes.

The councilmen gasped in amazement. What horror had
befallen her? Her jaw was bruised, and angry cuts crisscrossed
her arm. An abrasion the size and color of a wine-soaked host
defiled her shoulder.

The girl tossed her head and wiped her hair out of her
eyes. Her whole body trembled as she approached the mayor,
her father. She turned abruptly and stared into the distance, her
eyes glistening like emeralds. Through the shredded chemise
her skin shone white and smooth as marble.

"I have as much right as anyone to stand here in this circle of men! Even if a woman can't have a vote, she can have a voice!"

Esteban, the mayor, took her arm. "Daughter! Laurencia!"

"Don't call me your daughter!"

"But why . . . ?"

"I'll tell you why! Because you allowed that bastard to abuse me! Where were you when I needed someone to defend me? Fernán Gómez dragged me off before your very eyes, and what did you do? Nothing! None of you! What kind of shepherds are you, that you let the wolf invade your fields and carry off your lambs! And you call yourselves men! You're nothing but sheep!"

Eyes blazing, Laurencia flung her arms wildly. Her exquisite torso twisted and writhed, drawing attention to her smooth neck; her minuscule waist; her firm breasts, youthful and high.

Don Felipe held his breath. He couldn't take his eyes off her.

"No wonder they call this place Fuenteovejuna, the sheep well! You sheep! You cowards! You're no manlier than rabbits. You're barbarians, not Spaniards! Chickens! Why don't you dress up in skirts, with thimbles in your pockets? Why do you carry weapons if you're afraid to use them? Arm the women! We'd do a better job than you of protecting this village!"

Her voice rang through the theater like the bell of a cathedral, melodious and rich.

"Who is she? I have to have her," the king whispered to Olivares.

"María Inés Calderón. She's only sixteen."

"Get her for me."

Laurencia threw back her shoulders and lifted her chin.

The arch of her back sent tingles into His Majesty's groin.

"Give me stones, and the first ones I'll hurl them at are you cowards! Spinning girls! Sissies and faggots! Tomorrow we'll dress you in farthingales and bonnets. We'll paint your lips and powder your cheeks. The age of the Amazons will return! The women of Fuenteovejuna will give this town back its honor!"

The audience roared its approval. María Inés Calderón had once again thrilled the city of Madrid with her brilliant interpretation of the role of Laurencia in Lope de Vega's *Fuenteovejuna*. Only a consummate actress could play Laurencia, the peasant heroine who rebuffs the advances of the evil *comendador*, and then fights him off with tooth and claw when he tries to rape her.

Spectators leapt to their feet, applauding wildly, even those aristocrats who had more in common than they'd like to admit with the *comendador*. Lope had set the action in the times of King Ferdinand and Queen Isabella, more than a hundred years earlier, so that none of the noblemen in the audience could feel alluded to.

The afternoon when María Inés—La Calderona, as she was known— played Laurencia to a packed house, I was seated in the *cazuela*, the women's section, wholly engrossed in the show. By the end of the day, all Madrid was gossiping about what had happened at the Corral de la Cruz, not during the performance, but afterward. In every bodega and *mentidero* you could hear snorts and chortles and snickers as people invented and embellished details. Don Felipe had entered the theater incognito through a secret passage, along with his inseparable companion, the count-duke of Olivares. That in itself was unremarkable. The king and queen often attended performances, and they usually came in through a clandestine entrance to avoid being importuned by the mob. Nor was it unusual that by the final bows the king had fallen desperately in love with the leading lady. But what *was* extraordinary was that it took him less than an hour to get her flat on her back in his bed with her knees splayed and her future assured. I should say her immediate future, rather than her entire future because the king was notorious for tiring easily of his paramours.

By the next morning, the gossip mill was grinding full speed. According to—well, everyone—the breathtaking young actress had a very tight hymen—so tight, in fact, that it frustrated the king's efforts to enter her. In a frenzy, His Majesty called for the royal surgeon, who performed an emergency operation on the willing but impenetrable Calderona. Before she had even had the chance to heal, the king jumped on her and had his fun, which left the girl barely able to walk for an entire month— in spite of which she performed superbly every afternoon at the Corral de la Cruz for the run of the play.

For the city's scandal sheets, which at the time were gaining enormous popularity, La Calderona was a godsend. Madrileños reveled in the stories of her bedroom tricks, which, of course, they had no way of knowing. She was, they said, an extraordinary acrobat who could make love while doing a headstand, a sideward leg extension, or the splits upside down. Felipe and his Calderona were the subject of conversation for years, and the affair even figures in the chronicles.

Though I have no way of proving the stories of the girl's

sexual prowess, I can say with certainty—because I saw it with my own eyes—that within days of their encounter, La Calderona pushed her way into Court company, parading around as if she were a duchess, instead of the king's slut. She sashayed through the halls of the Alcázar in brocades and ermine, which only nobles were allowed to wear. She attended dinners and hunts. She showed up at bullfights and *cañas*. All of this was tolerated, until one day she went too far.

The occasion was a visit from an emissary of the House of Gonzaga, in Mantua. The Crown was bankrupt. Olivares had just announced the suspension of all payments to the palace staff, with the exception of Velázquez, who continued to receive his salary. Moneys owed to debtors would not be paid. Donations to the poor would be put on hold. In spite of this, the king ordered massive festivities to impress the Mantuan dignitary, with processions and dancing and *cañas* in the Plaza Mayor.

The spectacle was well underway when María Inés Calderón, flaunting a velvet fur-trimmed cape fastened with a diamond brooch the king had reputedly given her, sailed brazenly down one of the streets that edged the Plaza Mayor and then disappeared with her entourage into a building. Moments later she reappeared, chin high, eyes defiant, on one of the balconies overlooking the square.

The balconies were reserved for aristocrats—usually those who owned the houses on the Plaza Mayor, or the titled friends they invited to view royal celebrations from this privileged post. But there, in full view, was La Calderona. She smiled and waved to the crowd as though she were taking bows on a stage. No one knew who had invited her, but she was there nonetheless, flirting with her admirers from midair. She moved with the boldness and grace of a Laurencia, the character she played in Lope's *comedia*.

Suddenly, a hidden hand flung open the door behind her. A commotion erupted on the balcony. Royal guards appeared and shoved the actress to the side. La Calderona scanned the street, as though looking for an escape route. She couldn't exit through the balcony door, which was blocked by soldiers. She couldn't jump from the balcony, which was two floors above the street. Another girl might have trembled in terror, but La Calderona glared at the men defiantly. Sneering, she turned toward her admirers on the street, who cheered her on.

But then the gleeful hoorays stopped abruptly. The soldiers parted and another figure appeared on the balcony: a beautiful woman with regal bearing. She wore a sumptuous dress of brocade, heavily bejeweled, with a tight-fitting bodice and wide, flowing sleeves of a silk lighter in color than the bodice. The collar, white and trimmed in silver ribbon, was of the kind they call a Medici collar: raised in back and held in place by a wire form. It was the queen.

Isabel de Borbón was known to be an easy-going woman, jovial and tolerant of her husband's indiscretions. In fact, she reputedly had had an indiscretion or two herself early in their marriage. But in spite of her complacency, Isabel de Borbón had no intention of ignoring María Inés Calderón. The actress's presence at Court was an embarrassment, her brazenness an insult. Her relationship with the king was making Doña Isabel the butt of endless jokes in the *tertulias* and *mentideros* of Madrid. And now the cheeky girl had intruded into a space reserved for nobility. She, Isabel de Borbón, was not going to stand for it. She pushed through the soldiers and stood before La Calderona. If a moment before the actress was defiant, now she was flummoxed. She hesitated a moment, then bowed her head and curtsied deeply.

Isabel raised her left hand and pointed to the balcony door. She said only one word: *"Fuera!"*

María Inés disappeared. By the end of the day bad couplets were circulating about the incident all over Madrid. For example, this one:

> The *reina* took the *puta* by surprise
> And zapped her with a bolt from her eyes.

Or this one (and please excuse the vulgarity):

> The king's slut may be a good fuck,
> But now she's really out of luck.

From that day on everyone referred to the balcony as— and now, once again, I have to beg you to forgive me—the Balcony of Marisuperfuck, in honor of La Calderona's prowess.

Everyone thought the actress would hightail it out of town after that, but she did no such thing. Instead, she continued her career on the stage. She didn't have to work, of course. The king continued to give her everything, and he even secured her a permanent seat for Court celebrations on another balcony on the Plaza Mayor. But María Inés relished acting and the adulation of the crowd, and she wasn't about to give that up.

Some time in 1629 La Calderona gave Don Felipe a son, Juan de Austria. The king had high hopes for the boy and fulminated against any anyone who disparaged him for being illegitimate. After all, the illustrious Carlos V, the king's own great-grandfather, had also produced a bastard son, the first Juan de Austria, who had become one of Europe's greatest military leaders.

I remember the year of Don Juan's birth because not long afterward, on October 29, the queen gave birth to Prince Baltasar Carlos, Felipe's first legitimate son. All Spain rejoiced.

As for La Calderona, she realized that now that an heir to the throne existed, her moment of glory had passed. She begged the king to allow her to retire to a convent. Maybe he resisted. After all, she was still young and beautiful, and she had provided him with many hours of pleasure. Nevertheless, he let her go. The last I heard, she was abbess of some obscure nunnery in Alcarria. The king didn't release her child, of course. The royal couple had already lost several infants to disease, and he wasn't about to put all his eggs in the basket of legitimacy. He entrusted little Don Juan to a wet nurse and had him raised near the palace. But wait, I'm getting ahead of myself. Let's go back to the incident on the balcony.

Doña Juana rarely visited the *mentideros*, but that afternoon, she had been in the Plaza Mayor and had seen for herself the confrontation between the queen and the actress. Now she wanted to know what people were saying. She put on her black cape and a mantilla of the kind the authorities had banned over and over again to prevent women from doing exactly what Juana was doing now: sneaking out of the house incognito. As she and

Julia worked their way through the narrow streets, they pulled their veils across their faces and kept their gaze to the ground. She made her way to the steps of San Felipe and wandered around the crowd, ears cocked. "The cuckold queen," people were calling Isabel de Borbón. "The wronged wife, betrayed and discarded."

"Must be desperate, to shove her husband's lover off the balcony like that," opined an old woman.

"Must be a lousy lay, if you ask me," snickered another. "If he got what he needed at home, he wouldn't be out prowling at night with that pimp, the count-duke."

"All men prowl," growled the first. In front of the door of the cathedral a blind beggar sang:

> Poor Queen Isabel
> He's made her life
> A living hell.
> He won't come near her anymore.
> He'd rather fuck his actress whore.

The crowd yelped in glee and the poets among them launched their own round of verses. Before they got to the most vulgar of the couplets, Juana had made up her mind. It was time to put her plan into action. It was an audacious plan, but Juana was determined. After all, her own honor was at stake—hers and that of her daughter. If she did nothing, she risked becoming the butt of all kinds of jokes, just like Doña Isabel. Madrileños can be very cruel.

To obtain an audience with the queen of Spain is no simple thing, but Juana wasn't starting from nowhere. There was her husband's status, of course, and the many royal affairs she had attended with him. She had kept the company of countesses and chitchatted with ladies-in-waiting. She had even been presented to the queen once or twice, although she didn't expect Doña Isabel to remember her. Still, there was no chance that Juana would appeal to Fonseca or any of her other friends at Court for help, for what she was planning to do had to be done in secret. And the queen was well insulated, so she could not be easily approached.

Like all queens before her, Queen Isabel had her own staff, independent of the king's. Among Doña Isabel's many attendants were the *meninas*, referred to by the Portuguese word for "little girls" because they wore flat shoes, like children. These women were personal companions, whose job it was to accompany and entertain the queen. And then there were the *dueñas*, usually older women who served as second mothers to the queen, who, after all, lived far away from her own mother at the French Court. In addition, there were scores of personal servants—chambermaids, dressers, and hairdressers. There was an attendant in charge of the queen's jewels, another in charge of her clocks and watches, and still another in charge of her linen. There was a maid to bathe and perfume her and another to empty her chamber pot, and also countless minor servants, both male and female: cooks, assistant cooks, sweepers, scrubwomen, laundresses and ironers, not to mention carpenters, gardeners, blacksmiths, grooms, and stable boys.

How, Juana wondered, could she make her way through this human labyrinth to get to Doña Isabel? She could imagine the face of the third assistant majordomo when she, the wife of an artisan, asked for an audience with the queen. Petty bureaucrats like him loved to say no to women like her. In the end, she offered a gold coin to a chambermaid, who was reputedly sleeping with Majordomo Number Three, to get her an appointment with him. When she finally saw him, she gave him a thick gold chain to put her on the queen's calendar. It was expensive, but it worked.

When Juan de Fonseca scrunched up his mouth and looked out at the world through half-closed eyes—which is what he did when he was thinking—he looked more like a ferret than ever. On this day in May, 1629, a few weeks after the scandalous encounter on the balcony, he appeared so ferret-like that a dachshund might have hunted him down for his master to pelt. Velázquez wanted to go to Italy, and Fonseca knew that the boy's instincts were right—every great artist had to spend time in Italy. Tastes were changing, and a new, more elaborate style was developing—one that sought to capture moments of intense dramatism, of surprise or shock, one that was intensely psychological. The only way for his protégé to become a true luminary, thought Fonseca, was to learn the new approach through direct contact with Italian painters.

But the king balked. He wanted Velázquez to remain just where he was, so that he could paint Court portraits. Don Felipe depended on him to produce images of himself and his courtiers that would awe and inspire the people. Now that Rubens had left Spain, he didn't trust anyone else.

"But Your Highness," argued Fonseca, "how much better he will render your image when he has absorbed the new techniques. The boy is a genius. He will be the greatest painter in

Europe. Spain will be the envy of the world, not only for its splendid armies, but for its art."

"It's worth considering," he conceded, without making any further commitment.

Eventually, the king did decide to grant Velázquez a leave of absence and a stipend, but the old priest knew that the flimsiest contretemps could cause Don Felipe to change his mind. Fonseca had to be careful—he needed to manage the situation perfectly.

Fonseca rubbed his ferret eyes and looked wearily out the window. It was nearly nine in the evening, but the summer sun still hung low on the horizon, although shadows crept over the palace wall. Somewhere an anvil was pounding and a duck on the pond of the palace compound was squawking at its mate. Noise, thought Fonseca. There's too much noise.

To smooth Velázquez's path, Fonseca had begun procuring letters of introduction to Italy's rich and powerful, but even this operation was turning out to be tricky. One obstacle was Flavio Atti, emissary of the duchess of Parma to the Court of Felipe IV. "The fool," said Fonseca out loud as he watched a gaggle of ladies in farthingales make their way across the park. In the dusk he could only see their silhouettes, and in their wide skirts they reminded him of gray mushrooms gliding over the path. Word had reached him that Atti was dead set against Velázquez going to Italy because he was convinced that the painter was a spy, and that his trip to Italy was nothing more than a cover. Alvise Mocenigo, the Venetian ambassador, had been more cooperative. He was a jovial type, more concerned with good wine than with helping Velázquez, but he did agree to write a few letters presenting the Spaniard to people in high places.

Averardo de' Medici, the ambassador from Tuscany, was also a pain, thought Fonseca. The ambassador had advised the grand duke to be careful how he treated this *spagnolo basso*, this lowly Spaniard, with his pretensions to grandeur. It was true that Velázquez was the portraitist of the king of Spain—and therefore worthy of some consideration, but still, he was merely an artisan. Fortunately for Pacheco, the ambassador's amanuensis was easy to bribe. He gave the chaplain a full account of his missive for just a few *maravedíes*. A bargain, thought Fonseca. The intelligence from Tuscany was useful. It prompted the chaplain to pull a few strings and make a few contacts, so that even if the reception in Florence was chilly, elsewhere it would be at least tepid.

Still, one great obstacle remained: Doña Juana. She had lived apart from her husband during his first months at Court, and she was disinclined to let him out of her sight again. The poor child was insanely, absurdly jealous.

"It comes of being ugly," said Fonseca to himself. "She knows those Italian women are bombshells, and they fling off their clothes at the drop of a hat. After all, who poses for all those Venuses and Dianas?"

The truth was that when Velázquez had first brought up the possibility of a trip to Italy, Juana had carried on like a madwoman. She had cried and stomped and threatened to throw his bed linen out onto the street unless he took her with him. And now that Pacheco had gone back to Seville, she was more desperate than ever. She had no intention of staying alone with her daughter and servants in the big house on Calle de Convalescientes.

"The best thing about the priesthood," said Fonseca to himself, "is that you don't have to put up with women."

Something would have to be done about Juana—any tension would surely provoke the king to withdraw his support, and indeed, if she couldn't be brought around, Velázquez himself might balk, too. The young man, Fonseca thought, simply couldn't let his feelings for his family get in the way of his professional promise. She had, of course, been through a lot: being separated from her husband, being uprooted from Seville, losing her second child, and now the departure of her father for home. Even though Velázquez had managed to get Pacheco appointed Court painter, the old man longed for the sunlight of Andalusia. His departure, thought Fonseca, complicated the situation. Juana had grown melancholy, and Fonseca had to save Velázquez from his own sense of familial obligation. Of late, the boy had become more compassionate, noted Fonseca. Some might even say soft.

Juana was familiar with Court protocol, but she spent hours practicing her curtsey anyway. It had to be just right: low enough but not too low. Left hand on skirt, right hand on breast, eyes down. One wrong move could get you thrown out of the chamber.

On the day of the interview, Juana rose early. Arabela helped her dress, and Juana sat in front of the mirror for the maid to comb her hair. Arabela massaged her head with a light pomade and combed it through, while Juana scrutinized herself in the mirror. Her hair was a pretty, textured, soft brown color, but it was thin. All the dyes in the chemist's shop couldn't change that, and in fact, treating it had dried it out a bit. She

was twenty-eight years old, and the flush of youth was fading
from her cheeks. Her skin was still smooth and unfurrowed, but
it had lost some of its tautness. Cosmetics helped, but couldn't
give her a new complexion, after all. A terrible thought came to
her: the queen is a beautiful woman, La Calderona is a beautiful
woman, even Lidia is a beautiful woman, but I'm plain. In spite
of the creams and makeup, I'm homely.

The wind went out of her. Suddenly, she didn't want to go
to Court, and didn't want to see the queen. A thickness rose in
her throat. The container of *solimán* on her vanity table grew
blurry and watery-looking. Her chin trembled almost imperceptibly, but Arabela was quick-sighted.

"Don't be nervous, *señora*. They say the queen is cheerful
and warm. I'm sure you'll find her charming." Arabela knew
where Juana was off to that day, but didn't know why.

"It's not that. It's . . ."

A shriek, a giggle, and Paquita came flying into the room.
Nearly ten years old, she was a terror, not at all the decorous
señorita that moralists described in their conduct books.

"Let me fix your curls," ordered Arabela matter-of-factly,
"just as soon as I finish with your mother's hair."

"I can't stay. Mazo is teaching me to draw!" She was still
the apple of Pacheco's eye, and before he left Madrid, he had
asked Velázquez's assistant, Juan Bautista Martínez del Mazo,
to give her drawing lessons. "Mazo says that girls can learn, too.
Just look at the great Italian painter, Artemisia Gentileschi. The
king himself admires her work."

"Get me that pin, Doña Paca. No, not that one, the one
with the pearls. I'm going to put it in Doña Juana's hair, right
here. What do you think?"

"Oh, *Mamá*, you look beautiful!"

"Do you think so, Paquita?" Juana scrutinized her image in the mirror. Not beautiful, she thought—after all, can you take seriously the opinion of a child about her own mother?—but maybe not as awful as she felt.

"Oh, yes, *Mamá*! Absolutely *beautiful*! You know what, *Mamá*? *Abuelo* told me that someday I'm going to paint lovely pictures, and he'll hang them on the wall!" She let out another little shriek and disappeared out the door.

"I've tried to teach her to be ladylike, Doña Juana," said Arabela indifferently.

Why bother? thought Juana. It's not the ladies who satisfy the men.

What they said about the queen was true: she was a highly intelligent woman, far more intelligent than her husband. Three years Juana's junior, she had been engaged to Felipe IV in a strange diplomatic maneuver. Felipe III had attempted to secure peace with France by proposing double nuptials: his son would wed Princess Isabel, daughter of the French monarchs, while his daughter, Ana de Austria, would wed the dauphin. And so, in 1615 the Spanish princess made her way north, while the French princess traveled south. They met at the border, and then each went on to become a queen.

Doña Isabel turned out to be an excellent choice. She loved all things Spanish and cheered enthusiastically at bullfights. More important, she was a clever administrator, capable of carrying out government business while her husband was off hunting—or prowling. She was so efficient, in fact, that the king used to say that his favorite minister was not Olivares, but the queen.

When at last she found herself before Doña Isabel, Juana found her different from what she'd expected. She was as beautiful as they said, of course, and noticeably pregnant, but she was neither imperious nor condescending. Surrounded by ladies-in-waiting, she listened to Juana's statement with attention, remaining silent until she was certain the petitioner had finished. "Doña Juana, what evidence do you have that your husband is bedding this housemaid, this Lidia?"

"Your Highness, I have no hard evidence, but now that she's at Court, I fear the worst. She has been trying to seduce him for years, and the atmosphere here . . ."

"Yes, you're right. The atmosphere here is conducive to debauchery. Especially when influential older men contaminate younger men with their sordid habits." Juana knew she was referring to the count-duke.

"But still," continued Doña Isabel, "this girl is just a lowly washerwoman or something like that. I doubt Don Diego ever comes into contact with her at Court."

"I know he sees her. I saw her face in his painting, *The Expulsion of the Moriscos*." The minute she said it, Juana felt herself shrink into a tiny, squirmy worm. She didn't realize how preposterous her argument was until she had actually articulated it.

The queen laughed out loud. "What does that prove? Doña Constanza's face is in that painting, too."

Juana turned to look at the lovely young lady-in-waiting in mauve seated on a cushion at the queen's feet. She had seen the girl before, but had never known her name. Constanza stared back at her with wide, mocking eyes.

"If I were you," the queen went on, "I'd be warier of Doña Constanza than of some serving girl." Her tone wasn't scornful, but kindly and concerned—even sisterly. "Doña Juana, your husband is a painter, a portraitist. You can't be jealous of every woman he paints."

Juana pursed her lips and looked down. She prayed for the plush carpet beneath her feet to split in two, and for the floor beneath it to swallow her up.

"Are you jealous of me, Doña Juana?"

Juana looked at the queen. "Your Highness, of course not!"

"I've been posing for your husband every day for weeks. An equestrian."

Of course Juana knew that painters don't necessarily jump in the sack with every model who poses for them. Even when they paint a delicately erotic image, like the one I posed for, the body becomes nothing more than an object, with its own textures and shadows. I remember that Velázquez was absolutely clinical when painting. If he touched me during a session, it was to adjust the angle of my head or twist my torso to better capture the light on my skin.

"An equestrian," the queen was saying, but Juana was too humiliated to respond.

Doña Isabel sensed her pain. She closed her eyes, as though thinking, giving Juana time to regain her bearings.

"I'm sorry, Your Highness," whispered Juana finally. "I'm sorry to have taken up your time. I know Your Highness can't be concerned with my petty jealousies. It was ridiculous of me . . ." She backed away, head bowed, too mortified to say another word.

"Doña Juana," said the queen softly, "I cannot go searching for your former housemaid or her carpenter's apprentice husband. If I knew where she was, I would gladly send her off to some *sitio real* to get her out of the way, but in this gargantuan palace, there's no way for me to find her."

"Yes, Your Highness, I understand."

"But even so, I can promise you that she will soon be very far away from your husband. You won't need to worry about her at all."

"Thank you, Your Highness." Juana wasn't sure what the queen meant, but for the moment it didn't matter. All she wanted was to get out of that room, to leave the queen and her ladies-in-waiting—especially that Constanza, with her contemptuous sneer.

"But remember this, Doña Juana: Men are like bees. They buzz around and suck the honey from many flowers, but they always come back to their queen. And you are the queen of your own household."

A month later, Fonseca called for Juana and informed her that Velázquez would soon be leaving for Italy. The queen had advised him that she had already spoken with Don Diego's wife about the pending separation, and that she would have no objection. Fonseca was confused about the circumstances under which such a conversation had taken place, but Doña Isabel was such a kind soul, he thought, perhaps she had called for Juana in order to break the news to her gently. Fonseca knew better than to ask too many questions. The important thing, after all, was that Juana had agreed to let Velázquez go without a fuss. He asked her if she had anything to say.

"No, Don Juan," she answered calmly. "I understand that it is imperative for my husband to travel."

On August 10, 1629, Velázquez sailed from Barcelona with the famous Genoese general Ambrogio Spinola, who was to command the Spanish troops fighting in the Mantuan war. Juana would not see her husband again until January, 1631, and in the meantime, Lidia slipped out of her consciousness. The last Juana heard, the girl's carpenter husband had been sent off to work at the king's *sitio real* in Aranjuez. Good riddance, she thought. Out of sight, out of mind.

PART TWO

10

ADVENTURES AND ADVENTURERS
1629

Y OU SEE THEM IN THE PLAZA MAYOR. SOLDIERS HOME FROM
the wars. Some are missing a hand, a leg, an eye. Some are
missing a sense of who they are, where they were, why they
were there, why they are here. All are missing a livelihood.
There are no jobs for these men, so they lie on the steps of San
Felipe in the Puerta del Sol and moan. Or sleep. Or drink themselves into a stupor. Occasionally one will pull himself up long
enough to swagger around, brimming with bravado.

"Dutch bastards!" they cry. "We kicked their asses!"

"I shot a heretic right in the balls!"

"We routed those sons of bitches. Sent them right down
to hell, where they belong."

"Fucking Protestants!"

Perhaps they're remembering the triumphant siege of
Breda. It was around then that Olivares declared, "God is Spanish. He fights for Spain!"

When he said it, it seemed true enough. They called 1625

the *annus mirabilis* because everything seemed to be going our way. Not only did the Spaniards capture Breda, a key Dutch city, they drove the Dutch out of Brazil and chased France and Savoy out of the republic of Genoa, an important Spanish ally. And when the English tried to attack the port of Cádiz, our men clobbered them. The House of Austria, which had once been our rival, was now our firm ally, and in Central Europe, the Austrians won one victory after the other.

But then things began to go wrong. I can imagine the count-duke in his map room, bent over battle lines and strategy notes, trying to figure out the next move. In spite of all the pretty parades and rousing speeches, the show could not go on. The Crown was insolvent, and nobody had money to lend the government. Spain desperately needed a few years of peace to get its bearings and replenish its coffers. The Austrians had secured a shaky calm in Central Europe—they called it the *pax austriaca*—and it had to hold, thought Olivares, in order for Catholicism to survive and Europe to remain stable. I'm sure that Olivares and the king still found time for an occasional night at Cintia's, but more and more, they were concerned with statecraft, battling piranhas in the sea of international politics.

In those days, everyone was a piranha. England tried to gulp up Cádiz. The Republic of Venice nibbled at the sides of the Habsburg Empire. Pope Urban VIII, a truly ravenous piranha, devoured the duchy of Urbino and the fiefdom of the duke of Parma. Then, in 1627, when the duke of Mantua died without an heir, the toothy pope favored a Protestant over a Catholic to succeed him in order to increase his own political leverage in the area. And how would Olivares handle the Dutch, the largest piranha of all? They wanted independence, and they wanted their own religion. We had been fighting for decades to maintain Spanish rule and suppress Protestantism in the Low Countries. The war had sucked up every *blanca* in the royal coffers, as well as huge amounts of manpower. Now it was clear that we would lose the northern Low Countries, but Olivares hoped we could at least hold onto Flanders.

I can imagine Olivares pacing the room, puffing on his pipe, scratching his head. I see him plopping down on a chair, his fat belly quivering like jelly, his chest heaving in exhaustion. He calls for a servant, orders a brandy. He wishes that he could go to the theater, but he knows that he must stay and strategize. He gets up and once again pores over his maps. Finally, he comes up with an idea: He will try to compel Emperor Ferdinand of Austria to accept a formal alliance with Spain, to help in the war against the Dutch. But this won't be easy because nobody trusts Spain—not even its allies. To make the pill go down more smoothly, he will suggest that the emperor's son, Ferdinand of Hungary, marry the Infanta María Ana—the same María Ana who rejected Charles Stuart. So you see, we woman are good for more than a roll in the hay. We can also be used as political pawns if we're princesses or infantas.

Olivares did in fact propose an alliance between Spain and the princes of the Empire, Protestant as well as Catholic. If the Lutherans would side with Spain, Spain would side with them against the Calvinists. But even though the marriage between the infanta and her cousin took place, the plan unraveled. In Italy, where we had a strong presence, we suddenly lost face when a Protestant Frenchman took over Mantua, and with the pope's endorsement, at that. Olivares sent an army to Milan, but it was immediately obliterated, and everyone, including the pope, blamed the count-duke for the Catholic defeat. The war in Italy left us so poor that we couldn't support the troops in Flanders, which is what can happen when you try to fight two wars at the same time. Wallenstein, the Habsburg commander, was routed from the territories he'd occupied. Then the Dutch intercepted a boatload of Spanish silver, giving them the funds to take the offensive against our army in the Low Countries.

At home, everyone turned against Olivares. Prices were high and getting higher. Harvests were poor because of a drought. Exorbitant taxes were crippling business. And there was no work at all—not for returning soldiers, not for anyone. Without the expelled Morisco artisans, Spain had nothing to export. The towns were getting restless and threatening to revolt. Which explains why soldiers were lying around the Puerta del Sol. These were veterans of the wars in Flanders, Mantua, Cádiz. Hearing rumors of the desolation at home, some Spanish soldiers went to Rome, where they tried to pass themselves off as noblemen, even though they stank of sweat and urine. Velázquez saw them, and later told me how shameful he felt watching his countrymen behaving like common swindlers. These hucksters would find a wellborn lady to Court, and then, once in her good graces, steal her money and jewelry and disappear into the night.

People scurrying across the plaza don't stop to look at the soldiers, although these are the men who fought for the faith, for the glory of Spain. They're in a hurry, these people. The women carry straw baskets. They're going shopping. Maids and runners scamper behind them carrying packages. The men clutch portfolios—they have important business to attend to. And absolutely no one has time to talk to the soldiers, who spit out expletives, then sink back into melancholy. Some of these men were wounded by bullets, others were felled by disease. Typhus, scurvy, dysentery. In both the Low Countries and in Mantua they faced not only the Dutch, the French, and gangs of mercenaries, but also the bubonic plague. Some of them drool. Others cry, snot running out of their noses. They're disgusting, these men. That must be why no one stops to talk to them.

I close my eyes and I can see them. Even though this all happened decades ago, images of those battered soldiers still haunt my dreams. Their wailing still rings in my ears.

I *did* talk to them sometimes, even though I knew it wasn't the proper thing to do. A woman—I should say a lady accompanied by her maid—had no business talking to maimed old men. (They looked like old men, even though some of them couldn't have been more than thirty.) But I am Venus. I break rules.

His name was Carlos. Or perhaps it wasn't. You shouldn't ever trust what people say—you can't even trust your own eyes. That's one thing I learned from Velázquez. People can dress like counts and claim to have titles, when all they are is *picaros*, street scum. Anyhow, I called him Carlos. He was one of so many men strewn on the steps like bundles of garbage. Compared to many, he was lucky—he had both his hands and both his legs, both his eyes and both his ears. I didn't know if he had both his balls, but I imagined so. I almost stepped on his fingers one day on my way to the *mentidero*. He was leaning on one hand, holding a *bota* with cheap wine in the other.

"*Písame, no más,*" he snarled. "Go ahead and walk all over me."

I apologized. He burped.

We got to talking. It was unseemly, to be sure, but those men had memories, and I was eager to know Carlos's story. It wasn't the first time the men on the steps of San Felipe had seen me in conversation with one of their comrades. Some of them recognized me—some even nodded and smiled, or perhaps, grimaced would be a better word. But Carlos never smiled. He was angry—even enraged. Enraged and melancholic. He lashed out at people, then sank into sullenness. I wanted to know what was behind all that fury. I knew he had fought in Flanders. He had seen action. He had killed men and was proud of it. "Heretics!" he snarled. "Heretics who set fire to Catholic churches where innocent women and children were praying!" People who did such evil things deserved to die, he said. They captured Catholics, and then impaled and disemboweled them. He had seen the bloodless heads of his countrymen atop poles in town squares. He whimpered as he cursed them. "Bastards! Protestant vermin!"

Even when the money from the Crown stopped flowing, the men kept on fighting. What else could they do? There was no food, no firewood, no new ammunition. But they fought on. They marched, marched in the driving snow, their teeth chattering, their soaked uniforms sticking to their bodies, lumbering northward toward the Dutch territories.

"It was so cold that the piss froze on the horses' dicks," he said. "So cold some of us dropped to our knees and prayed death would take us right there, right then. All we wanted was to drift into sleep, slowly and gently. First, your fingers and toes go numb, then your hands and feet. Your breathing slows down and you lose consciousness and then you freeze. I've seen it happen, and it couldn't be worse than having your head shattered by a bullet. Or starving."

I knelt beside him. Decent people stared. A lady kneeling on the steps! It was an outrage!

"Were you really starving?"

He looked at me as though I were an idiot.

"Why did you join up in the first place?" I asked him.

"How else can a poor man get ahead? I didn't want to be a farmer like my father. To break your back working another man's land? My father left Soria when he was a young man. Made his way south to Andalusia to get work in the orange groves. But he died of disease. I didn't want to relive his life. A good fighter can get a promotion, move up, make something of himself. Only it's impossible to be a good fighter when you haven't eaten for days and have no bullets for your gun.

"I joined when I was twelve. At first, it was fine. Noblemen were still leading the charge. It was a matter of honor for the great families to have a son or two in command of a regiment. And where there are nobles, there's food and shelter for their troops. So I joined to get ahead and, ha!, to keep from starving. Funny, isn't it! I joined to keep from starving and wound up starving. Life is so stupid."

I nodded in agreement.

"In the beginning there was always food. The nobleman saw to it that his commanders and their men were well fed. And then, occasionally you'd ravage a town and take whatever you wanted. Food, money, girls to fuck, animals to slaughter . . . But then the great families no longer had money to support a regiment. The nobles lost interest. One by one they abandoned the fight. And then there were just poor slobs in command. Poor slobs who had risen in the ranks but who didn't have powerful families behind them. Slobs no better than me. And the king—what can you expect from the king? He has no money. What he has, he spends on the campaign in Italy."

"But what about your pension?"

"Yes, yes, we're all supposed to have one. But it's not for deserters."

"You . . . ?"

"I don't want to talk about it."

He sat with his head between his hands. I could see his eyes were bloodshot. He kept swallowing saliva over and over again, as though his throat were so dry he needed to lubricate it. I thought he had forgotten I was there. I was about to get up when he began to speak again.

"We were marching north. I was so hungry that my head was pounding. I could hear the drums . . . brmmm brmmm . . . and it was as though they were battering my brain. We were so hungry that when we slept—which was almost never because it's almost impossible to sleep when your guts are screaming with hunger—but when we did manage to sleep, our jaws moved up and down, up and down. We chewed our saliva, dreaming of food. Sometimes I'd watch my comrades gnawing at their tongues in their sleep and I'd want to bludgeon them to put them out of their misery. You don't want to hear this story, *señora*. What's a lady like you want to hear this story for? Go on and gossip with other *damas* in fluffy skirts."

"Go on. You were marching. The drums were beating."

"In the distance I saw a farmhouse. I said to the guy next to me, my pal Vivaldo, 'Let's go. We can be there and back in a half hour. Then we can catch up with the others.' 'They'll shoot us,' he said. 'Not if they don't catch us,' I answered."

"So you took off and never came back."

"You already know the story, lady? Then you tell it and I'll just lie here and chug my drink."

"No, I'm sorry. Please go on."

"It was hard going in the snow. Curtains of white opened and closed depending on the wind. Sometimes we could see the house in the distance, and sometimes we couldn't. As we drew nearer, it became more steadily visible. We trudged on and on for what seemed like hours. Finally we reached it. Vivaldo checked to see if there was a back door, but there wasn't. The front door was locked, but not bolted. We kicked it open, the way we always did. We had plenty of experience. When we took a village, we spread out in front of the houses. Then we just kicked in doors and hauled out the people. Sometimes we shot them, but usually we let them run away. Then we just took what we wanted."

"Was there anybody inside?"

"There was no one. Maybe they saw us coming and hid. I don't know. Maybe they were out attending to the animals. Even in a storm, animals have to eat, you know. In Flanders the animals eat better than Spanish soldiers. Anyhow, I didn't see anyone. If there'd been a woman, I swear I would've raped her. But I didn't see a soul. There were four loaves of bread on the table."

"And you took them."

"Yes, we took them. Vivaldo took two and hid them under his rags, and I took the other two. Then we set out toward the road."

"Did you reach your platoon?"

"We were plodding along. The drifts were so high, they were like barricades. We made it back to the road, though, the warm loaves pressing against our bodies. They felt so good, like a heating stone. And the aroma, how can I describe it? Like the scent of vanilla candles at Christmastime. Like heaven itself. The snow started to let up a bit, and we turned in the direction our men had taken. There was no one around. No sound. No shadow.

"Suddenly a child appeared. He was standing right in our path—a blond boy, ragged and tired-looking. He had a face like a cherub, but he had snot coming out of his nose and he was hacking like he had consumption. His lips were bloody from the cough. But no, he was a pretty child in spite of all that. Something about him reminded me of the sea. Big green eyes, so deep you could swim in them. Skin as pale as sand. A merman, that's what he was. As beautiful and seductive as a mermaid, except he was a boy. There was something eerie about him. Something almost—I don't know, translucent. He was shivering horribly."

"How old was he?"

"Maybe eight or ten. He was so blond. I've never seen hair so fair on a child. It was like white gold, the way it glistened."

"So you gave him your bread!"

"You know what, lady, if you already know the story, get the hell out of here and let me drink myself dumb!"

"I'm sorry," I whispered. "Please go on."

He closed his eyes, trying to remember. He didn't speak again until I started to get up because I was sure he'd fallen asleep.

"He was staring at us," Carlos said finally. "At Vivaldo and me. At the loaves of bread that were peeping out through our shirts."

I sat back down.

"His eyes were glued to our torsos. Those enormous, emerald, watery eyes. He was working his mouth, salivating and swallowing spit, the way soldiers do in their sleep. He kept staring, staring. I was sure he was going to lunge. He took a step towards me, as if to grab my loaves."

I held my breath. Carlos began to tremble. He thrust out

his arm like a wild man. His hand slapped the air, as if he had no control of it.

"We'd trudged all the way to hell and back for those loaves. I wasn't going to give up mine, not even to a kid with a face like a sea sprite. I reached out to shove him away, but he was quicker. He sprang at me. He had something in his hand—I saw it flickering in the white morning glare. It was a knife!"

Tears were trickling down Carlos's jowl. His whole body was quivering.

"He was almost on top of me, at no more than a finger's distance. He drew back his elbow for the plunge. I thought I was a dead man. And then suddenly, inexplicably, he fell back into the snow."

Carlos paused, took a breath, shuddered, and then went on. "I stared at him. He was nothing but a crumpled mass of brains and blood. "

I inhaled sharply. "What?" I whispered.

"Vivaldo saw the blade before I did. He raised his sword and split the kid's skull open like a pomegranate. His face was no longer a face. Blood oozed everywhere. It seeped into the snow. It formed little puddles, then, like juice seeping into a flavored ice, disappeared under the surface. Crimson, vermillion, pink, lighter and lighter until it almost blended into the white of the snow. I stared at the crumpled form. I couldn't force myself to move. I just stood there, frozen."

I didn't say anything about it at that moment, but Carlos's description of the fading color of blood seemed bizarrely precise.

"Vivaldo wiped his sword in the snow. Then he gave me a push. 'Get going,' he hissed. 'We have to get out of here.' 'But the kid!' I said. 'We can't just leave him on the road!' 'Why not? It's just one more dead heretic! We've killed plenty of these bastards before. What difference does one more make?' I let him drag me along the road. I could feel urine trickling out of my body and freezing on my leg. It burned and made me want to scream. 'I can't,' I cried. 'I can't go on!' 'You have to go on, asshole!' I sucked back sobs. I felt as though I had a lump of coal smoldering in my throat. 'But what about his mother? What if she finds him like that?' 'For Christ's sake!' snarled Vivaldo. 'He's just Protestant scum. He was going to rot in hell anyhow. He was dying of consumption, or didn't you notice? I did him a favor, spared him a lot of suffering.'

"I tripped along until we could see our men in the distance. They were heading toward a wood, probably to rest in a more concealed area. It had stopped snowing, and the ground was a smooth sheet of ice that glistened in the frail winter sunlight. I felt as though I were walking on a mirror. My reflection moved before me, a formless blotch of indistinct color. I am dead, I thought. I am a ghost, like all the other ghosts that float over this blood-soaked, godforsaken land.

"'Eat that bread,' snapped Vivaldo.

"I didn't want to eat it. I was ravenous, but the image of that child discharging his brains into the snow made me nauseous.

"Vivaldo insisted: 'Eat it now. If the others see it, they'll grab it away from you. Not only that, they'll know we broke rank.' The plan was to slip back into the formation without being noticed, but the bread would be a giveaway that we'd been gone.

"He was already tearing into his, pulling out fat chunks and stuffing them into his mouth. I felt as though I were seeing it through a haze. I wanted to vomit. 'Eat!' he snarled. 'Or I'll eat mine and yours, too.'

"I choked it down. It felt like raw dough in my stomach. My gut tightened as we hurried our step. I wanted to take a crap, but there was no time. Finally, we caught up with our men. No one said anything about our being gone.

"Images of the child's mother flashed through my mind. I imagined her blond and emerald-eyed, like her son. Her horror when she found him, her screams, her wails. What if he were an only child? He was sick, it's true, but maybe he would have recovered. Maybe he would have brought her solace in her old age. Maybe he wanted to steal my bread for her. Poor kid. Sure, he was a Protestant, but he was just a child . . . What did he know about the sanctity of the pope and the intercession of saints and all that stuff? Suddenly the sermons of the priests, about how Protestants were going to hell because they didn't believe in transubstantiation seemed—I don't know. I know it's a sin to say it, but it all seemed senseless." Carlos was weeping again, softly, pitifully.

"Rest a while," I whispered. I wanted to put my hand on his, but didn't dare, not because of the scandal it would provoke, but because he would have felt diminished to be comforted by a woman. After all, he was a man, a soldier, a Spaniard.

"No," he sighed miserably. "I've told it this far. Better just to get it all out." He took a swig and then went on.

"When we got to the woods, we took a break. Then we formed ranks and resumed our march northward. Some men were so famished that they fainted. We stepped over them and left them to their fate. I was so numb from the cold I couldn't see straight. The backs of the soldiers in front of me seemed to blend together and quiver, as though seen through glass. I wished I would collapse, so that I could just die on the road. Vivaldo, on the other hand, seemed refreshed.

"We marched and marched. I lost track of the days. When we finally came to a village, we kicked in doors, raped the farm girls, and replenished our provisions." Carlos shook his head. "My heart wasn't in it, though. I wanted to go home."

I stifled the urge to ask him if that was when he deserted. "Where was home?" I asked instead.

"I don't know," he whispered. "After my father died, my mother went to live in Seville. Maybe she's still there." He was calm now. His breath was even, controlled.

I wanted to ask his mother's name, but it seemed silly. Seville is a huge city, and there was no way I would know the mother of this poor soldier.

"We must have been fairly close to the border when suddenly we heard the pounding of hooves and the shriek of men in agony. Our men. Blood was spurting all around me, and curses sliced the air. Fighters in the front lines fell back. Horses lay on the snow, their legs churning, their insides oozing from gaping wounds in their sides. The Dutch were skilled at ambush, and our men were too weak to fight. I saw Vivaldo parry and lunge, then stumble and crumple almost comically, a sword stuck hideously in his heart. A Dutch soldier pulled it out and then whacked off his head.

"I was trembling. Every part of my body wanted to move in a different direction. I felt like a broken puppet. I took a step backward, then another, then another. I was watching the Dutch soldier to see if he would come after me. At first I thought he didn't see me, that his mind was set on lopping off the heads of fallen Spaniards. But then I caught his eye, yellow, like a tiger's—or the way I imagine a tiger's eye must be, anyway. He was staring at me, and he looked ready to pounce. I felt trapped in his gaze like startled prey. I tried to take another step backward, but my legs were frozen. His tiger's eyes were focused on my coward's eyes, my deserter's eyes. I was sure he was going to spring.

"But he must have decided I wasn't worth the effort because he only sneered, threw back his head, and turned away. In a moment he was back in the fray.

"Paralyzed, I forced myself to focus on the gore before me. I knew it was only seconds before some other Dutchman caught sight of me and ran me through. I turned and ran. I ran as fast as I could with my wooden legs on the frozen ground. Behind me I heard the thumping of boots. 'I can't slip,' I kept telling myself. 'I can't fall. They're right behind me.'

"My knees throbbed. My blistered feet screamed with pain. Still, I ran. I ran and ran and ran until the hurt began to dissipate. Finally, I felt nothing. My whole body was numb. I stopped in my tracks. 'Let them kill me,' I whispered. 'I'd rather be dead.' I turned to face my enemy. There was no one there.

"I squinted at the whiteness. Nothing. No sound. No Dutchman. I turned back toward the road. I spotted an old farmhouse in the distance and trudged toward it. I was still armed. I could kill the farmer and steal his food.

"But it turned out to be abandoned. I spent the night there and then took off, traveling south. I stole some eggs from a chicken coop, and I stole a chicken, too. I avoided people until I reached Brussels. There I begged a night's stay at the Carmelite monastery. The friars there were kindly. I confessed the murder of the child to an energetic young priest, and he told me I was innocent. 'You can't be guilty of a crime committed by another man,' he told me. 'If your friend was guilty—and I'm not sure that he was, after all, the boy came at you with a knife—then God punished him.'

"The friars were poor. Their supper consisted of a piece of stale bread, a turnip, an onion, and a slice of moldy cheese. Nevertheless, they fed me as well as they could. They supplied me with whatever provisions they could find and a new set of clothes that one of them had kept from the days before he entered the monastery. At the French border I met a convoy of merchants and accompanied them all the way to Paris. From there I joined a band of Spanish Jesuits returning home from a stint at the University of Paris. I remember crossing the Pyrenees into Spain. Home, I thought. Finally. We crossed the fields of Castile in the late spring. It's dry land, bad for growing crops, but the sky was gorgeous, clear, and cerulean."

"Cerulean," I echoed. I stared at him a moment and noticed, for the first time, that he was rather handsome. I knew I shouldn't ask—I didn't want him to think I was mocking him— but I couldn't contain my curiosity. "Carlos," I said finally, "I'm sorry to interrupt, but. . . . vermillion, crimson, cerulean—where would a soldier learn words like that?"

He looked at me askance. "What do you mean?"

"Those are poets' words, painters' words."

"I don't know. I've always known them." He thought a moment. "When I was little, after my father died, my mother went to work in the home of a painter."

"In Seville?"

"Yes, I told you she went to Seville."

"Do you remember the name of the painter?"

"I don't. But I do remember that he was very precise about the names of colors. Anyhow, when I was about six or seven, I went to apprentice with a chandler in a village outside the city. I only saw my mother a couple of times after that."

"But you didn't become a chandler."

"I hated the man I was apprenticed to. He was stingy and impatient. He whipped me when I dripped wax on the floor. I knew I'd never have a future making candles, so when the king's regiments passed through the city, I ran away and joined up. I was twelve. The army promised a salary, regular meals, adventure. If I had only known . . ." Carlos was quiet a while, lost in a labyrinth of memories. "What I don't understand," he said finally, "is why it's our job to kill them."

"Kill whom? What do you mean?"

"If the Protestants are going to go to hell anyway, why can't we just let God's will be done without getting involved? Let them believe whatever they want. If God condemns them to hell, it's their problem, not mine."

I thought about it. "You might be right," I said, although what he had said was probably a sacrilege. Anyway, I was thinking about something else he had mentioned. "The house you lived in as a small child, did it by any chance belong to a man named Pacheco?"

"I don't know. What difference does it make?"

"Carlos, was your mother's name Arabela?"

He put down his *bota* and looked at me, eyes wide, lips parted. But then his expression changed. His jaw grew tense, his eyes small. He nearly spat out the words: "Who are you?" he snarled. "Who the hell are you?"

11

ACROSS THE PLAZA
1629 – 1630

ORKMEN LUGGED BEAMS AND TOOLS ACROSS THE PUERTA del Sol, oblivious to the soldiers sprawled over the steps of San Felipe. Spain at last had an heir to the crown, and the king was determined that the baptism of Prince Baltasar Carlos would be the most spectacular event Spain had ever seen. At the moment, the veterans of the wars against the Dutch were the farthest thing from his mind.

The king hunched over the large marble table in the blue room of his private apartments and knit his brow. The sketches submitted by his architects were splendid, but to turn them into reality would cost money. No matter. He could always borrow gold and raise taxes. He was prepared to spend thousands of *maravedís* he didn't have on a massive renovation of the Alcázar. The ugly old building had once been a fortress, and it had retained its heavy, utilitarian look. It's true that the main facade, which was adorned with marble and gold, gave the place an air of elegance, and the bulkiness of the exterior walls was offset by the surrounding parks and gardens. Still, the Alcázar was clearly too shabby for the baptism of the future king of Spain.

I can imagine His Majesty on a walking tour of the palace with his architects, stopping in this courtyard and that entrance hall, chin in hand, clucking and nodding. The architects take notes, make measurements, and click their tongues. This wouldn't be a simple project. The main body of the building had two upper floors, each with three large balconies. The south facade boasted twenty-eight balconies on each floor. A massive main door was reserved for official acts and ceremonies, while a smaller door served for everyday use. In order to ease palace traffic and facilitate access to the main hall for the baptismal celebrations, the king wanted a majestic staircase that extended from the large balconies to the principal entrance. The architects squinted at their carefully lettered notes and asked how much he was prepared to spend. Damn the cost! exploded the king. This was for the baptism of his newborn son! The architects bit their lips, bowed their head, and sighed. They knew they had to carry out orders, although they also knew they'd never get paid.

After he had decided on structural changes, Don Felipe turned his attention to the furnishings. The walls of the Alcázar clearly needed attention. The king sent his courtiers to El Escorial and the *sitios reales*, the smaller royal palaces and lodges he maintained throughout Spain, with orders to bring back the finest tapestries in his possession. The most gorgeous would hang in the newly refurbished Alcázar. He instructed Olivares to purchase mirrors and vases to decorate the corridors. He ordered a chandelier of Murano glass and an exquisite bust of Christ from Montelupo for his private chapel. He procured thousands of flowers to adorn every part of the interior. It was

November, but the king had to have his flowers, so somehow, they appeared.

Although Velázquez was getting his monthly allowance, everyone else—from the scrubwoman to the royal dresser—had to do without; no one had been paid for months. Yet there was little grumbling, and the reason was obvious. For too long, Spain had been without a male heir, which meant we were vulnerable: if there was no Spanish successor, the French would surely make a play for the Spanish crown. But now there was no need to worry. With the birth of Prince Baltasar Carlos, our future was guaranteed. The baptism would be attended by monarchs from all over Europe—damn the wars, plagues, and bankruptcies ravaging the continent! All Spaniards, not just the king, wanted the Alcázar to gleam. This was a matter of Spanish honor!

Juana was as excited as everyone else about the upcoming festivities, but there was a problem. Her husband was in Italy and her father, back in Seville. All of Madrid had been invited to the Plaza Mayor, where there would be music, dancing, acrobats, magicians, jugglers, and trained monkeys. But Juana was not one of the common people. She was the wife of the usher of the privy chamber and had been summoned to the palace itself. But who would accompany her? A lady couldn't attend an important event at Court unescorted.

"Surely the *señora* can go with her maid," suggested Arabela. Then, so that Juana wouldn't think she was angling for an invitation, she added, "Julia will be happy to accompany you.

She loves the merriment of the Court, and I know she's looking forward to the baptism of our dear little prince."

"You and Julia will both go with me. Paquita is going, so of course, you must be there. But we need a male escort. How will it look for a gaggle of women show up without a gentleman?"

"I should think . . ."

"It must be someone whose presence won't provoke gossip." Juana sat down by the brazier and picked up her embroidery.

"What about Fonseca?"

Juana pulled her needle through the cloth and looked up at the maid. "The royal chaplain? Surely you must be joking, Arabela."

"He's a priest, *señora*. No one will think ill of you for appearing in public with a celibate man of the cloth!"

"That's silly, Arabela. Fonseca's services will be needed at the baptism. He won't be free to attend to guests. We have to think of someone else. Someone distinguished, who fits in at the palace."

Paquita erupted into the room like a cannon ball. "*Mamá, Mamá!* I have something to show you!"

"Is there no way to teach this child manners, Arabela? Does she always have to *burst* into places? Why can't she just walk through doors like a normal person?" But Juana couldn't keep from laughing. She was delighted that her daughter wasn't a porcelain doll who tiptoed and curtsied like most girls her age. "Francisca," she said with mock gruffness, "will you please restrain yourself?"

"Look, *Mamá!*" squealed Paquita. "This is a painting I made! All by myself! Juan Bautista says I have talent!"

"Of course he does, darling. You're the boss's daughter."

Paquita pretended to pout. "That's not nice, *Mamá*. I think Juan Bautista is sincere."

"Now, there's an idea, Doña Juana," mused Arabela. "Juan Bautista Martínez del Mazo! He could accompany you to the baptism. He's only seventeen, *señora*. It's unlikely anyone would take him for your lover, and Doña Francisca is only ten, so I doubt anyone would take him for hers. He's a well-mannered young man from a good provincial family, and in the Maestro's absence it would be natural for him to fulfill these social duties."

"Oh, yes, *Mamá*! That's a wonderful idea. Let him come, please!"

Juana gazed at her daughter and raised a brow. The girl seemed rather too fond of her painting tutor. Soon she would be of marriageable age. It was unseemly for her to show so much enthusiasm for a young man. "I don't know," said Juana. "I'd say a handsome seventeen-year-old can indeed set off tongue-wagging. But I'll think about it."

In the end, Mazo did accompany them. The only alternative was to stay home, and no one favored that. For the occasion, Juana chose her finest frocks, with emeralds and pearls dripping from her earlobes. Paquita dressed discreetly, as became a virgin, but Juana made sure she flashed a couple of strategically placed jewels, to make clear that she was from a wealthy family. After all, she would soon have to find Paquita a husband, and although she had no intention of pretending that her daughter was high aristocracy, she certainly wanted to attract an appropriate suitor. Arabela wore a flannel dress with small ruffs as befitted her station, but Juana had the rose-colored gown she had worn to the last Calderón play remade for Julia, who loved to mingle with the other ladies' maids at Court.

"Really, Julia," said Juana, "you look better than I do in that dress."

"Nothing would make me happier than to follow in your footsteps, *señora.*"

Juana wasn't quite sure what the maid meant by this, but she decided to brush it aside.

Juan Baptista had a knack for color combinations that were at once catchy and tasteful, and he cut a dashing figure in an ochre coat with bright red trimming and a *golilla*, a small, stiff, raised collar. His *greguescos*—the voluminous, short pants that were in style at the time—were chocolate-colored with gold and silver threads running from waist to knee. I have no idea where he found the money for such lavish outfits.

Crowds gathered outside the Alcázar hours before the ceremony began. As you might expect, the baptismal procession was a splendorous affair. The Countess of Olivares, seated on a sedan chair of rock crystal, carried the baby into the church in her arms, accompanied by the godparents, his aunt María Ana, the future queen of Hungary, and his uncle, the *infante* Don Carlos. Dignitaries from near and far approached with costly gifts for the new prince. The ladies wore magnificent brocades with diamond brooches and headdresses of gold. They crowded into the women's section of the chapel, elbowing each other discreetly for the best seats. They sat with painstaking care so as not to send their petticoats over their heads. They gossiped unobtrusively, remarking on everyone else's outfit, their skirts caressing their neighbors like the hands of unabashed lovers. The men were no less regally adorned, with heavy chains and medallions and enormous emerald rings. They prayed with great piety, squinting surreptitiously at the bosoms in the women's gallery. It was all stunningly ornate—like theater brought to life, and the combination of music, incense, candles, and perfume made me heady.

And yet even that opulence paled in comparison with the dinner! Normally the king and queen ate separately, attended only by their private entourage, but for this historic event they both ate in the great hall, although at separate tables. A long, elegant Oriental carpet had been laid out for the occasion, and an elaborately embroidered canopy had been installed over the king's chair, while a smaller one hung over the queen's. Once the guests were present and standing at their places, the serving ceremony began. Accompanied by the royal guard, the dining room personnel entered in order of rank, carrying glasses, pitchers, terrines, salt and pepper containers, tablecloths, silver, wines, and bread. With military precision they passed the items from hand to hand, placing each on the table. Finally the king and queen entered the hall and took their positions. Fonseca, to the king's right, gave thanks and blessed the meal.

"¡A la vianda, caballeros!" announced the king, and the guests sat. While we ate, musicians in the balcony played music for our enjoyment, while on the main floor, jugglers, acrobats, dwarves, and jesters circulated.

Each dish and condiment was prepared by a specialist: the *panetero* made breads, the saucer made sauces. The royal chef, Francisco Fernández Montiño, was known not only for his culinary expertise, but also for the beauty of his presentations. Every dish was a work of art: golden squab breasts surrounded by crimson love apples and sprigs of cilantro, all sitting in baskets of crisp potato shavings; partridges floating in a stew of prunes and raisins; baked capons adorned with sprigs of parsley and florets of carrots all basking in butter and garlic. Every presentation was more spectacular than the previous one; every concoction was served in the king's own gold monogrammed porcelain. The waiters paraded in with immense fanfare provided by Court musicians and circled the tables before laying their terrines in front of the guests. It took hours and hours to present the dishes, eat, and then remove the plates for the next round.

After a long rest period, the elegantly attired staff reappeared with sweets: apricots, strawberries (in winter, just imagine!), red cherries, white cherries, limes, raisins, walnuts, almonds, and preserves of all types. Waiters balanced mountains of cheese on silver trays and returned with creams, puddings, tarts, flaky cakes, and mounds of frothy cream whipped into peaks and decorated with berries and comfitures.

The following day, the Puerta del Sol was cleared temporarily of soldiers—they were too visible a reminder of reality, and anyway, they would get in the way of the day of dancing arranged for the common folks. In the streets, women flirted shamelessly with men they would never see again. Rumor had it that a young veiled coquette caught the attention of a prowling caballero, who didn't recognize his own sister behind the long, black mantilla! When he tried to follow her, she took off through a side street and lost him. Hours later, the frustrated lothario dragged himself home, where he found his sister in her room, pretending she'd been at her prayers the whole time. When he bemoaned his rotten luck, she scolded, "That's what you get for trying to pick up veiled women! Who knows what kind of a floozy she was!"

No one who was in Madrid in the winter of 1629 would ever forget those nine days of total excess. Party after party. Nine days of partying in all. Early in December, the king ordered bull-fights in the Plaza Mayor, which were followed by *cañas*, in which the king and the count-duke rode together in the same quadrille. More silks and satins, gold and emeralds. And for ordinary Madrileños, more fun and merriment in the streets. The baptismal celebrations ended with one final grand dinner and ball to mark the departure of María Ana, Queen of Hungary, for her new realm.

The truth is, I hated the whole thing. During the banquets, the balls, the bullfights, and the *cañas*, all I could think about was the poor soldier Carlos. Images of Carlos pursued me through the cream-soaked, sugar-dusted, diamond-studded hours. Carlos chewing the air in his dreams; Carlos sucking saliva and ice to stave off hunger; Carlos stealing bread to stay alive; Carlos wading in pools of blood and mud and shit; Carlos cowering in an abandoned farmhouse. Soldiers freezing. Soldiers falling. Soldiers dying.

Soldiers scattered over the steps of San Felipe in the Puerta del Sol, shivering and sobbing, while the king and his guests savored fresh fruit and tortes and fine liqueurs.

Velázquez never wrote to his wife the whole time he was in Italy. But many years later, I came upon the following letter to Pacheco folded, like Fonseca's letter from many years earlier, between the pages of *El arte de la pintura*. It's not dated, but it must have been composed around September, 1630.

Dear Father-in-Law,

God be with you. I have been working and traveling inces-
santly since I came to this country of excess and confusion. Upon
my arrival I went immediately to Venice to see the Titians. The
Spanish ambassador received me amiably, but I was anxious to
get to Rome, so I left after only about a week. On my way I spent
a couple of days in Ferrara with Cardinal Giulio Sacchetti, whom
I had met when he was papal nuncio in Madrid. He was kind
enough to introduce me to many of his friends, so many in fact
that I don't remember all their names. I then left for Rome, where
Cardinal Francesco Barberini put me up in some rooms of the
Vatican Palace on the outskirts of Rome. He was surprisingly gra-
cious considering how aloof he was when he was in Madrid. At
the time he said my painting was dull and static, but maybe he
views my anxiousness to learn from the Italian masters as a sign
of promise.

Cardinal Barberini is a great patron of the arts and has
many friends among artists. Through him I have met the Frenchmen Claude Lorrain and Nicolas Poussin. The former is quite
young, but has already made a reputation for himself as a landscape artist. The latter is especially popular here among connois-
seurs who appreciate the clarity of his lines and the drama of his
images. I also met the great Gianlorenzo Bernini, an astonishing
artist who excels at all three plastic arts: painting, architecture,
and sculpture. This man is a genius, Don Francisco. He combines
the precision, symmetry, and elegance of classical sculpture with
the dramatic natural realism of the baroque, creating limbs out
of cold marble that seem to quiver and pulse. Truly, they take your
breath away. This is what I came for, my dear father-in law, to be

surrounded by brilliance, old and new. To learn and observe, and to take it all back to Spain with me.

I devoted my first months in Rome to the frescoes. I would have to be a poet to describe them, and God knows, I am not so very adept at painting pictures with words. The Sistine Chapel is a marvel, especially Michelangelo's ceiling. Standing beneath the images, you feel as though you could actually stretch up and touch them. In "The Creation of Adam," God reaches out to touch the first man, who is so beautiful and vibrant that he really seems at that very moment to receive the breath of life from his Creator. They say Michelangelo painted this masterpiece in a single day, just as God created man in a single day. It is indeed a marvel.

But there is much more than that in this hall. "The Last Judgment," on the sanctuary wall, also by Michelangelo, left me gaping. The paintings by Botticelli and Perugino are magnificent, as are the tapestries by Raphael. Now I see clearly what Barberini meant when he complained that my painting wasn't dynamic enough.

I spent weeks copying the frescoes, and for the first time I truly understood the power of the human figure to convey an idea. The body, my dear Pacheco, is one of God's most exquisite creations. We must not fear it or shun it, as our rabid moralists do in Spain. Here figure painting is highly regarded and models are easy to find through the guilds. Even female models. Through the body, painters express every emotion—lust, surely in some cases, but also devotion, spiritual yearning, and the love of beauty. These paintings shock no one. Surely not Barberini, and he is a prince of the Church.

At the end of spring I changed abode, for the vernal heat was getting to be too much for me. With the help of the Spanish ambassador, the Count of Monterrey, I was able to move to the Villa Medici, where I spent two pleasant months copying Italian statues. However, at the beginning of September I fell ill with a fever. The Count had me moved to a house near his residence so his physician could care for me. I have been here for a fortnight. At first, I was terrified I had been stricken with the plague and would die far from you, my wife and daughter, and especially my beloved country, but now I am beginning to recover and no longer fear the worst.

Dear Pacheco, please make sure Doña Juana is properly cared for. Write to little Francisca and tell her Papá sends her a kiss.

Your unworthy servant and devoted son-in-law,
Don Diego Rodríguez de Silva y Velázquez

If Doña Juana had read this letter at the time it was received, she would have noticed two things: that her husband was painting nude female models and that his country was more "beloved" to him than she and Francisca.

12

Venus interrupta
1660: 1630 — 1632

THERE WAS A TIME, NOT THAT LONG AGO, WHEN I LOVED nothing more than sitting in the convent garden and sketching roses. The rose! A symbol of beauty and perfection—its multilayered, overlapping petals enfolding the divine center, the treasure, the jewel. We have a magnificent bush that in summer throbs with bloodred roses. The Prioress, Mother Augustina, calls it "a symbol of Our Lord Jesus Christ and His love for humanity." I know to keep my mouth shut. I don't mention that the red rose is also a symbol of sex.

I hardly sketch anymore. My sight is going. It's as though I'm seeing everything through milky glass. From time to time, little black cobwebs float over my field of vision. Venturo Almedina (not the old midwife—he's long dead—but his son) came to see me the other day. He says there's nothing I can do about my eyes. It's just old age, he says. Young Venturo is a doctor, too. He lives and works here in Madrid, and he comes to see me a couple of times a month, always bringing candy or ices. He's a good man—

kind and attentive—just like his father. Old Almedina looked like a prune, with a brownish-red face all wrinkled and squishy. He even smelled like a prune! Very old people have a kind of putrid-sweet odor about them, the odor of rotting flesh. I hope that I don't smell like that, but perhaps I do. I can't be sure.

I used to sit for hours by the roses, sketching and sketching. Velázquez himself had taught me, though I don't recall him ever complimenting me on my work, except once. But no matter what he said—or didn't say—I think that some of my roses were quite real-looking, with delicate, silky petals and sharp, threatening thorns. I am Venus, the rose, and now I "lie hidden / in sad, dark shadows that prevent me / from seeing the glorious face of the sun . . ." I see the world from behind a hazy shield that grows denser by the day.

Velázquez started back to Spain in August, 1630, stopping in Naples to paint a portrait of King Felipe's sister, María Ana, who was making the trek north to meet her new husband, Ferdinand III of Hungary. Everyone who saw the portrait loved it. It was a refined work, people said, warm and rich with color—russets, gray-greens, golden browns. The new queen's face looked firm and astute, her gaze direct and engaging. To render the clothing, Velázquez used a looser technique—one he had been developing in Italy—that combined strokes of different lengths and uneven layers of paint. He was now a mature painter, as accomplished as any in Europe. The trip to Italy had been a success. "Money well spent," the king must have told himself.

Velázquez reached Madrid in January. count-duke Olivares received him like a prince and gave an elaborate reception
in his honor. I was there, of course, and I saw how they fawned
over him.

"His Majesty allowed no one to paint either him or the
prince while I was gone," he told me proudly. Clearly, the flat-
tery was going to his head.

He hadn't forgotten his wife and daughter during his trav-
els, even though he hadn't found time to write. For Juana he
brought a lovely necklace of Murano beads, a cameo brooch,
an elaborate Italian petticoat, and a porcelain vase, and for
Paquita he brought a porcelain crucifix to hang on her wall.
There were gifts for the servants, too—a delicate silver rosary
from Rome for Arabela and a silk coif for Julia. He kissed Juana
tenderly when she thanked him for the gifts, but shared few
details about his trip. Maybe he thought that she wouldn't
understand the intricacies of the new techniques he had mas-
tered or maybe he thought she wouldn't be interested. But Juana
was disappointed.

Before long Velázquez had painted a delicate painting of
Prince Baltasar Carlos that made old ladies coo and sigh and
grown men puff out their chests with Spanish pride. It was different from anything Velázquez had ever done before. In the
painting, the royal toddler wears a black and gold dress with a
frilly collar and a red sash. He stands next to a dwarf child, one
of his tiny playmates. The diminutive prince wears a sword and
carries a dagger with a gold, bejeweled hilt. His companion
appears to be sneaking out of the room with the royal rattle and
an apple, but the future king doesn't look perturbed at all. He gazes
out at us with an air of tranquility—perhaps because he doesn't

need toys any more. The Cortes—that is, the national assembly—
has just sworn fealty to him, and his future seems certain. Toddler and dwarf are framed by richly textured burgundy curtains;
beneath their feet, a carpet of crimsons and oranges. The prince
sparkles like a diamond among so many heavy textiles, his forehead and lace catching the light and marking the peak of a tri-
angle formed by his face, the dwarf's white apron, and a hat
plume lying on the floor.

This was a new Velázquez, buzzed the Court, one who offered something fresh and vibrant instead of the usual stiff, drab
royal portraits. This was a virtuoso! He had learned from the Italians, but didn't imitate them. His technique and thoughtfulness
placed him apart, and Olivares and Fonseca were thrilled.

The paint had barely dried on his portrait of the prince
when Velázquez turned his attention back to the little boy's father. Within weeks, the protégé had produced a new portrait of
the king in a brown suit adorned in silver brocade. It was as if
the needlework had come alive. Velázquez had managed to capture the light dancing off the threads through a radically inno-
vative technique: sketch-like strokes of thickly applied paint that
made the brocade appear to float above the brown base of Don
Felipe's outfit, making the silver seem to glitter. The first time I
saw it, I could hardly believe it was made of pigments on canvas.
I was so awed by his vision—and by how much progress he'd
made—that if he had asked me to pose at that moment, I would
have abandoned all decency and thrown off my clothes in a
heartbeat!

What I couldn't have known at the time was that Venus
was already taking shape in his mind. Some aristocrat—to this
day, I'm not quite sure who he was, although I have my suspi-

cions—had offered him an extraordinary amount of money for a female nude. Did Velázquez hesitate? I doubt it. It was rumored at Court that he had painted nudes in Italy, and this would be a chance to bring his new aesthetic to Spain. His new style was already causing a frenzy, so why not introduce new subject matter as well? He wanted to paint as freely in Madrid as he had in Rome. And now a noble had offered him money to do it.

And besides, you know what they say about forbidden fruit. Moralists continued to rant about the vulgarity seeping out of Rome and Florence and disintegrating morals here at home. With this painting, Velázquez could thumb his nose at those tiresome old men and also earn some points with the king, whose appetites hadn't diminished at all with the birth of his heir.

I know now that he already had someone in mind to model: a delicate twenty-two-year-old with porcelain skin and flirtatious eyes, soft brown hair, and a neck as smooth as alabaster. A sassy girl, even brazen. She'd married a few years before and already had three children, but her waist was still as slender as a twig. I'm speaking, of course, of Doña Constanza Enríquez y Castro. When they had first met and she asked if Velázquez would paint her, he had turned her down. He had wanted to, though, and since then he *had* managed to paint her several times. She was a face in the crowd of *The Expulsion of the Moriscos* and a lady-in-waiting in a Court scene. He had done other paintings of Constanza, too—anonymous formal portraits, that sort of thing—but never a nude.

When he approached her, she giggled. He coaxed. She demurred. He insisted. Finally, she agreed. They would meet at the home of an unidentified patron. He would need her services for less than two weeks.

"That long?" she asked.

He explained that he would be working on other assignments at the same time.

"But everyone will recognize me. What about my husband's honor?"

This could be a problem, of course. Her husband, Don Basilio de Valdepeña y Fajardo, was a dimwit, and yet like all Spanish men, he was obsessed with honor. If someone whispered to him that his wife was stretching out on a divan in the buff for an artist, he would feel obligated to do something about it. The rules were clear. If your wife was cheating, or even appeared to be cheating, you got rid of her. This was no joke. A few years back, a certain Don Gutierre got it into his head that his wife was sleeping with a high-placed courtier. She was innocent, but no matter. The mere suspicion was enough to push Gutierre over the edge: he claimed she was sick and called a surgeon, then paid him to open her veins and bleed her to death. Velázquez had to be careful. He would paint her from the back, he said, and no one would be the wiser. He would call her Venus, which would confer an air of mystery and anonymity on her. He didn't say anything about the mirror—perhaps it hadn't even occurred to him yet to put a mirror in her hand.

"And what about the Inquisition?" Constanza wanted to know. What about the strictures against painting nudes? She wasn't afraid to do whatever he asked, she insisted. Indeed, she was looking forward to posing. But she didn't want to get herself killed in the process.

Velázquez smiled indulgently. He had thought through all

of these possibilities, he explained. His client had promised that the canvas would be kept in a private vault. No one would see it but a select group of friends—sophisticated men who appreciated this kind of art. The identity of both the painter and the model would remain secret.

They fixed a date. He described the location of the patron's house—a large mansion of the type they call a *palacio*. He told her to dress plainly to attract as little attention as possible and to come in through the servants' entrance. The door would be open, and no one would be there to receive her. She was to walk through the servants' hallway, turn right at the first door, go up the stairs, and enter the large room straight ahead. He would be waiting for her.

But mere days before the artist was due to begin, the project was delayed. Two people were to blame. The first was the count-duke of Olivares, whose reputation was deteriorating precipitously. The government was losing prestige both abroad and at home. Things were going from bad to worse, and the nation blamed Olivares. Spain was oozing blood and treasure all over the continent. Taxes were high, inflation was soaring, unemployment was rampant, and the national debt was enormous. Revolts were brewing in Catalonia and Portugal, and uprisings had started in the Basque country. On top of everything, the war in Mantua had ended with a treaty favorable to the French and so devastating for us that everyone said it was worse than surrender. People in high places were losing patience. Queen Isabel of Bourbon was a smart woman who knew about affairs of state, and she was convinced that Olivares was making a mess of things. Furthermore, Doña Isabel was still reeling from the scandal over La Calderona, for which she held Olivares responsible.

But the count-duke had an idea—one that he was sure would restore glory to both him and the king. The Crown's reputation, he knew, depended on Spain's economic prosperity. From the Austrian emperor to the poorest dirt farmer, nobody respected a monarchy that appeared destitute. If you weren't rich, at least you had to *appear* rich. To Olivares, appearances were just as good as reality, or perhaps they were the same thing. Many years before, Felipe II had built a delightful park near the Alcázar called El Retiro, with ponds and fountains and lovely tree-lined avenues. But now when Olivares looked at the park, he envisioned something far grander—great halls, ballrooms, galleries, chapels, theaters, courtyards, orchards, riding paths, woods for hunting, exotic gardens, a zoo, an aviary, and even an artificial lake for mock naval battles and aquatic exercises—a true pleasure palace, where the king could take his recreation without leaving Madrid. It would surely make Don Felipe the envy of every monarch in Europe, and Olivares a hero. He had to change the Crown's image before it was too late.

But it *was* too late. When Madrileños witnessed the hordes of carpenters and masons (whom the Crown had no money to pay) streaming onto the grounds, they were furious. In the midst of so much poverty and deprivation, thousands of men were building . . . a royal aviary? Should housing exotic birds really be the priority of a monarch whose realm was on the verge of ruin? Within days, the aviary, nicknamed *El Gallinero*, the Henhouse, became a symbol of Olivares's whole harebrained project and the distorted values that prevailed at Court.

Olivares was in such a rush to get the new pleasure palace done that everything was assembled in a slipshod way. The king's fabulous aviary was held together with chicken wire. The great Olivares, chief administrator of a country drowning in debt, put together a fantasy of glitter and glamour with chicken wire! Spain became the laughingstock of Europe. What had appeared to be a great nation was now exposed as a crumbling facade. Richelieu threatened to send all of France's chicken coop builders across the Pyrenees to help Olivares fill Madrid with strands of metal. At home, broadsheets depicting Don Gaspar in a decrepit cage fondling hens appeared on every wall.

In an effort to change public opinion Olivares named the place the Royal House of the Buen Retiro, which was supposed to suggest a religious retreat as well as a place of withdrawal from the cares of the world. Meditating mystics. Contemplative courtiers. That sort of thing. But it didn't catch on, at least not in Olivares's lifetime. Through it all, Velázquez painted. He painted portraits and more portraits, and occasionally a religious allegory. What he didn't paint was Venus because there was no time. Olivares's crowning achievement was to be the *salón del Buen Retiro,* a fabulous hall, the most significant in the palace, which would eventually serve as a throne room where the king presided over Court ceremonies. It would be known as the Hall of Realms, and it would be decorated with twelve large battle paintings commissioned from Court artists, as well as five royal equestrian portraits painted by Velázquez—a project so demanding it would keep the king's favorite painter busy for months.

But as I mentioned, Olivares wasn't the only one to blame for the delay. Pesky rumors had started to surface shortly after his return from Italy—a sideward glance, a raised eyebrow—but at first, Velázquez didn't pay much attention. One day, after he had finished the equestrians and was putting the final touches on a monumental painting of Saint Anthony, Constanza tiptoed into the studio. She wasn't supposed to be there, but he didn't bother throwing her out. He had work to finish, and he didn't want a row.

"I care about you, Diego," she began. "*She* doesn't. Otherwise she wouldn't be making a fool out of you."

Velázquez frowned as he dipped his brush into a tiny pot. "Well, I was abroad and she needed someone."

"How can you remain so unruffled? Everyone's whispering. It makes you look terrible."

"Don't worry. I'll take care of it."

"Will you? Will you get rid of her? That way, you and I could . . ."

"I told you—I'll take care of it."

Constanza arched her back and stuck out the tip of her tongue like a kitten. If people were talking, he had to do *something*. At the very least, he could confine Juana to their home, or move her to an obscure corner of the city. Perhaps he'd even send her back to Seville or put her in a convent. Which would mean that he'd have more time for Constanza.

She didn't actually say these things out loud, but Velázquez sensed that she was thinking them.

"Do you promise?" she purred.

"I'm working, Constanza," he said. "I'll think about it. Please leave now."

Velázquez was troubled, of course. What man wouldn't be? Especially a man like him. After all, he was a courtier, not just a painter. There was talk of making him royal wardrobe assistant—a highly enviable position. He was beginning to dare to hope that he would someday be named a Knight of the Order of Santiago, one of the most elite societies in Spain. Maybe it was sheer fantasy, yet one could wish. But a scandal concerning his wife would ruin everything.

Velázquez pursed his lips as he applied swaths of gray-green to the background. Trees and forests appeared magically behind Saint Anthony, who stood resolutely facing the Devil. Velázquez put down his brush and stepped away from the canvas. He stared at his character, old and infirm, yet strong before danger. Saint Anthony was a tough man, thought Velázquez, not because he attacked his enemy with cunning and stealth, but because he looked him in the eye. Rather than sneak around and spy on his wife like a cuckold in a *comedia*, Velázquez decided to do what characters in plays never did: he would simply ask Juana to explain what happened.

Mazo came in and began mixing pigment in a corner. Suddenly, he looked up. The two men locked eyes. Velázquez's breathing had become jagged.

Mazo looked around as though he thought he might find something appropriate to say floating up by the moldings. "Forgive me . . ." he began. "Forgive me, Don Diego, but you look troubled. Is there anything I can do for you?"

The younger man glided across the room cautiously, so as not to spill any paint. Then he picked up a brush and began to fill in the mountains Velázquez had outlined above the forest.

"Don Diego?" Mazo said without looking away from his work.

Velázquez smiled. "Yes," he said softly, "I believe there *is* something you can do for me."

That night, Velázquez found Juana sitting by the brazier in her *estrado*, Paquita crouched on a cushion in front of her. Both of them were squinting into the flickering light and laughing. Instead of the dainty giggle of a Court lady, Paquita had the full-throated chortle of a farm girl. On a nearby table, an oil lamp sputtered and glimmered. Juana had laid her embroidery on her lap in order to give her full attention to her daughter.

Velázquez stood in the doorway. Paquita was a satisfying child, he thought—boisterous and unladylike, but smart, good-natured, and disarming. He would have liked to have a son, yes, but God, he knew, distributed riches in unpredictable ways. Some are blessed with children, some with wealth, and some with talent. It's true that some have everything, but most don't, and he had no reason to complain. He was the king's favorite painter, and he was on his way to a promotion. Still, he felt deeply burdened that evening, as if a heavy ball of wax had lodged itself in his stomach. He had no taste for what he knew he had to do.

His eyes passed from his wife to his daughter. He had been wrong, he realized. Paquita wasn't a child, but a young woman. She was only twelve, but her breasts heaved under her bodice, and her movements revealed the confidence and carriage of a young lady. Yes, she could be silly, but what woman is above silliness? And Juana? Velázquez searched her face for signs of betrayal, but there, in the shimmer of the flame, he saw only candor.

"Paquita," said Velázquez pleasantly, "would you mind giving your *señora madre* and me a moment alone? We need to speak about a private matter." He sat down on a stool by the window as Paquita hurried out.

"What is it?" asked Juana after the girl had closed the door.

Velázquez noted that his wife seemed perfectly composed. He knew, of course, that women could be cunning where adultery was involved, and yet Juana gave no sign of nerves.

"Doña Juana," he began. "People are talking . . ."

"About what?" She picked up her embroidery and began to cover a white handkerchief with tiny blue petals.

"About the prince's baptism, Juana." He made his voice as soft and gentle as he could, as unthreatening as possible. If he was going to catch her in a lie, the worst thing he could do was alarm her.

"Still? Whatever for? That was nearly two years ago. I can't imagine there's anything left to say."

Did she sound a bit testy? Velázquez pondered the possibility. A bit defensive? "Nevertheless, Juana, many are still talking about the baptism, at least as it concerns me."

"*You*? You weren't even here! You were in Italy." Juana was looking at him as though he were out of his mind.

"That's precisely the point, Juana. I wasn't here, but you went anyway."

"What did you expect me to do? Stay at home for the biggest event of the social season? What would their Majesties have thought if Velázquez hadn't been represented at the event of the decade?"

"You went with another man!" He struggled to strike a delicate balance in his tone—he wanted to sound emphatic, but not accusatory.

Juana looked at him for a long time, and Velázquez stared back, trying to read her expression. All of a sudden, she burst out laughing.

"Another man! I went with your apprentice, Juan Bautista Martínez del Mazo! I hardly kept it a secret, Diego. I myself told you about it."

"The point is, Juana, he's a man, you're a woman, and people draw conclusions."

"*Virgen santísima*, husband. I'm a married woman, thirty-two years old. Mazo is a child."

Velázquez knew there was no point in delving further. Juana had gone to the affair accompanied by her daughter and two maids, not only by Mazo. She had walked into the church with him in full view of the Court. She wasn't a brazen woman—if she had had something to hide, she would have been far more subtle in her behavior. He knew all of this—he had always known it, and he felt foolish for forcing this conversation on her, but even so, if people were impugning his honor, he had to set the situation right.

"They're gossiping about it at Court, Juana. They look at me askance."

"I see . . ." She knew the rules as well as he did. If a man became the subject of public chatter, he had to cleanse his name. Still, she couldn't bring herself to believe that her husband would actually harm her. "What do you propose?"

"I've been thinking . . ."

"About running me through with a sword?"

"I've been thinking about Paquita. She's nearly thirteen."

"Oh, Diego, no. She's just a baby."

"If you went to the baptism accompanied by your daughter's fiancé, no one would think anything of it."

"Fiancé. You mean Mazo."

"It makes sense, doesn't it? I married my painting master's daughter. It's logical that my apprentice would marry Paquita."

Juana put down her embroidery and sighed. Tiny wrinkles were forming by her eyes, and in the flicker of the fire, her skin looked rough in spite of the pomades of animal fat she rubbed on her cheeks every night. "Well . . . She likes him, I know that much." Juana paused and looked into the flame. "He told her she had talent."

"She does, it's true, but she won't have much need for it once she starts having babies. I'll talk to him, and if he agrees, you can talk to her. Where's Arabela? It will be up to her to prepare Paquita's trousseau."

"Oh! I forgot to tell you. Arabela had a visitor today. A young man. Looked like a soldier. Shabby and scruffy."

"If he's looking for work, we don't have anything."

"I don't think he was looking for work. He wanted to talk to Arabela. He asked for her by name."

"At her age?"

"Why are you so suspicious today? I have the impression he's a relative."

"I didn't know Arabela had family. Who does she say he is?"

"I haven't seen her. In fact, she might still be downstairs talking to him. Although maybe not. It's pretty late. Should I call for her?"

"No, let me talk to Mazo first. Then, if he agrees, we can start planning."

"Well, I don't think he'll need much convincing," Juana said to herself, grinning slightly.

13

Family Business
1633 – 1635

"I WAS CAREFUL. I DIDN'T WANT TO FRIGHTEN HER. I WASHED my shirt and my feet. The shirt is so threadbare in places that my chest hairs stick out of it, but it's the only one I have. I'd have liked her to see me in a new suit of clothes with no patches or tears, but you have what you have. I didn't want to disappoint her, but I did."

"I'm sure she didn't care about your clothes."

"'We used to know each other,' I said to her. 'A long time ago.' She didn't say anything for a long time. Then she . . . I don't know to explain it . . . she kind of moved her mouth without speaking and caught her breath. I thought she might faint, but she didn't. She just sort of crumpled onto a stool. She's not ugly, you know. I mean, for a woman her age. I thought she'd be all wrinkled, crags from her nose to her lips. She has creases around her eyes, of course, and furrows over her brow, but she's not a hag."

"Of course not, Carlos," I said. "Arabela was a pretty woman when she was young, and she's aged well."

"Finally she said to me: 'In Seville? Did I know you in Seville?'

"'Yes,' I said, 'but I looked different then. I was a child.' She blinked at me and her jaw tightened. I could see her straining to figure it out. Then her gaze shifted. She stared down at the floorboards and moved her foot as though she were mashing ashes into the ground. When she finally lifted her eyes, she fixed them on the wall behind me. I knew then that she understood. What did I expect her to do? Jump up and hug me? No, that's not our way. We're reserved. 'Are you . . . a chandler?' she asked finally.

"'No. I was apprenticed to a chandler, but I ran away and became a soldier.' She mulled over this new piece of information."

"Remember, Carlos," I interjected. "This was a shock for her. She hadn't seen you in decades."

"But she didn't seem shocked," Carlos said. "She just sat there, hunched over on her stool. It was as though she'd always known I'd come back, but hadn't decided how she'd react when I did. 'I was in the Low Countries,' I told her, 'fighting Protestants for His Majesty, King Felipe IV.' I opened my shirt and showed her my shoulder. 'See this, Mother?' I said. 'It's a bullet wound. It's healed, though.'

"All of a sudden, her features hardened. 'You look poor,' she growled. 'I can't give you anything. I'm poor myself. Born poor, die poor, that's how it is for people like me.'

"'You live in a nice house, Mother,' I said.

"'It's not my house,' she snapped. 'I don't have anything of my own. Once in a while the *señora* gives me an old dress or a pair of shoes. But I have nothing to share.'"

Carlos must have felt as though she'd booted him in the gut, but all he said to me was: "I told her it didn't matter, I was going away again."

"Are you?" I asked him.

"Yes, I am. I'm going to Peru. I told my Mother: 'In the New World a man like me can make a future for himself. I'm still young. I know how to fight. If you win territory for the king, he'll make you a gentleman. He'll give you land and all the Indians in it. There are opportunities in the colonies, Mother. If I say here, I'll starve.'

"'You may starve anyway,' she said. I laughed. I assumed it was a joke, but even so, I felt uneasy. After that, I shut up. The explosion of words had worn me out. I wanted to leave, but I didn't know how to end the conversation. 'What about a wife?' she asked suddenly. 'Are you going to take an Indian woman?' My mother is a servant, but she's proud of her Old Christian blood. She didn't want half-breed grandchildren — even if they were halfway around the world.

"'The king sends boatloads of Spanish women to the colonies every year,' I told her, 'just so Spanish men won't marry Indians. Don't worry, Mother. I'll be waiting by the dock when the ships come in with Christian *señoritas*.'

"'Probably damaged goods,' retorted Arabela. 'Ugly or deflowered or dowerless. Or else some lovechild someone wants to get out of the way.'

"'It doesn't matter,' I told her. 'In the New World, nobody knows where you came from. And I'll make enough money that I won't need a dowry. As for whether or not she's a beauty . . . well, sometimes you have to take what you can get. I'm old enough to know that.'"

Carlos asked Arabela for his blessing, and she gave it to him. I suppose that she had never really known her son, and so she didn't miss him when he left. At least, nobody ever heard her crying. He appeared in her life suddenly, and he left the same way. It wasn't until years later that she found out what happened to him.

It is just before dawn, during the spectral hour before things take on color. Houses, horses, coaches, and fountains that shine bronze in the daylight are nothing more than monochrome shadows at dawn. The air reeks of rotting leaves and piss from chamber pots. Cold grips your temples like pincers. Your nostrils stick together and your throat burns raw. I see you, a silhouette gliding over dull cobblestones. You shouldn't be out alone, not without a maid. You shouldn't be floating like a ghost through the dark. But Velázquez has called for you. He says he must speak to you. He has something urgent to tell you. You can't wait for daybreak. You know that he and Mazo are already in the studio. They arrive before dawn to prepare for the day's work. They clean brushes by candlelight and stretch canvases. They perform those tasks that don't require natural light.

I can see you in my mind's eye, even though I'm crouching here by the window of my cell with paper and quill. I'm supposed to be shelling peas in the convent kitchen. I'll go down and finish my tasks as soon as I write these few lines. I see you, even though we're separated by time and space. I see you now and I see you when I work alone in the kitchen—Cintia never helps with the household chores—and I close my eyes and remember. I see you climbing the stairs, opening the door, entering the studio. You slip off your cape and wait for instructions. Velázquez nods at Mazo, and the younger man leaves the room.

"When do we begin?" you whisper.

"Not yet," he responds. "Not today and, quite frankly, not for a while."

"But I thought . . . You said you wanted to see me."

"You didn't have to come before dawn. I only wanted to tell you we're going to have to wait. I have too much work right now, and what with Paquita's wedding . . ."

"You said it wasn't going to be a grandiose affair."

"It isn't, but there are decisions to be made. The dress is of primary importance. I'm going to pick out the fabrics myself, and it will be an involved process."

". . . But surely the mother . . ."

". . . No, I'm going to do it. It's an investment. The fabric will have to be resold afterward. I can't let Juana do it on her own."

I see you scrunching up your face. Squinting and puckering your lips. You're prepared to pout and sniff, but Velázquez raises his hand and halts the show, the way he always does when he senses a storm brewing. "I have no time for tantrums, Constanza." By now light is streaming through the window, the low, pale light of an autumn daybreak. As soon as the angle and intensity are right, he'll want to get to work. You should leave. "I have this canvas to finish, and afterward the king wants a painting commemorating the siege of Breda. I'll have to leave before dusk because the seamstress is coming by the house. Juana and Paquita will have something to say about the style, of course, but I will oversee the cloth and trims."

"A year has gone by since we first talked about the painting. By the time you get to it, I'll be old and fat!"

"I'll find someone else, then," says Velázquez cruelly. He is already engrossed in his work. If you say something else, he won't hear you.

"I hate you!" you blurt out. Maybe you stomp out of the room or maybe you hold back, weeping softly, praying he'll change his mind.

Velázquez told me about that encounter many years after it happened, Constanza. When I think about it, I can't help but pity you. I didn't really know you back then, but I'd seen you at Court flirting with the handsome young men who went hunting with the king. People talked about you. Courtiers had seen you and Velázquez at one of the royal lodges. You followed Velázquez around like a hound puppy, even though your husband was right there in the tracking party. Ah yes, Constanza, you were hunting, but not for boar. What happened at that lodge? In those days, I saw you as a rival—how could I not?— but now I feel pity for you. You wanted so much to be Venus. You were such a pretty girl, so full of ambition. Why did things have to end so badly?

Back at the house on Calle de Convalescientes, Juana and Paquita huddled over bolts of fabric and fashion engravings with the dressmaker.

"*Papá* says he will make the final decision," grumbled Paquita, "but that doesn't seem fair. I'm the one who's going to be wearing the dress."

"We can look at the cloth and see what we like," said Juana. "But he's going to pay for it, so he makes the final decision."

"I imagine you'll want a bell farthingale," said the dressmaker importantly. "The *verdugado redondo* is very stylish." She opened a fashion book with pictures of wide hoop contraptions, and pointed to the *verdugado*, a stiff petticoat cinched tightly at the waist that gave form to the overskirt.

By the time Velázquez arrived for the midday meal, Paquita had set aside four or five bolts of fabric to show her father: a peach-colored silk, a flesh-colored satin, a pale pink figured gauze with an elaborate pomegranate design. Brocade was out of the question — the new sumptuary laws forbade it.

Velázquez vetoed the print the minute he saw it. "That one is too fragile," he observed. "It'll fall apart when you take out the stitching."

"But these pomegranate and artichoke motifs are fashionable right now!"

"Well, see if there's one that isn't so flimsy."

After the wedding, the dress would be disassembled, and every part of it, from the fabric to the trim to the buttons and hooks, would be sold, so that Velázquez could recuperate his outlay. That's what everyone did. Otherwise, how could a man afford to marry off a daughter?

In the end he chose a soft coral silk. The following week, the dressmaker appeared with drawings of a funnel skirt with a close bodice cut low and square to allow for a huge collar and a velvet vest of a deeper shade, long and pointed to extend the torso. Paquita peered at the sketches. From underneath, a salmon-colored crinoline petticoat peeked out, repeating the motif of the lace ruff, which was stiffened to extend at the sides and back. Although a wealthier man might have ordered ornate embroidery incrusted with jewels, Velázquez settled for silver braid trimming. Paquita insisted on fashionably tight sleeves with over-sleeves of rose printed satin with gauzy blush-hued cuffs. Although the feet would be invisible, Velázquez picked out a silk high-heeled shoe, open at the back and adorned with rhinestones.

"How will I walk in this petticoat?" exclaimed Paquita. "To sit down I'll have to take it off and hold it in my hand!"

Arrangements for the betrothal hadn't been complicated. Mazo lived in a small room in Velázquez's house, and he shared Velázquez's studio at Court. Nothing much would change, except that the young couple would move to a sunny suite facing the street on an upper floor. Eventually, perhaps, Mazo would be able to purchase his own house, but for the moment, this would do. Velázquez offered a dowry of ten thousand ducats.

The wedding was set for late September, after the summer's stifling heat and before the sad pageants of All Souls' Day and the Day of the Dead. Earlier in the month, Velázquez painted a lovely wedding portrait of Paquita, a testament as much to the loveliness of the child as to the magnificent finery her father had provided. She wore a long, gold necklace that had been Juana's and would now be part of her dowry, as well as jewels she borrowed from friends. In the Italian style, she carried a little brown and white spaniel for the portrait. It appeared in the picture with blue bows on its ears and tiny diamond earrings. Paquita hadn't actually posed with the dog—Velázquez was terrified that if she did, it would rip the subtle stitching to shreds. Instead, he quickly sketched the puppy of one of the Court ladies and integrated it into the painting afterward.

Not six months after the betrothal ceremony, the wedding party set off from Velázquez's house on Convalescientes to the neighborhood church where the couple was to be married. A small band of friends and relatives lined up in the foyer. It was Sunday, of course, and church bells filled the air—the cathedral bells with their rich, baritone clang; the parish bells with their tenor chime; the tiny bells of the monastery chapel, with their dainty tinkle. Although Madrid can be rainy in the fall, the sun peeked out from a somber firmament and the clouds held their moisture.

The musicians waited outside the house with their pipes and their drums. When the lead piper gave the signal, they began their slow march through the streets of the city. The bride followed, accompanied by girls carrying rosemary and garlands of wheat tied in colorful satin ribbons. Next came the groom and his companions, all dressed in bright colors and elegant plumes. As they wound their way through the city, people called out to the betrothed from their balconies. "May you be rich and healthy!" "May you have a dozen sons!"

Velázquez and Juana waited inside the church—he in the men's section, and she in the women's. His entourage was composed of the count-duke, courtiers, and painters, as well as Mazo's father, brothers, uncles, and male cousins. Hers was made up of Mazo's mother and female relatives, a handful of friends, Arabela, and Julia.

After the ceremony, Paquita and her party gathered at Velázquez's house, where a notary was waiting. He was a tall, thin man with a ruddy complexion, and he wore a long burgundy cape and a red cap encircled by a ribbon. In his official outfit, he looked like a giant rhubarb carrying a large book.

Shortly afterward, Mazo appeared with his entourage. The notary took his place at one end of the *sala* and adopted an imposing stance. The bride and groom stood at either side of the room. He cleared his throat and turned toward Paquita.

"Do you, Doña Francisca, take Don Juan to be your lawful husband freely and without duress?" he asked, repeating the question the priest had asked in the church.

"Yes, I do," whispered Paquita, blushing.

Then, turning toward Mazo, he said, "And you, Don Juan, do you take Doña Francisca to be your lawful wife freely and without duress?"

"Yes, sir. I do."

Arabela was sobbing like a Magdalene. She had watched her son walk out of her life without shedding a tear, but this was different. Paquita had grown up clinging to Arabela's skirts. It was Arabela, not Juana, who had swaddled her and changed her diapers, who had brushed and bathed her. Arabela had nursed her through fevers and through her mother's melancholia after the death of baby Ignacia. She had watched Paquita grow into a young woman, with gentle curves, smooth skin, and tresses the color of almond kernels. And now, Paquita was getting married, even though she still played with a cup and ball.

After the notary had received the couple's statement of mutual consent, he tipped his leafy head toward Paquita and walked toward her holding out his hand. He led her to her new husband, and the bride and groom exchanged rings before their parents and guests. Everyone cheered, but sedately, as behooved courtiers. The guests then moved into the dining room for the wedding banquet.

The company sat at two long tables, the men with Mazo and the women with Paquita. It was mushroom season, and most of the huge platters that servants brought in were filled with mushrooms in one form or another—in stews, pies, soups. Afterward there were fruits and cakes and spiced wine for the ladies, and brandy for the men. Musicians circulated through the room enlivening the atmosphere. Sometime before the guests left, Paquita and Mazo snuck upstairs to their new living quarters.

Juana watched them go. She hadn't cried all evening, but now, suddenly, a tempest welled up inside her.

"The baby," she whispered to Velázquez. "Our baby. I remember the day she was born. Old Almedina delivered her." Her voice sounded throaty to her own ear, and her hands quivered like aspen leaves in the breeze.

Velázquez laid his hand on her shoulder. He was still a handsome young man of thirty-four, with untamed black hair, a gallant mustache, and a neatly trimmed beard. His swarthy skin, glistened with perspiration. It had been a nerve-wracking day, and although it wasn't hot, the strain of receiving guests and the heavy party clothes left him drenched. Still, he appeared composed as he steadied his wife, one hand under her elbow and one around her back.

Juana sobbed into his fine velvet sleeve. Quiet, constrained little sobs. "I can't help thinking . . ."

Velázquez stroked her cheek. "Don't torture yourself, Juana. God's ways will always remain mysterious to us."

"But if she had lived . . ."

"I know, Juana," he whispered.

"If she had lived, we'd be planning her wedding soon, too."

"She's with God now—what else is there to say?"

"I miss her, Diego. I miss my little Ignacia."

"I miss her too," he whispered.

I suspect that he was lying. The truth is, I don't think that Velázquez ever thought of Ignacia. He lived for his work, after all, and he was driven by ambition.

"It was a lovely wedding," said Velázquez, as he deposited Juana in her suite.

"Except . . ."

"Yes, except Ignacia . . ."

"Ignacia and *Papá*."

Pacheco had written a fortnight earlier. He just couldn't come to the wedding, he said. He was too old and too infirm. His right hip hurt, and his knees ached. He could no longer sit in a carriage for hours on end—the jarring thud of wagon wheels against the rocky, mountain road were too much for him. I understand what he meant. Now that I'm old, everything hurts me, too, especially my fingers, my wrist, and my right shoulder. That's what happens when you get to be my age. There isn't a single part of your body that doesn't torture you once in a while, except . . . well, except those parts that torture you all the time.

I'm too tired to copy down Pacheco's entire letter. My eyes are bothering me and the joints of my fingers are swollen. On top of everything, my head is throbbing. I'll just copy down a paragraph, and then I'll go back to my room and pray to Saint Teresa, the patron saint of headaches.

I'm truly sorry to miss the wedding of my only granddaughter, but as I explained above, I simply can't travel anymore. And I have another piece of sad news to relate to you, my dearest Juana. Our cherished Sister Inmaculada, spiritual director to us all, passed from this valley of tears just one week ago today. The Carmelite sisters gave her a lovely burial. They have the voices of angels, these dear women, and they sang so beautifully at her funeral mass. I know you haven't seen her in years, but she never failed to ask about you. She loved you very much, Juana, just as she loved your blessed mother. We will miss her sorely.

The night of Paquita's wedding, Juana wept for her daughter's bygone girlhood, and for her own impending old age. She was still in her early thirties, but soon she would be a grandmother, which meant she would be old. She wept for her dead baby Ignacia, gone to eternal life before she had known the joy and bitterness of this one. She wept for her father's absence and his infirmities, and for the passing of her old friend Sister Inmaculada, who had comforted her after she'd lost her mother. She crumpled into her chair and wept until her eyes stung, a broken carcass of sorrow.

Juana wanted to go to her husband. She wanted to lie in his arms and feel the warmth of his chest and his breath on her cheek. She wanted to feel his touch, his fingers on her aching temples. Only Velázquez could breathe life into her wrecked body. So she rose from her chair, put on her shawl, lit a candle, and made her way down the hall.

Spring followed winter and summer followed spring. Day blended into day, sunrise into daylight, dusk into dark. Time is mystifying. Some incidents you remember in stark detail, but then whole months or even years go by in a blur.

For example, Velázquez did in fact become royal wardrobe assistant, and he passed his usher's title to Mazo. There must have been a ceremony or at least an announcement, but I don't remember. And he finished *The Surrender of Breda*. I'm sure there was an unveiling, but it's a blank in my mind. Still, the painting's there, hanging in the Hall of Realms. War broke out with France, the Pope condemned Galileo as a heretic, Calderón wrote his marvelous new play *Life Is a Dream*—everybody knows these things happened. But what was I doing? I can't tell you. It's a fog. It's strange how you get lost in the day-to-day and forget that outside your little world things are happening.

The next thing I remember with any clarity took place three years after the wedding, on a brisk fall afternoon. Juana was rocking baby Ana while Arabela amused two-year-old Juanita with a cat's cradle. Juana had taken the baby from her nurse for the sheer pleasure of holding her. It wasn't her place to be rocking the infant, of course—Velázquez thought it unseemly for a grandmother to perform such duties herself—but Juana refused to be deterred. The sensation of a squirming newborn against her breast, the sweet perfume of freshly scented swaddling clothes—these were joys she had no wish to forgo. Juanita would be sent away soon enough to a convent school or farmed out to a petty noblewoman to be educated in reading, writing, and the feminine arts of spinning and embroidery, as was customary for the offspring of courtiers. While the children were nearby, she would enjoy them.

"Ana, Anita," she cooed. "La la la Anita." The tiny body was a warm, moist sponge against her body. She held the child closer, and the baby gurgled.

"Don't you want to put her in the cradle, *señora*? She might get accustomed to being held."

Juana closed her eyes and breathed deeply. "What of it, Arabela?" she murmured. "What of it?"

Sapphire shadows crept across the walls, the familiar harbingers of evening. Forms grew indistinct—the cradle, the cot, the pile of diapers, Arabela's furrowed brow and slackening jaw. The rocking chair creaked, its irregular, whiny music somehow reassuring.

The nursery door cracked and a silhouette appeared in the doorway. It was Julia.

"There's someone to see you, *señora*." Juana had never seen her fair-skinned maid look so flustered. Julia's voice was low and uncertain, as though she were hiding something. She looked down at her apron. "It's Lidia," she whispered. "Lidia, the housemaid . . . the one who used to work here."

Juana's gaze met Arabela's.

"Lidia . . . it can't be." Juana felt her arms go rubbery. Alarmed that she might drop the baby, she stumbled out of the chair, clutching it against her. Arabela took the child and laid her in the cradle. "Say I'm not here! The nerve! How dare she set foot in this house!"

Julia pursed her lips. She stared at the floorboards. "*Señora*," she stammered. "Forgive me . . . but I think you should see her."

"You go," snapped Juana, clamping her eyes on Arabela.

The old woman gathered up her shawl and slipped out of the room behind Julia.

Ten minutes later, she was back.

"You have to go, Doña Juana," she said calmly.

"But . . ."

"You have to go."

14
Appearances
1636–1638

"Lidia," Juana hissed under her breath. "Lidia!" Lidia, with her delicate frame, her curvaceous hips, and gazelle-like neck. With her soft brown hair. Her irritating habit of placing flowers in Juana's room. Her more irritating habit of hovering over Juana's husband. She had posed for his first painting of the Virgin! Lidia—the Virgin! What about Lidia the slut who couldn't take her eyes off another woman's man!

Lidia hadn't occupied Juana's thoughts for years. The last thing Juana had heard was that the girl's husband had been promoted to carpenter and shipped off to one of the *sitios reales*, where His Majesty and his men chased boars all day, danced all night, and slept with every woman in sight. "What does she want in this house?" Juana asked herself as she trudged down the stairs.

Juana approached the servants' entrance with the regal bearing of Empress Leonora of the Holy Roman Empire. She thrust out her chest, raised her chin, and prepared to issue a command: "Get out of this house!"

But at the sight of Lidia, she deflated. This was not the sassy housemaid she remembered. This woman looked old, at least twenty years older than Juana. Her face was filthy and wadded like a clump of grimy cobwebs. And where were the tiny breasts and waist? This ghoul had a torso like a lumpy pillow. She moved unsteadily, limping and in obvious pain. Her lower lip was swollen and her jaw had turned a nauseating yellow-tinged blue. Juana gulped air and stared. The visitor stared back out of watery eyes.

Yes, Juana decided after a moment, this actually was Lidia. Behind the damaged exterior she detected a trace of Lidia's old sultry fierceness, her defiant determination. The woman was a bruised flower, but noxious and barbed, like a thorn apple blossom. The bundle in Lidia's arms shifted position and whimpered. The baby looked to be eight or ten months old and seemed out of place. Juana was afraid Lidia would drop it and beckoned to her to sit down, but the former maid remained standing

"*Gracias, señora,* thank you for seeing me." Her voice seemed obstructed. She could hardly push out the words.

Juana signaled to Julia to take the baby. Julia scowled as if such a task were beneath her. Her job was to accompany her mistress to Court, her crinkled brow seemed to say, not play nanny to a battered carpenter's wife.

"Sit down there, on that bench by the fire. I'll have them bring you some broth from the kitchen," said Juana. Then, anticipating protests, she added: "Don't argue with me."

"*Gracias, señora.*" In spite of herself, Lidia cowered under Juana's gaze.

With an unsteady hand, she sucked the broth through swollen lips. The warmth of it seemed to soothe her. Tears trickled from her eyes, and Juana looked away. Lidia reminded her of a storm-battered kitten she had once pulled out from a clump of bushes. Pacheco had told her to get rid of it, but the animal was scrappy and feisty and determined to survive, so she kept it anyway, in the kitchen and out of sight, where it grew into a fine, fat mouser. Would this woman recover as the cat had? Juana had hated this woman, wished her dead, but now she felt an unexpected compassion—and admiration for that boldness that had brought her out of whatever messy situation she was in and back to the place that had been her home. What could have happened to her? Juana thought it would be insensitive to press for an explanation just yet, so when Lidia had finished her broth, Juana ordered Julia to find a place for her and her child in the servants' quarters and let her rest.

It wasn't until two weeks later that Juana saw her again. She was struggling to help the cook, Bárbara, carry provisions into the kitchen. She limped in pain, but it was clear she wanted to make herself useful. Bárbara was not an overly patient woman. She had a household to provide food for, and she preferred to dispatch her tasks as quickly and efficiently as possible. Marketing at dawn, peeling, shelling, cutting, mixing, stewing, and baking in the mid to late morning to prepare for the midday meal. Then more peeling and shelling for the light repast at dusk and another in late evening. Still, she waited without comment as Lidia lugged bundles of vegetables, jugs of oil, animal carcasses, and condiment pouches across the patio with the help of Andrés, the houseboy. Lidia worked in silence, always with her baby nestled in a sling snug against her back.

"He kept his rage close, like a dog on a tether," she whispered by way of beginning when she was finally ready to tell her story. It was a beautiful day in early spring, and Juana was relaxing in a rocking chair by her brazier, embroidering. Arabela sat on a cushion by the flame, tatting lace, and Julia crouched next to her, sewing a gown for Ana.

"Go on, Lidia."

"You won't send me away, will you, *señora?*"

"No, I won't send you away." She sighed. She had been thinking about a childhood story of a snake caught under a rock. A farmer saw the creature squirming and writhing, so he took pity and freed it. No sooner had the farmer moved the rock and freed the snake than it reared up his head and hissed. Then it bit the farmer on the ankle.

"How can you pay a good deed with evil?" gasped the farmer right before he died.

"It's your fault," laughed the snake, "for being stupid enough to trust a viper!"

Would Lidia do the same to her? wondered Juana. Would she turn out to be a faithful family servant, like the cat she had rescued, or would she turn out to be a serpent under a rock?

"I won't send you away," Juana repeated . . . but with misgivings. Lidia had already regained her color. How long before she turned back into the spirited minx she had once been?

"His rage was like a dog," Lidia began again. "It was always with him, an inseparable companion. He nurtured it. It slept by our mat and waited in a corner when he ate. He cherished his rage."

Sancho hadn't been averse to marriage. He knew it was the fate of men, whether noble or common, just like bowel movements and death. What he had resented was the heavy-handed way in which Emilio, the master carpenter, had decided the matter without even consulting him.

"I have a wife for you," he had said. "A maid in the house of Velázquez, the painter. She's too good for you, really, but old Pacheco seems in a hurry to get rid of her. He offered two hundred *maravedís*, fifty for you and one fifty for me. Now sandpaper those boards, and don't stop until you're done."

Sancho was glad to get the money, so he said nothing. Carpenters hadn't been paid for months, and apprentices weren't paid at all. Sancho depended on Basilio for sustenance, and so if Emilio had nothing, Sancho had even less. Any amount of cash, no matter how small, was welcome.

Lidia loved life at Court. She was put to work in the laundry, where she scrubbed, rubbed, wrung, and hung out to dry the table linen and bedsheets of lords and ladies. The scent of lilac water intoxicated her. Folding dainty embroidered hand towels thrilled her. Just knowing that the fabric in her fingers had touched the flesh of dukes and countesses made her feel significant. She lived in their realm and breathed the same air.

Before long she learned her way around the Alcázar and discovered ways to sneak out from among the piles of cloth. She tiptoed like a thief through the corridors pretending to do her job and spying on her betters. Finally, she discovered what she was looking for: Velázquez's studio.

Juana could imagine her stealing in, smiling coyly, curtseying, and handing Velázquez a sweet-smelling hand towel, pretending to be flustered at his amazement—"Oh, Don Diego, I must be in the wrong place . . . I thought . . ." Juana could imagine her giggling and turning to run out, dropping a cloth and bending to retrieve it, wiggling her little bottom in provocation. Naturally, she didn't tell Juana everything. She did reveal that after she found him, she saw the painter again. How often and under what circumstances, Juana could guess, but Lidia didn't elaborate. She treaded carefully. She lowered her eyes appropriately and offered feeble explanations: "I was so happy to see someone from home!" She knew she couldn't leave Velázquez out of her story entirely because everyone had seen her likeness in *The Expulsion of the Moriscos*. But she didn't dwell on it. She didn't gloat.

The one thing she didn't like about Court life was her husband, Sancho. She had dreamed of a handsome, dark-haired lover, someone debonair and worldly. (She had dreamed of Velázquez, although of course she didn't say so.) Sancho was everything she'd never dreamed of, not even in nightmares. Short and stocky, with a chunky neck and uneven teeth, he was bearishly ugly. To Lidia, he looked liked a weather-beaten keg placed over thick, stumpy logs. He reeked of garlic and farted like a cannon firing rotten eggs. When he ate, he reminded her of a hyena from the king's menagerie—the way he tore his food apart with grubby claws and stuffed it into his mouth. And he liked his wine, too. Maybe she'd have gotten used to his nauseating face and manners if he'd at least been gentle, or if he didn't gamble away the few *blancas* he managed to get his hands on. But Sancho was brutish and irresponsible and as thin-skinned as an onion. He took offense at a sideward glance, and he was suspicious of his own shadow.

"Before running out to the laundry early in the morning, I'd primp and preen. I'd lick my finger and rub it over my eyebrows to make them smooth, and I'd pinch my cheeks to give them color. Then I'd put on my cap and apron and scurry out of the room without saying good-bye. I couldn't wait to get away from him and to get to the wash and the day's gossip. I wanted to find out which foreign prince was coming to visit, what the ladies were wearing, who was going out in whose carriage. That was my world, not Sancho. I didn't care about him—he was there, but he wasn't part of my life."

Carpenter is not a lowly occupation. A carpenter is a respected artisan who belongs to a guild and (unless he works for a bankrupt king) earns a decent salary. But it must have seemed to Sancho that Lidia wasn't showing him any respect at all. He may have heard rumors about how she lingered by Velázquez's studio. Perhaps someone had even mentioned that she had posed for the artist. One day, when she came back chattering about Lady This One and Lord That One, he lifted his hand behind his head as though he were going to toss a log, then smacked her so hard across the face that she flew clear across the room and banged her head against the wall. He was a strong man, don't forget. A man used to carrying beams and furniture.

That cuffing opened her eyes. She learned to play the part of the obedient wife, even as she flitted and flirted around the palace. She set food before Sancho at dinnertime, and she lifted her skirts for him whenever he wanted it, which was always. Night after night he would ride her like a mule and then collapse into a drunken daze by her side. By the end of the first half-year she knew two things: that she was pregnant and that she loathed him.

The order to leave Madrid came as abruptly as the order to marry. Emilio turned to Sancho one day as they were repairing the moldings in one of the palace alcoves.

"Congratulations, my boy," he said with a snicker. "You've been promoted. You're ready to take the test to enter the guild. You can do it in Aranjuez."

"Aranjuez?"

"That's where they're sending you. To the *sitio real* in Aranjuez. Tell your wife. You leave in three days."

Aranjuez is a lovely place, famous in all Europe for its luxuriant forests and exuberant gardens. It's not far from Madrid, and the hunting is plentiful, so the king spends a lot of time in this beautiful "rustic" palace, whose galleries overlook undulating meadows, shady lanes, intricate gazebos, and graceful fountains. There are exotic plants—elms from England, cotton from America, and a clump of mandrake. He planted them all on an island in the River Tajo, the famous *Jardín de la Isla*, where he also built a menagerie to compete with the one at El Buen Retiro and filled it with exotic animals: tropical birds, monkeys, camels, gazelles, jaguars, hyenas, and buffalo that produced milk from which the *quesadero* made delicious cheeses. It's a marvelous place, a land of dreams and fantasies. But Lidia didn't want to go there. And once she got there, she detested it.

Sancho didn't like it either, which put him in an even fouler mood than usual. The king constantly ordered renovations and repairs, so there was a lot of work to do, and even an occasional payment for doing it. But Sancho hated being far from his favorite taverns and his *tertulia*—the men he drank, gossiped, and played cards with. He hated the refined environment of the place—the *mozárabe* ceilings with their three-dimensional *trompe l'oeil* mosaics that made the rooms look twice as enormous as they already were, the gold leaf moldings, the artificial ponds and artificially stocked woods. Everything about the place was false. But most of all, he hated that his wife was pretty and might attract attention.

"He didn't know that I was pregnant yet," said Lidia. "And I wouldn't have told him if we had stayed in Madrid. I would have gotten rid of it. There was an herbalist in the laundry, and sometimes she helped girls. But we left for Aranjuez before I could go to her. So I finally did tell him. I told him so that he'd leave me alone. 'Get off me, you pig! I'm pregnant!' I screamed it in his ear one night when I could no longer bear the weight of his body or the stink of rotten garlic.

"'Good,' he screamed, 'because that's just the way I want you. Pregnant *all the time*! I don't care if the brats live or die, just as long as you've got a big belly!' And he made good on his word. I got pregnant six times in five years and carried four babies to term, including a pair of twins—all boys, except this one." She held up little María Jesús. "Well, after he told me that, he ran out to find some poor goatherd to roll dice with! Gambling! Rich men, poor men, they all do it! When I was at Court, I heard of rich men who lost fortunes at the gaming tables. And for a wretch like me, a poor woman, to have a husband who gambles . . ." She was trembling with rage.

"Relax for a while," whispered Juana. "You can tell us the rest tomorrow."

But Lidia wanted to go on.

"One day," she began again, "we heard that the king was coming to spend a fortnight at Aranjuez. He was going to bring a large group of friends with him, including Velázquez." She became cautious again, weighing each word. "I thought it would be so nice to see a familiar face," she said, "someone who remembered me from . . . happier times."

By then Lidia was heavy with her fourth child, little María Jesús. She wasn't allowed to work at the palace—the king wouldn't want a pregnant maid in his line of vision. So Lidia was confined to her room, forbidden to go out.

"But I snuck out anyway," she told Juana. "I spied on them. I wanted to see the ladies in their riding dresses. I wanted Don Diego to smile at me, just once . . . because . . . you see . . . he was my former . . . my former employer."

Lidia's eyes went dreamy. "Every afternoon, after the hunt and the midday meal, the ladies and gentlemen would take their siesta under trees with leafy branches that stretched out to form a parasol. They would remove their shoes and doze peacefully in the breeze. They liked to play at being rustics. The ladies wore dresses that were simple, like those of country girls, yet made of fine silk. And they wore jewels like no country girl has ever seen—pearl necklaces, emerald hair ornaments, diamond earrings, ruby rings . . . They were so lovely, these ladies. I wished I could serve one of them, instead of living in a pigsty with a pig. They'd line up on the meadow for tug-of-war, or else some of them would hide and the others would try to find them. Sometimes they'd pick flowers and weave garlands. Even Don Gaspar came for a few days. Imagine the count-duke in his bare feet braiding flower stems! You'd have thought he didn't have a care in the world! I knew Don Gaspar was busy in the war room most of the time, but here he seemed as relaxed as can be.

"I stayed hidden. I made sure they didn't see me. I saw Velázquez speaking with many elegant ladies and powerful men, but only from a distance.

"Then, one day, I saw some of the guests' servants carrying trunks to an awaiting coach. 'Is your master getting ready to leave?' I asked a squire. 'Day after tomorrow, they're all going home.' And then, when he saw my belly, 'Stuffed like a partridge, are you? Get back in your hole, where you belong.'

"That's when I knew I had to take a chance. They were going to leave soon, and I had to talk to Don Diego. I just had to. I wanted to tell him how unhappy I was, how badly things had gone for me. I didn't want anything from him"—here, she looked warily at Juana—"only that he ask if they would take me back in the palace laundry. Or maybe that he help me find some other place to run away to after the baby was born.

"Pretty soon the king's party came along. They were all lined up in hunting formation, hat plumes and horses' manes quivering in the morning air. Velázquez looked as graceful as ever in his crimson riding jacket and lace collar. Spain had just won an important victory over the French at Fuenterrabía, and they were celebrating with one last kill. The king was an excellent hunter, renowned for his skill with the crossbow. Don Diego was deep in conversation with a man I heard everyone call Don Luis. A moment later, Don Luis rode ahead to speak with some other gentleman."

Don Luis de Haro, Marquis of Carpio, was the man who would soon replace the count-duke of Olivares as the king's confidant, and the man whom I suspect of commissioning my portrait—that is, the painting of Venus. Either him or his son.

"I had brought my basket with me," Lidia went on, "so I could pretend I was picking berries if anyone saw me. I stationed myself behind a thick oak tree and watched them. They were coming toward me, trotting toward the woods. Velázquez was toward the rear of the party. I waited for the king and his closest friends to pass before I budged. Just as Velázquez approached, I stepped out into sight and held my breath.

"He looked right at me. My heart skipped a beat . . . I mean because his face was so familiar and welcome to me . . . his smile was like a soft breeze on my cheek." Lidia began to stammer. She paused, but quickly pulled herself together. "He looked right into my eyes . . . but . . ." she looked down. Her voice became low, throaty, and forced. "But he didn't see me. It was as though I were invisible. It's not as though he found me . . . ugly or . . . disgusting . . . with my huge belly . . . It's not that he turned away or snarled at me the way the squire had. It's as though . . . I just weren't there." She began to weep softly. "Nobody sees me," she whispered. "It's as though I were dead."

"Lidia," said Juana. "Go rest now. It's enough for one day."

"No, *señora*, let me get it all out. Let me get it over with." Arabela handed her a cup of water and she drank it. She sat quietly a while, as though lost in memory. She was breathing deeply, as though she might faint.

"After that, I lost all hope of ever getting away from Sancho," she said finally. Tears trickled in spurts over her still-bruised cheeks. "There was clump of mandrake in the *Jardín de la Isla*, and I began to sneak in there every once in a while to gather plants. I don't know if you've ever used mandrake. The leaves have a nasty odor, but they're good for curing skin irritations, so I was glad to find the plants on the property. With children, there's always a rash or a scrape that needs attention.

"But mandrake is good for something else as well. If you squeeze the juice from the bark of the roots, you get a foul-smelling liquid, but the stink goes away after a while. Essence of mandrake bark is a strong sleeping drug. It makes you fall into a slumber so deep that you don't wake up for hours, even if the house falls in. People say it drives the Devil out of the soul of a possessed person, but if you use it all the time as a sleeping potion, the Devil learns to resist it, and then he comes back with a vengeance. I started dribbling a few drops into Sancho's drink at supper. By the time I stretched out on the sleeping mat, he was too dead to the world to roll on top of me and demand I open my legs. Sometimes the Devil would come to him in his dreams. Sancho began to complain of nightmares, but I didn't care how much the Devil taunted him. Every night I dripped the mandrake juice into his cup from a vial I kept in the sleeve of my blouse."

"Oh my God!" exclaimed Juana. "Did you poison him?"

"No, I didn't poison him. If I'd been at Court I could have gotten hold of some arsenic and made fast work of it, but no, mandrake just makes you sleep . . . nothing worse.

"One night he came back from the carpentry shop a little early. I had just given birth to María Jesús a couple of months before. I was still eating with the children, seated on a mat on the floor. Usually the little ones were fast asleep by the time he was home for supper. I'd serve him his meal, and he'd sit alone, stuffing food into his mouth, burping and grunting and farting like a pig. But that night I wasn't ready when he got home.

"'Where's my food,' he growled.

"'Just as soon as we're done here,' I said. I only had bread and cheese for the little ones, but I had made a fine lentil stew for him, with a bit of bacon and onions. 'I have something nice for you,' I added.

"'Now!' he screamed. 'When I get home, I want my supper. I want it *now*!'

"I got up and took the baby off my breast and laid her in

the cradle," said Lidia. "She started to scream. 'Hush,' I told her. 'Hush, Jesusita, *Papá* wants his dinner.'

"Sancho stood there staring at me, trying to steady himself. His eyes were bloodshot and runny. He belched loudly, and the stench of rancid wine filled the room. Suddenly he lunged at my oldest boy and yanked the bread out of his mouth, then threw it on the ground. Sanchito is only four years old, *señora*. He was terrified. The twins started to wail, too. It all happened so quickly then . . . I crouched down to pick up the bread—we don't have bread to waste—and suddenly I felt a sharp pain in my . . . female parts . . . and my rump. He kicked me so hard, two, maybe three times, that I felt as though my guts would spill out onto the floor. I tipped over in pain, clutching my knees, even though that wasn't what hurt.

"'It's *my* food that matters, not your brats'.'

"I pulled myself up. The children were crying louder now. One of the twins started to scream. Sharp, piercing screams, like the bursts of a whistle, the kind of screams that give you a stabbing headache."

Sancho lifted his hand to slap the boy, but Lidia pushed the child out of the way. "Run!" she yelled. "Run!" All three disappeared out the door.

Sancho grabbed her by the arm and twisted, trying to dislocate her shoulder. Lidia stepped on his foot and wriggled away from him. He grabbed her again and raised his hand high behind his head, so high it seemed to detach itself from his body. She saw it coming down toward her cheek, down, down, as if in slow motion, but this time she couldn't get away.

"Then he hit me on the chest so hard, I thought my nipples would burst. I stumbled, and he hit me across the face. I could taste blood in my mouth. One of my teeth was wobbling around under my tongue. I could feel my lip swelling up as though a bee had stung it. The baby was screaming and screaming. He turned to the cradle and looked at her with such hatred, I was afraid he would kill her.

"'Stop!' I begged. 'Please stop! Let me get you your dinner.' I hobbled to the kettle, scooped lentils into a bowl, and placed it on the mat with a half-loaf of bread. He sat down on a stool and brought the bowl to his lap.

"'Wine!' he thundered. I didn't have money for wine, and the water from the well had a funny smell, but I had collected some rainwater in a jug from a morning shower.

"'I'm sorry,' I said. 'This is all I have.' I collapsed on a bench by the door. It was dark out and the children were who knows where? I rubbed my arm. It ached horribly."

Juana had put her embroidery to the side. She was weeping softly, dabbing her eyes with a lace handkerchief. "Don't go on, Lidia," she whispered. "Don't go on."

"I'm almost done, *señora*." Lidia breathed deeply, as though preparing for a terrible ordeal.

"I was sitting on the bench, terrified to move. I wanted to go out and call the children, but I was afraid. They're probably safer out there among the wolves, I thought. So I didn't budge.

"'Why are you sitting!' he snarled. 'How dare you sit there while I'm eating! Get up and serve me wine.'

"'I don't have any . . .'

"'What? I can't hear you.'

"'I don't have any,' I said louder. I tried to stay very still, very calm. I tried not to shift positions. I stopped rubbing my arm. I was afraid that any gesture, even a swallow, might irritate him. The baby was still whining and I was frightened for her.

"He jumped up and moved toward me. Instinctively, I shrank back against the wall and lifted my hands to cover my face. 'You whore! You bitch!' he screamed. 'Don't think I don't know what you did when those palace big shits were here, those *cacas grandes*. You ran out to see them, didn't you? You ran out to see that painter! A painter's no better than a carpenter, but you think he is, don't you, you tramp! You slut! But he isn't. He's a worker, just like me.' I'm sorry, *señora*, but that's what he said.

"I was trembling. I kept looking toward the cradle. I wanted to grab the baby and run. I didn't see him raise his foot, but the next thing I knew, my shin exploded! It felt as though it were splintering. A pain like lightning jolted through my leg, from the arch of my foot to my knee to my hip. He had kicked me so hard that I staggered to the basin and threw up. I remember the smell of vomit, the awful liquid, gray-green and mucous tinged, spewing into the bowl. My head pounded. My eyes throbbed. Everything went blurry and I thought I might lose my balance. I steadied myself against the wall and tried to breathe. I couldn't pass out. I couldn't lose consciousness because if I did, who knows what he might have done to the baby.

"All of a sudden, he burst out laughing: a high-pitched giggle like the hyenas in the king's menagerie when they fight over food.

"After a long pause—I don't know how long—but long, I got my breath back. 'I have some juice from the berries in the garden,' I stammered. 'Would you like some of that?'

"At first he didn't answer, but then he grunted, and I pulled myself up and limped out the door. 'Where are you going?' he demanded.

"'To get the juice. It's in a jug by the front step.' He was watching me, but it was dark. I bent down with my back toward him and quick as a bolt slipped some mandrake juice into the mug—a big dose, huge. Tonight, I thought . . . tonight will be the last time . . . the very last time.

"He staggered onto the sleeping mat and fell into a deep sleep. I slipped out the door and called softly to the children. They had been hiding behind the bushes, not ten paces from the hut. 'Go to sleep,' I whispered.

"'Let's run away, *Mamá*,' whimpered Sanchito.

"'No,' I said. 'He'd only find us and kill us. Go to sleep.'

"'But . . .'

"'Do as I tell you. He's going away. He won't ever bother us again.'

"When I was sure they were asleep, I went out to the shed and grabbed a pitchfork. I stood there with it in my hand and looked down at Sancho, snoring and grunting in his sleep. I hoped the Devil was torturing him. I hoped he was dreaming of being stabbed to death. But after I'd thought about it a while, I put the pitchfork down. Driving the prongs through his heart would leave a terrible mess. There would be blood, and the Santa Hermandad would surely hunt me down and hang me into the town square, just like they did my mother."

Arabela looked up from her handwork and squinted. Lidia lowered her voice, as if confiding a secret. "My mother killed a man who battered her," she murmured. "I don't know whether or not he was my father. I was very little when it happened, but I do remember the Holy Brothers, with their black hoods and powerful horses. They grabbed her and dragged her off . . . I remember them tying a rag over her head and slipping a noose over her neck . . ."

Juana stared at her, wide-eyed. "She did what she had to," said Juana. The other women turned to her and gasped, but then nodded. "Good for her."

Lidia took a deep breath and went on. "Well, that wasn't going to happen to me. I looked around for some rags, but all I had were the clothes on my back, so I took them off and wadded them into a bundle. Then I placed them over Sancho's face and sat on them. I straddled him. I was careful that no air should get in. I hugged his filthy head with my knees. He squirmed for a while. I tightened my grip. Finally, he was still.

"I stood over him a long time, searching for signs of life. I held an onion skin in front of his nose to see if it fluttered. Then I slipped my fingers under his shirt. His skin was clammy and repulsive. His heart wasn't beating, but just in case, I pushed the bundle of clothes into his mouth and nose one more time and sat there a while longer. Then I got dressed and waited for dawn.

"The night was eerily quiet. The air was fresh, and the moon hung high and opaque in the sky. I felt strangely giddy. At first light I limped to the carpenters' shop. The carpenters begin work early, but no one was there yet, so I hobbled to the hut where one of them lived. The door was open, and his wife was already at work kneading dough. She eyed me suspiciously. 'Why are you here at this hour?' she asked. 'The men aren't out of the house yet.'

"'Something's wrong!' I told her. 'I can't wake up Sancho. He went to bed at the usual time, but this morning he hasn't stirred.'

"'She studied my face. I could see her taking it all in—the swollen lip, the angry bruises on my jaw and cheek. 'Why are you limping?' she asked.

"She caught me off guard. 'I . . . I fell . . . trying to . . . trying to . . .'

"'I know what happened,' she said matter-of-factly. I froze. 'Sancho's heart, it gave out,' she went on. 'It just gave out. It happens.' She was staring right into my eyes. 'He died of a heart problem.'

"'Yes,' I said, 'maybe . . .'

"'Definitely.' She placed dough on a board and began to shape it into a loaf. 'Where are your children?'

"'Still sleeping.'

"'Bring me your children. I can't take care of them myself, but there are farm families around here that would be happy to have an extra boy. Sanchito will soon be old enough to work and earn his keep, and the twins are healthy; they'll grow. You take the baby, the girl. You can leave her in a convent if you can't keep her.'

"'What about the burial?' I asked.

"'I'll take care of it. Do you have people?'

"'In Madrid.'

"'Some of the farmers are taking produce into the city today. See if one of them will take you in his wagon. You can hardly walk with that limp.'

"I stammered my thanks and turned to leave. 'One more thing,' she called after me. I turned around to face her. 'You did the right thing,' she said. 'Don't worry about the children. Just get out of here.'"

Juana was sobbing hard now. Heavy, disconsolate sobs. She could hardly catch her breath. Finally, she buried her face in her hands and shook her head. Her whole body pitched and heaved as though it would break. "Holy Virgin Mother," she stammered, "protect this woman."

"*Señora*," said Lidia with bowed head. "Please let me stay here forever. I promise I'll never give you reason to regret it."

Juana wiped her eyes and thought about it a moment. The cat or the snake? Would Lidia turn out to be the cat or the snake? Juana took a deep breath. In front of three witnesses Lidia had just confessed a crime that could send her to the gallows. In so doing, she had given Juana complete power over her. She had furnished Juana with a guarantee of loyalty. Arabela and Julia stared at their laps, each one lost in soundless prayer. Only the crackling of the brazier was audible. Finally, almost imperceptibly, she nodded yes.

Years later, she would remember that she had had a choice, and that she had made the right one.

It wasn't too long after Lidia came back to live at the house on Convalescientes that Velázquez began to turn his attention once again to Venus. Is this what he and Haro were talking about at the *sitio real* in Aranjuez? I can't be sure, but I do know that at about that time Velázquez started looking around for another model. Lidia was out of the question. Not only was she no longer the lissome girl she had been, but her new elusiveness made her impossible to approach. She and her baby pretty much stuck to the kitchen, where she now worked as Bárbara's assistant.

Constanza was also out of the question because Constanza was dead — another gloomy story. At Court people had been gossiping for years about the ongoing friendship between the queen's pretty lady-in-waiting and the king's new wardrobe assistant. They had been seen together at the bullfights in Medina, which Velázquez had attended in the party of the count-duke; at the *sitio real* El Pardo, where Velázquez had gone to paint hunting scenes; and at El Escorial. There were rumors that he was going to paint a female nude, Italian-style, and that she was going to pose for him.

Constanza's husband may have been an obtuse old man, but the buzz was too loud and too persistent to escape his notice. His wife's conduct had become a public embarrassment, and he knew he had to do something—but what? He could corner Constanza and the insolent little painter and run them through with a sword, but that would create a public scandal. He could lure them out to his country estate and burn down the house, the way the honor heroes did in Calderón's dramas, but to be absolutely honest, he didn't have the stomach for murder. After some deliberation, he decided that he would get her pregnant again. By the third month, Velázquez wouldn't want her. And by the time she got her figure back, the painter would have found another model. Problem solved.

Don Basilio set his plan in motion. He had been rather lax about his bedroom appearances for a while (after all, there were so many flowers to choose from in the king's garden), but circumstances had changed. Although Constanza found her husband repulsive, she knew what her wifely duties were, and within eight weeks, she knew she was expecting. Not long after that, she began to show. One morning, well before her due date, she noticed a blood stain on her shift. She called for the midwife, who examined her and declared that it was nothing—a routine discharge. But by evening, Constanza was bleeding profusely, and it was clear that something was wrong. The queen summoned her own physician, an old *converso* named Marcos de Montemayor, whose medical skill outweighed his impure blood in Her Majesty's mind.

"I don't know," he muttered. "She's lost a lot of blood."

The queen sent one of her favorite ladies-in-waiting, Doña Milagros de Rodríguez, to sit by Constanza's side all night, and to call for the doctor if the patient took a turn for the worse. Around midnight, Constanza began to drift into delirium. Doña Milagros called for the queen's doctor and for a male midwife to deliver the fetus, which she was certain was doomed.

The baby survived a couple of hours. It was a tiny, feeble mass of tissue that hardly resembled a human child. The poor thing struggled heroically to breathe, but finally had to give up. By the time it expired, Constanza was already gone—another woman dead in childbirth, one of thousands, maybe tens of thousands, lost every year.

The next morning, Don Basilio made quite a spectacle of his grief at Court. Velázquez had been busy at work in his studio since dawn and had missed the commotion. When Mazo entered the workspace a little before noon and told his father-in-law the news, Velázquez didn't say a word. Instead, he stood in front of his canvas for a long time, staring straight ahead. Then he picked up his brush and began to paint.

15

The birth of venus
1660:1644:1660

"HE HAD A CHILD, YOU KNOW."

"Yes," I respond evenly. "I know."

"A son. The son he'd always wanted. In Italy."

"Why are you telling me this?"

Cintia wraps her shawl more tightly around her shoulders. The air has grown chilly, but it's still more comfortable in the garden than in the house, where moisture settles into the crevices of the stone walls and gives the atmosphere a dank feel.

"Oh, no particular reason. I didn't think you knew—that's all. She was a model."

"Who was?"

"The mother. At least, that's what I heard."

"What kind of a model?"

"I'm not sure. Maybe a nude model. Juan told me he painted a lot of nudes during his second trip to Italy. There's one in the collection of . . ."

"Juan?"

"Juan de Pareja."

"Oh."

"The Morisco."

"He was a good painter in his own right. I've seen his work."

"You know how those Italian women are, always looking for an excuse to drop their petticoats. She must have been posing, and then, well . . . one thing led to another. It's only natural. A woman lying around with her pussy exposed. What do you expect? Men are animals and women are stupid enough to want to please them. Whether a woman is covered from head to toe like a nun or an Arab or sprawled out naked on a bed, it's all the same thing. She's doing it because of some man. Why, Velázquez was just . . ."

"I'd really rather not discuss this."

"Why not? He's dead now. Of course, *she* probably isn't. She must have been much younger. Artists don't paint old women nude."

My head feels like a vessel with a wasp trapped inside. I can hardly stand the buzzing.

"I'm going in now. I don't feel like having this conversation. Anyway, you don't know anything about any of this. You're inventing . . ."

"All right, I won't mention it again." Cintia chews her gums, the way old women do. Spidery veins stretch across her cheeks to the sides of her nose. Her skin is tawny and as tough as hide, in spite of the bacon grease she rubs on her face to make it smooth. All she manages to do with her beauty regimen is make herself stinky. She runs her sandaled foot through the dead leaves, then kicks them aside to expose the sleeping earth below. "His name was Antonio."

"Whose?"

"The boy. Antonio de Velázquez. He gave him his own surname. Surprising, under the circumstances, isn't it?"

I stand up to leave.

"Oh, sit down. Don't be so tight-assed." She yanks on my sleeve and pulls me back to the bench. She gropes in the pocket of her habit and brings out a pipe, and then two small gray stones.

"What's that?"

"Flint."

"You can't smoke here, Cintia. Mother Augustina will see you."

But she's already puffing away on her pipe, spitting and coughing like a soldier. "I could have made a fortune in Rome, you know." She blows tiny circles of smoke into the cool autumn air. "Whoring is a much more respectable profession there than here. I could have had my pick of girls. And so many powerful men with money. Dukes, cardinals . . . If I'd gone to Rome, I could have been a rich woman."

"You didn't do so badly for yourself, Cintia. You made plenty."

"Yes," she says, gulping smoke, "I suppose I did." She pauses reflectively. "Well, not really. Don Felipe and Olivares were cheapskates. The count-duke deserved what happened to him."

"Maybe, but not because he was stingy with whores, Cintia."

"Why then? Because he refused to take orders from the queen?"

"Queen Isabel hated him. She wanted peace with

France—she was French, after all—but Olivares brought nothing but war."

"I think she hated him because he brought Don Felipe to my house."

"Don't flatter yourself, Cintia. Doña Isabel had more important things to think about. Those were terrible years. Plague, crop failures, inflation, and those interminable wars that Olivares started. And Doña Isabel struggling through it all to keep the country together. When Catalonia rebelled and the king went to put down the uprising, she saw her chance to go after Olivares. Anyhow, by then he was nuts."

"They say he lost his mind after his daughter and her baby died."

"He picked fights with everybody. He couldn't govern anymore."

"Well, at least he was a steady customer. It was good while it lasted."

I close my eyes and listen to the leaves crackle under Cintia's feet. The cold bites my cheeks and my ears. I look at my hands and see that they're quivering. Cintia taps her pipe against the edge of the bench, and a little mound of tobacco falls to the ground. She spits on it and wipes her mouth on her sleeve. She's a vulgar woman, that Cintia, but what can you expect from a whoremonger?

It was a day like this one when Velázquez set out for Italy for the second time with his slave and disciple, Juan de Pareja. By then Melgar was dead, and Pareja had replaced him. Velázquez was fond of Pareja. Sometimes he had him finish off the details in his work—repetitive patterns in clothes, that sort of thing. When they were in Rome, Velazquez signed the papers to give Juan his freedom. He also painted his portrait, which was displayed at a big exhibition at the Pantheon. Velazquez was proud of the painting. It was the first time he'd been able to create such interesting optical effects through the use of variations in surface. Pareja's suit is gray, but changes subtly from warmer to cooler tones to create a sense of light dancing on the cloth. I never saw it, of course, but Velázquez described it.

"Juan was a customer of mine," says Cintia, bursting into my thoughts. "He was swarthy, but the girls liked him. Anyway, that's why I know about the boy. Velázquez's love child, I mean."

"Shut up, Cintia."

"It must have been about 1649 when they left. I remember it was right before the outbreak of the second great plague."

Cintia pauses and hunches down against the wind. The October air slices at you like a knife. Leaves swirl in little circles—brown, red, orange, and yellow whirligigs spun by invisible hands.

I mean to get up but instead settle back onto the bench. The mention of the plague brings back memories. Sickness and death everywhere. It was even worse than the pestilence in Seville at the turn of the century. "It must have been right before they threw out Olivares, and Haro came in. Everything was falling apart. Haro just wasn't a favorite in the same way the count-duke had been."

"By then the king had fallen under the spell of Sister María de Ágreda," Cintia says.

"María de Ágreda . . . The flying nun."

"I never believed those stories about how she flew through the air without ever leaving her cell to preach to the Indians in Texas and New Mexico. That's bullshit."

"With God's help, anything is possible."

Don Felipe had met María de Ágreda on one of his trips to Aragon in 1643. I remember it was in 1643 because it was the same year that Pacheco died. She was the abbess of the Convent of the Immaculate Conception, and they said she bilocated: she could be in the American territories and in her convent in Ágreda at the same time.

"I hated that old nun," says Cintia. "She made the king feel guilty about his innocent pleasures. But that's stupid. Brothels keep poor girls in decent clothes and give men something to do in their leisure. Besides, it's a natural thing . . . but anyway, King Felipe was feeling guilty, so he stopped coming."

"The king was getting married, Cintia."

"So he was getting married! That's no reason to give up whoring!"

"What a selfish woman you are!"

"I remember Queen Isabel's funeral. A cortège from here to the moon and months of national mourning. I'm telling you, everything contrived against me, a poor old woman just trying to keep bread on her table. What I remember most is that they closed the theaters. That was María de Ágreda's idea. Men like to go to the theater in the afternoon, then have a nice fuck afterward. But the old nun insisted performances be suspended during the mourning period. The best plays are the ones about girls who lose the jewel. The heroine dresses up as a man so she can go look for the cad who screwed her and trap him into marriage. My customers would see those actresses parading around in britches, showing off their legs. They'd come out of the theater all worked up, and I'd make a killing. On a good night, the ducats would pile up like shit in the gutters. But María de Ágreda . . ."

"Don't be vulgar, Cintia."

"Why not? I'm a whoremonger. The king was in Zaragoza when he got the news that the queen had a fever. He was headed for the campaign in Catalonia, but he turned around and headed home. Six royal doctors attended her. They gave her potions and bled her, but she died anyway. They say the king just fell apart. He didn't even want to see the body. He hid at the *sitio real* in El Pardo. Prince Baltasar Carlos rode out to be with him. Don Felipe wrote long letters to María de Ágreda looking for consolation."

"Funny how these unfaithful husbands get so religious when their wives die," I say.

"Bah, it's a natural thing."

"You see everything through the dished glass of your brothel window, Cintia."

"My brothel didn't have glass windows. I was just a poor workingwoman, don't forget. Anyway, everyone sees things through distorted glass. That's the way of the world."

"Velázquez was at the height of his career when he went back to Italy. He'd just been named Superintendent of Royal Works, and he was in charge of furnishing El Buen Retiro. In spite of the fact that his coffers were empty, Don Felipe raised Velázquez's stipend to seven hundred ducats. Velázquez thought he might even be named a Knight of Santiago. In Italy, he bought paintings for the king—works by Titian, Tintoretto, Veronese . . ."

"I don't know them," growls Cintia. "If they don't pay me, I don't know them." She puffs on her pipe and spits.

"The duke of Modena treated him like royalty. He even painted a portrait of Pope Innocent X while he was in Rome."

"No shit! The pope?"

"That's when Velázquez developed his new style, what they call the *manera abreviada*. It's bolder and sharper than his earlier style. They say the portrait shows such ruthlessness in the eyes of the pontiff that everyone thought he'd throw Velázquez out, but instead he gave him a gold chain!"

"Did Velázquez tell you about the boy?"

I want to punch her. An image flashes through my mind: Cintia crumpled over on the ground, starbursts of pain radiating through her chest. Instead, I take a deep breath and stare at the leaves drifting and fluttering like wounded birds. "Of course not," I say.

"Who told you?"

I purse my lips.

"Anyway," she snickers, "I'm more interested in his Venus. Now *that* is a *real* scandal."

I feel my fingers go numb, and my arms hug my body as if preparing for an assault. "Venus?" I utter feebly.

"Don't you know about Venus? Everyone knows that he painted nudes while he was in Italy, but Venus is the only one he brought back with him. Some of my customers saw it."

"Where?"

"At Gaspar de Haro's house—you know, the son of Luis de Haro."

"Gaspar de Haro? Did you . . . I mean . . . did anyone ever say anything about the model?" I feel as though I've been pierced in the gut with a knitting needle.

"Ah, now you're interested. I thought you would be. She was a young girl, by the looks of her body and the face in the mirror. Maybe she's the . . ."

"What mirror?" I know what mirror, of course, but I want to make sure we're talking about the same painting.

"According to what I heard, Venus is lying with her back toward the painter and admiring her face in a mirror held by a cherub. Maybe she's the mother of the . . ."

"Cupid. The cherub's name is Cupid."

"How do you know?" Cintia squints at me through the sweet smoke of her pipe.

"They always show Venus with her son Cupid. He's the Roman god of physical love, Cintia. You should know that."

"I don't know anything about love gods. I don't care about them, either. Anyhow, the woman is thin and graceful, with round buttocks and brown hair. A vixen, all right. I wish I'd known that girl. I'd have had her come and work for me."

"Just because she posed like that doesn't mean that she's a prostitute, Cintia. In Italy they have professional models."

Cintia snorts and runs her hand over her brow. The mole on her chin transforms itself into a bug—a tick preparing to spring at me and bore into my skin.

"Well, she was gorgeous, that's all I know. All the men wanted to take her from behind." She smirks and locks eyes with me to see if I cringe, and I do. "She's lounging, admiring herself in a mirror. Very sensual. Very enticing." Cintia is needling me. "Cupid, that sex god you were talking about, he's standing over her, looking at her while she's sprawled out on the sheets. She knows she's luscious. She knows men want her. She knows they can't see what they want to see because her back is turned toward them. But they can glimpse her face in the mirror. It's as though she's winking at them over her shoulder. She lazes there, teasing them . . ."

"Go to hell, Cintia!"

"What's the matter with you? It's just a painting that he did while he was in a foreign country, far from his wife and family. What do you care? All men fuck around. Velázquez was better behaved than most, but a man is just a man. That woman meant nothing to him. All the painters in Italy were painting naked women, so of course he wanted to try it, too. And maybe one thing *did* lead to another. Maybe she *is* the mother of his brat. What of it? The king produced a gaggle of bastards! Did you expect Velázquez to behave like a mushroom or a doorknob or a stone while he was spending the days staring at some Italian girl's bare rump? He's a man, *un hombre de carne y hueso*, and when he's in some exotic place, he's going to want to sample the wares. And if a kid pops out, what's the big deal?"

Her words course through my head and the horrible buzzing gets louder. I know Velázquez didn't paint Venus in Italy, of course, but I bite my tongue. How can I tell her I know for certain the model is *not* Italian and is *not* the mother of Velázquez's son?

I take off toward the house. The path is strewn with leaves, and I feel them crunch under my sandals. All I can see is a blur of yellows and browns. The breeze whirls and spins, lifting dry foliage from one little pile and depositing it in another. I slow down as I approach the back door, which opens onto a porch accessed by a set of steps. In my diseased eyes, one stair dissolves into another, but I've negotiated these steps so many times that they usually give me no problem. Still, I grab the handrail and take them one at a time. Once inside, I hug the walls. It's getting harder and harder to make my way around the convent, even though I know the layout perfectly. I only hope I won't run into anybody. The buzzing in my head has turned into pounding. Cintia's words pummel my brain.

Once back in my cell I look around for my breviary because I desperately need to pray. It's not in the pocket of my habit, but I won't go look for it. I'll stay here, in my room. The *recreo* will be starting soon. Nuns will be pouring into the yard to chat and relax. Some will stroll up the path. Others will play games under the trees, twiggy and bare. I don't want to run into them. I lie down and close my eyes, and I remember:

I am reclining on the divan facing the wall, my back to the artist. Gossamer sunbeams caress my left shoulder and buttocks. He has posed me looking away from the window, but I can feel the fingers of light warming my body. They stretch over my arm toward the plush red curtain that hangs around the foot of the bed. I lie on a maroon-colored silk sheet that will eventually turn charcoal, the better to show off my mother-of-pearl skin. The luster of flesh against the sheen of the cloth fills the scene with light and creates an atmosphere of luxurious intimacy. That's what he says: "luxurious intimacy." He's a well-spoken man. He is, after all, a courtier.

I feel his eyes sweep my body. For the first time in all the years we have been making love, I am truly the object of his gaze. He scrutinizes my form, discerns curves and lines, colors and shadows. I am not a person, but a thing to be measured and dissected into shapes—circles, ovals, rectangles. I am a figure composed of cream and rose, beige and blue. Every detail, from the indentation at the shoulder of my extended arm to the shadow between my buttocks, is worthy of his attention. His stare is cold, but the image, that emerges on the canvas is warm and tangible.

He has reinvented me. He has elongated my limbs and made my torso luscious and smooth. He has restored a raw sensu-

ality I no longer possess. My waist is slim and delicate and inviting. My buttocks are two juicy melons. Look at Venus lounging insouciantly on luxurious sheets. You want to run your hand along the arch of her silhouette from the knee to her graceful hip, then into the concavity of her waist and up her back. She's relaxing in her private boudoir with a naked Cupid, a winged boy who holds a mirror to her trunk, and you are there. You have snuck into her private chamber. You're a spectator, a voyeur. Your thirst is awakened, and you drink her in. The atmosphere is charged with eroticism, and you are heady with it.

I lie staring at the curtain, at the spot where Cupid will kneel when Velázquez paints him in. Sunlight spills in ribbons over my body. It's hard not to move. A frisson shoots through my leg. I feel as though someone had strewn feathers over me. They tickle my toes, the arches of my feet, my calves and knees and thighs. I feel them on my haunches and between my cheeks. Soft, downy feathers that drift like snowflakes and settle on every part of me. The tickle works its way up between my legs and into my body. I want Velázquez to put down his brush and touch me. I want him to run his fingers over my earlobes and bend down to kiss me.

"Stop fidgeting!" he barks.

I bite my lip and force myself to hold still.

Why do terrible things always happen in October? Maybe it's because October leads up to November, which begins with All Saints Day and All Souls' Day. It's a time to think of death, to remember the dead, to visit cemeteries and pray for souls in purgatory. The convent grounds are a needlepoint of oranges, browns, and yellows—the colors of death. It's beautiful in the way funerals are beautiful. There is splendor in the rituals of death—the dazzling candles of the *capilla ardiente*, the funeral carriage pulled by black horses, the chanting and the prayers. There is solace in the hope that the deceased has gone to everlasting life and is resting in God's embrace—or will, after he has done his time in purgatory.

It was a gloomy day in 1646 when Velázquez asked me to pose for him. Gloomy not because of overcast skies, but because Madrid was in mourning. The sky was diaphanous—at least at first—and the air as crisp as an ice flake, but the cortège that wound its way from El Buen Retiro all the way around the city had made the atmosphere grim. People were not only morose, but also frightened, for no one knew what would come next. Who would rule? What would the future bring? Olivares was gone, his replacement Haro was ineffective, and Don Felipe couldn't last forever. A black void filled the hearts of Madrileños.

Prince Baltasar Carlos had been his father's greatest treasure—his heart's desire, his constant companion. As the boy approached adulthood, Don Felipe thought it essential to teach him the art of governance. The king had always considered his wife his most trusted advisor after Olivares, but now that he had lost both of them, Don Felipe needed a new political ally. The prince was bright and energetic. He was curious about affairs of state and disposed to serve. And like his mother, he loved the Spanish people in spite of his Bourbon blood. He would make a fine ruler, thought Don Felipe. And this wasn't just fatherly pride. Anyone could see that Baltasar Carlos was gifted: handsome, chivalrous, athletic, and prudent.

Father and son started visiting the regional assemblies around the time the prince started to grow a mustache. First they set off for Zaragoza so that the Cortes of Aragon could swear allegiance to him. The following year they went to Pamplona to allow the Cortes of Navarra to do the same. But on this second trip, Baltasar Carlos fell seriously ill. A wave of panic rippled through the king's entourage, and the news quickly reached the Court. The envoys from Aragon were urging the king to lead the resistance against the French, who were pushing south through the mountains into Lérida, but Don Felipe refused to leave his son.

It wasn't until two months later that physicians deemed the prince well enough to travel. Don Felipe was overjoyed. He admitted he had been frightened, but thanks be to God, Baltasar Carlos had come through. His Majesty ordered that their bags be packed, and he and the prince left for Zaragoza in order to attend to the hostilities with the French. After a few weeks and a visit to the pillar where the Virgin once appeared to James the Apostle, doctors stated confidently that Baltasar Carlos had fully recovered. The king—and his nation—heaved a sigh of relief.

Two days later, father and son attended a mass commemorating the second anniversary of Queen Isabel's death. During the service, the prince began to sweat and sway, and the doctors carried him off. They fingered and prodded him and determined he had a raging fever. They bled him three times, but Baltasar Carlos continued to lose color and grow weaker. The king sat by his bed and sobbed. He wrote to María de Ágreda, his faithful correspondent, mentor, and spiritual guide. Now he needed her more than ever because deep in his heart the poor king knew that all he could do for his ailing son was call the priest to administer last rites. The boy wasn't yet seventeen years old.

Some said he died of smallpox, but others said it was appendicitis. There were also insinuations that like his father, he prowled around so much that he'd caught what they called *el mal francés*, syphilis. There were even those who insisted that ambitious courtiers, jealous of the prince's growing influence on his father, had poisoned him. But what difference did it make? The boy was dead and the king had no heir. The disconsolate father was mad with grief. Poor Don Felipe. Choir boy and libertine. María de Ágreda had warned him to mend his ways or God would punish him.

As soon as the body arrived in El Escorial, Hieronymite friars dressed it in a plain tunic, shrouded it, placed it in a lead casket, and lay a wooden cross on Don Baltasar Carlos's breast. The friars said masses for the repose of his soul in every chapel of the huge compound, and the next morning, the prior celebrated a solemn requiem mass at the high altar. In the afternoon, vigils with prayers were held throughout the Escorial. At six in the evening, pallbearers carried the coffin from the sacristy to the main cloister. Scores of friars followed the casket, carrying candles and chanting a low, gloomy dirge. The cortège wound its way around the perimeter of the Escorial to the south entrance of the basilica and into the sanctuary, where the air was heavy with incense and flowers, and thousands of candles glowed mournfully.

The bereaved father was so unsteady on his feet that he had to be propped up by Luis de Haro and the Court chaplain, Crispín de Valdivieso. The king and his attendants, who were all dressed in traditional hooded mourning robes and carried candles, led the procession. Then came the Hieronymites in their white tunics, brown hooded scapulars, and brown mantles, followed by a throng of courtiers, Velázquez among them. Hundreds of paid mourners brought up the rear, moaning and yowling for a boy they never knew.

The cortège advanced sluggishly. The mourners intoned *posas* and *reponsos,* psalms sung responsorially:

Libera me, Domine, de morte aeterna, in die illa tremenda:
Quando caeli movendi sunt et terra.
Dum veneris judicare saeculum per ignem.
Tremens factus sum ego, et timeo, dum discussio venerit, atque
ventura ira.
Quando caeli movendi sunt et terra.
Dies illa, dies irae, calamitatis et miseriae, dies magna et amara valde.
Dum veneris judicare saeculum per ignem.
Requiem aeternam dona eis, Domine: et lux perpetua luceat eis.

Deliver me, O Lord, from death eternal on that fearful day,
when the heavens and the earth shall be moved,
I am made to tremble, and I fear, till the judgment be upon us,
and the coming wrath,
when the heavens and the earth shall be moved.
That day, day of wrath, calamity, and misery, day of great and
exceeding bitterness,
when thou shalt come to judge the world by fire
Rest eternal grant unto them, O Lord: and let light perpetual
shine upon them.

The scents, the smoke, the glow—I feel faint as I try to imagine it. Velázquez went to the funeral and described it to me, but I stayed back at El Buen Retiro with the *damas* and their maids, and together we watched the black-garbed throngs wailing and swaying and praying in the street. Funeral rituals were going on all over Madrid, all over Spain for that matter. Priests were saying mass in every church, and processions wound through every boulevard and alley.

Velázquez told me that during the two-hour requiem mass, the archbishop wept so hard he was overcome with a fit of coughing and could hardly get through the service. Afterward, another cortège made its way to the burial vault directly below the high altar of the basilica. Don Felipe insisted on accompanying the cadaver of his beloved son to its final resting place and watching as they placed it in the family burial chamber next to his mother. The experience brought him closer to God, he said. Like Our Father, he knew what it meant to lose a son.

The realm was deep in mourning when Velázquez approached me that day in the Retiro park, somewhere between the zebras and the orangutans. The air was redolent with the sweet, nauseating odor of animal feces. The sun had disappeared behind the clouds, turning the sky from luminous to menacing. We were glad to be together, glad to talk about something besides death.

"We should take cover now, before it starts," said Velázquez, urging me toward a canopy. I hiked my skirt up above the ankle and bolted. An instant later, raindrops like crystal goblets began to fall, shatter on the cobblestone walk, and splinter.

"Are you cold?" he asked.

"No, not especially," I lied, wrapping my cape more tightly.

"Let's go inside."

We found our way to one of the small parlors near Velázquez's studio. A fire sweetened by lavender stalks was burning in the chimney. The fragrance filled my nostrils, making me feel inebriated and sleepy. I settled back on a cushion and closed my eyes.

"You look very lovely this afternoon, my dear."

He rarely called me "my dear." "Don't be silly," I snapped. "I'm old." And then I added, "We'd better be going. No one should find us here."

"What difference does it make if someone finds us here?"

"It's clear that someone was intending to use this room. Otherwise, why would the fire be lit? We should leave before they come."

"I need to speak with you about something," he said, without moving. "I have a commission—a very important one. A private one."

"Oh?"

"And I need your help."

I looked at him, confused. He was nearly fifty and still very handsome. His hair was black and thick despite his years, and his upturned mustache curled fetchingly over his lip. He'd become a bit stouter, as all men do, but he was as dashing as ever in his black velvet doublet and simple ruche.

"I want you to pose," he said calmly.

I was taken aback. "Why?" I asked. "There are plenty of other women willing to pose for you. You've painted every duchess and lady-in-waiting at Court."

"No, this is different. I can't ask anyone else to do this."

"But why? You've never asked me to model before."

"Because . . ." He looked around nervously. "Because it's for a nude."

I burst out laughing. "A nude! Are you mad? You can't paint me nude! It would be—why, it would be unseemly. What would people think?"

"The patron wants a female nude, and it's very difficult to find models in Spain."

"I'm sure there are women in this city who . . ."

"I have to be very be careful. There are laws . . . and there's the Inquisition. And people are watching me. People who are jealous of my success, and who would love nothing more than to have a reason to accuse me of indecency."

"Who commissioned this painting?"

"I'm not at liberty to say."

"He doesn't care that our beloved prince is dead and that we're all in mourning?" I sat looking at my hands in my lap. "I don't know," I said after a long pause. "I'm not young."

"You're still slim and supple, and with paint . . ."

"You can create an illusion."

"It's all about illusion. On a flat surface, you create three dimensions. You create depth with paint and shadows. All I need is the outline of your body. I need the dimensions and the shading. I need to see how the light falls on your skin and what hues are visible in the refraction. I need to see the foundation colors and the contrasts. It shouldn't take too long." He made it sound so simple.

I shook my head.

"You needn't worry—it won't be a perfect likeness. It will be a Venus for an aristocratic libertine. But it won't be lewd, *mi amor*, I promise."

I smiled. Velázquez so rarely called me "*mi amor.*"

I thought about it for a while. "I'd want something in return," I said coyly.

"Anything," he said without hesitation. "Tell me. The patron is a rich man. He'll give me whatever I ask for."

I laughed. "No, I don't want money," I said. "I want something else."

"Tell me!"

"I want you to teach me to draw and paint."

"But, *mi amor,* whatever for?"

"I want to see what it's like . . . to do what you do. I want to learn to see the world as you see it. Oh, I know I'll never be a real painter, but . . . I want to try!"

He sighed. "It's a strange request. I admit it's not at all what I expected. But if that's what you want, *mi amor,* I can arrange to have Mazo give you lessons."

"No, not Mazo, you. I want *you* to give me lessons."

I had him where I wanted him. He was in no position to argue, so of course he agreed. But, I wondered at the time, would he keep his promise or, after he got his painting, would he forget all about it?

I was as nervous as a Jew in the chapel of the grand inquisitor as I made my way through the streets of Madrid. I was on my way to the house of some unknown nobleman, and it seemed to me that every fishmonger and carpenter hurrying along in the haze of early dawn squinted at me wryly. I had worn my plainest dress and covered it with a simple, black hooded cape in order not to attract attention, but a lady alone in the street, especially at that odd hour, was always suspect. I kept to the lanes and alleys to avoid the watchful eyes of the *aguacil.*

I found the *palacio* of the patron without difficulty and followed Velázquez's instructions about entering. He had been extremely precise: Do not stop at the front gate. Come in through servants' entrance—the door will be open—and climb the stairs to your left. Follow the corridor nearly to the end and enter the door to your right. Do not speak to anyone or tell anyone where you're going.

Velázquez was waiting for me in a large room, which would soon fill with sunlight. I expected him to kiss me, to thank me profusely for doing him the great favor of posing for his painting. Instead, he hardly looked up from his palette.

"Disrobe and put on the dressing gown I left for you behind the screen," he said matter-of-factly. "I'll position you as soon as the light is right."

"It's chilly in here," I commented.

He didn't answer. It was clear he didn't want to chat.

When he was ready, I threw the gown aside. I could feel his eyes on me as I moved toward the bed and stretched out on the sheets. I giggled nervously, but he seemed not to notice. He slid his hand under my right hip and positioned my torso, then moved my right shoulder slightly forward. I trembled to his touch and caught my breath. I wanted him to stroke my back or to say something soothing, but instead, he took his place behind his easel.

"No one saw me leave the house," I said, to dispel my nervousness.

"Don't talk!" he snapped. "Now I have to reposition you."

He took my chin in his hand and adjusted my head. He

was treating me like an object—a bowl of fruit or a vase. My jaw tensed—imperceptibly, I thought—and I bit my lip.

Velázquez sighed, annoyed. "You've changed the angle of your head," he chided. "I wish I had a professional model."

"So do I!"

He lightened his touch. "I'm sorry, *mi amor*, but your body reflects your feelings, and even the slightest movement changes everything. Try to relax your facial muscles."

I did as he asked. He walked toward the foot of the bed and observed me from different angles. I caught sight of his face from the corner of my eye. His gaze was detached, cold. I concentrated on the sounds in the street in order to keep myself from moving.

After a while I grew used to lying there naked. The room no longer felt chilly. I no longer felt uncomfortable. Slowly I began to understand that posing for Velázquez was important. He would immortalize my figure. He would transform me into Venus.

The bell is ringing to call us to vespers. Cintia's sordid remarks about Velázquez's son and his frolic in Italy left me feeling foul, but I must take my place in line to process into the chapel. If I don't go, Mother Augustina will send someone to look for me. I drag myself to my feet and grope for the bedpan. Then I pour water onto my hands from a jug and dry them on a rag. I make my way out into the hall and follow the shuffle of feet. The nuns move in silence, like disembodied spirits—black silhouettes gliding noiselessly through the shadows. The boarders stand at the rear and enter after the others. I squint, searching for Cintia. Her scent gives her away. She reeks of tobacco and bacon grease. She smiles faintly when she sees me, and then takes her place among the professed nuns. Her maid Trinidad is very devout and prays more loudly than either of us. I bow my head and follow them into the chapel.

> *Deus, in adiutorium meum intende.*
> *Domine, ad adiuvandum me festina.*
> *Gloria Patri, et Filio, et Spiritui Sancto.*
> *Sicut erat in principio, et nunc et semper,*
> *et in saecula saeculorum. Amen. Alleluia.*

> O God, come to my assistance.
> O Lord, make haste to help me.
> Glory to the Father, and to the Son, and to the Holy Spirit.
> As it was in the beginning is now and ever shall be
> world without end. Amen. Hallelujah.

The prayer flows like liquid over my body, and I am washed clean.

16

THE FACE IN THE MIRROR
1652:1660

"PSST, HAVE YOU HEARD?"

"Have you heard about Velázquez?"

"Have you heard about Velázquez's new painting?"

"Have you heard about Velázquez's scandalous new painting?"

"No one but Velázquez could get away with it."

"Now that he's the *aposentador mayor*, he can do as he pleases."

"He has the protection of the king, the *valido*, and the *Espíritu Santo!*"

"The strictures of the Holy Inquisition mean nothing to him!"

Gossip: a trickle, a stream, and then a gush. The female nude had turned up in an inventory of Gaspar de Haro's paintings, and although few had seen it, in the *mentidero* no one could talk about anything else.

"He's so full of himself, he thinks he's the last egg in the basket!"

"Well, we all know that people who are too big for their britches are exposed in the end."

"*She's* the one with her end exposed. *He* may be immune, but *she's* going to get it right where it hurts."

"And what about Haro, that womanizer? The way he carries on!"

The rumormongers couldn't get enough of young Haro, son of the king's counselor. They claimed that he lived in a pleasure palace filled with indecent images of frolicking nymphs that fueled his prodigious appetites. Everyone knew that by the time he was fourteen, Gaspar de Haro was a renowned *tenorio* with a penchant for actresses, courtesans, and foreign-born whores, and that he squandered his father's enormous fortune at breakneck speed.

At twenty-one, he'd married Antonia María de la Cerda, daughter of one of the most powerful men in Spain. Doña Antonia was reputedly the most beautiful woman in Spain—slim and graceful, all cream and roses, with silky brown hair and emerald eyes. But in spite of his own wife's physical charm, Don Gaspar was relentless in his pursuit of pleasure. And Doña Antonia was just as bad, according to the tattlers. In fact, some whispered that the face in Venus's mirror bore an uncanny resemblance to Haro's bride.

But what everyone really wanted to know was how Velázquez got drawn into all of this. There had, of course, been a *galanteo* or two when he was young, and there was talk of a bastard baby in Italy, but he had always been careful to avoid outright scandal. What mattered to him, people agreed, was to solidify his position at Court. A consummate social climber, he knew better than to make waves.

As Court painter, Velázquez had always known that above all else, his job was to promote a sense of the king's majesty. It was not Velázquez's role to publicize the aristocracy's taste for flesh. So why had he so boldly wandered into scandal, and so soon after his promotion to *aposentador mayor*?

To be honest, I was as wound up over the situation as everyone else. People said that Velázquez had overstepped his bounds. After all, they whispered, you are what you're born into, and it was only a matter of time before this artisan stepped on the wrong toes and was sent flying into the gutter, where he belonged.

And where did this all leave me? Now that he had painted my smooth white body, he'd almost forgotten all about me. I was risking my life for him—the day the inquisitors confiscated that painting, I'd be in the bonfire. Perhaps Velázquez really was untouchable, but those black-robed ogres would have no qualms at all about reaching out their claws and grabbing me.

Every passing day brought more anguish. The longer the gossip churned, the more vulnerable I felt. Velázquez hadn't made a move to teach me to paint, and, I thought, in view of all I was going through on his behalf, the least he could do was to make good on that promise! It seemed that it had slipped his mind, but I was determined to refresh his memory. I thought that maybe painting would distract me from the hell I was going through—the sleepless nights, the stomach pains. I started begging for lessons, and I wasn't going to let him pass the job on to his son-in-law Mazo!

But it wasn't just that I needed a diversion. I was determined to keep Velázquez away from El Buen Retiro—away from the questioning eyes of inquisitive courtiers. I was convinced that it was dangerous for him to spend so much time among those scavengers. A couple of glasses of wine and a good cigar, and he'd spill the beans and land me on the rack. But most important, I wanted him near me. Since his appointment as *aposentador mayor*, he hardly had time to paint. And he hardly had time for me.

Sometimes I'd lie in bed and think about him making love to that Italian woman, the one who had his baby. She was a soft brunette, or maybe a dusty blond, with supple skin and round buttocks. I could feel him kiss her brow as though it were my brow, run his fingers over her shoulder as though it were my shoulder. She shivered at his touch. I shivered. She held his hand to her groin. He moved his thumb across her sex and then covered her with his body. I slipped my hand between my legs and wept.

Not everyone agreed about the face in the mirror. The model was Italian, argued the defenders of Doña Antonia, Haro's bride. The painting had to have been done in Italy because no Spanish woman would do something so disgusting, so depraved, so decadent as pose like that for an artist. Especially not a lady of the duchess's standing. The very idea, harrumphed the bad-tempered old ladies with their high black collars and their modest white coifs. The Spanish inquisitors, unlike their Italian counterparts, enforced the rules, they said. Our fine inquisitors would have seized the work and jailed not only the artist but also his model. Would a duke's daughter risk such a thing?

If the painter was Diego de Velázquez, darling of His Majesty Felipe IV, and the model the powerful Duchess de la Cerda, countered the gossips, anything was possible. Besides, they argued, the painting couldn't have been done abroad because Haro's inventory was completed early in June, 1651. Velázquez didn't return to Spain from Italy until the end of June.

He could have shipped it, countered the other side.

The anti-Antonia contingent insisted that the painting was done in Spain and that the Duchess was the model, while the pro-Antonia forces argued that it had to have been done in Rome. Where tittle-tattle is concerned, who cares about facts? Positions hardened, arguments grew virulent, and the scandal intensified until all Madrid was buzzing. I listened to the gossip in the *mentideros* and never said a word. One compromising remark and I'd have the Inquisition on my tail. I had to be very, very careful.

Doña Juana kept her distance from Court as much as she could, and Arabela wasn't surprised. Whether the face in the mirror belonged to Doña Antonia or to some Italian hussy, the *señora* was being made to look like a fool. And then there was the news about the Maestro's love child! No wonder the *señora* had gone into near-seclusion.

The once-lowly painter now had everything he'd ever dreamed of: a shockingly large salary plus income from the estate of Pacheco; a position at Court so secure he could give the fig to the censors; and now, a son of his own. But what of Doña Juana? Arabela shook her head and grimaced. The girl she had nursed and raised was now a woman of over fifty. As the wife of the *aposentador mayor*, she should have been basking in glory. But instead, she was hanging her head in shame. Velázquez had embarrassed the entire household. Even Julia seemed agitated of late. Usually, she jumped at any opportunity to accompany the *señora* to El Buen Retiro, but now she hung behind, spinning and sewing. She seemed to take no joy at all in the new gowns Doña Juana gave her.

"Corruption, corruption, decadence and corruption," muttered Arabela under her breath. "He thinks that just because those lecherous sons of bitches smile at him, they've accepted him. Doesn't he know they're snickering behind his back?"

Arabela was an old woman. She had aged dramatically in the years since Carlos had left. Her hair was ashen and limp, and when she tried to embroider, her hands trembled like sparrows in the snow. She no longer attended to Paquita's children—there were six of them now, and even the youngest was pretty well grown—but she did her best to remain useful. Juana urged her to sit by the fire and rest, but Arabela still puttered around the *estrado*, barking orders at younger maids and finding fault with their dusting. Nevertheless, it was hard for her to putter—hard for her to do much at all—when her darling Juanita seemed so wilted and morose. She dragged herself around like an adulteress about to be stoned.

At that moment Juana was running her fingers over a plush velvet bodice. The luxuriousness of the fabric took her breath away. She was careful to stroke with the grain so as not to leave any signs of her touch. In contrast with the supple cloth, the silver trim was stiff and scratchy. It would, she thought, make the dress heavy and uncomfortable to wear.

"It seems excessive," she muttered, "when so many are wanting for food."

"*Señora*, you have to dress the part," said Arabela firmly. "You're the wife of a high-ranking Court official, and you must look stylish."

"I don't want to look stylish. I don't even want to go."

"I don't either," echoed Julia. "There are too many parties! Too much hubbub!"

Arabela sighed. Julia had never married, but instead had spent her entire life by Juana's side. And she adored the pomp and glitter of the Court. "I'd rather be a servant to a lady than a slave to some garlic-breathed lout," she said. That's why to Arabela, Julia's sudden balkiness sounded suspicious.

"The queen is having a birthday party, and the *señora* has to go," snapped Arabela. "I'm too old, and she needs an attendant. That's you, Julia—who else would it be? What's the matter with you?"

"Nothing," moaned Julia. "I don't know. I just feel like everyone will . . ."

"Will be staring at the *señora?*" whispered Arabela.

Julia directed her gaze to the floor tiles. Outside, a lattice of ice formed on the window.

"Well?" hissed Arabela, too low for Juana to hear. "Is that it?"

Julia looked at the pane as though she wished she could fly through it, like the nun María de Ágreda.

"I want to stay home," Juana said meekly. But she knew that Arabela was right about the party. She not only had to go, she also had to fit in. She could hardly show up in burlap.

"Doña Juana, it's a great honor to be invited to the birthday celebration of Her Majesty, Queen Mariana," said Arabela with feigned patience. "Isn't it, Julia?"

"*Sí, señora,*" said Julia dutifully. "A great honor."

Of course, Juana recognized that the queen was the queen, and that it was a privilege merely to breathe the same air as she. She was a divine creature, after all—chosen by God to produce an heir to the kingdom. She had already given birth to a baby—a girl, to everyone's disappointment, but a boy would surely follow.

The king's new wife was a child, really, only sixteen years old. She'd been destined to marry Baltasar Carlos, her first cousin, but when he died and Don Felipe suddenly found himself with no consort and no male heir, he decided to marry her himself. He was used to young flesh, snickered the gossips. His defenders countered that he was simply meeting his responsibility: the kingdom needed a new prince. Between Velázquez's painting and the king's new bride, the Court, the taverns, and the *mentideros* hummed like beehives.

"Get dressed, *señora*," said Arabela with the authority of a mother.

Julia held up the stiff wide farthingale for Juana to step into. Juana stood in the middle of the room and went through the motions. One foot and then the other. One clasp and then another. Her limbs moved as though controlled by some unseen puppet master.

"Now the *basquiña*," said Arabela, "and now the *saya*. The hairdresser will be in soon. You shouldn't put on the lace collar until after you've had your hair done."

"I'm tired," moaned Juana, ignoring the billowy, white pleated collar in Julia's hand. "I want to rest a while."

"Sit then," commanded Arabela. "You can't lie down in those clothes."

After the hairdresser had come and gone, Julia attended to the makeup: first, the chalk-like *solimán* for the face to achieve the pallid tone so fashionable at Court, and then the bright red paste for the cheeks and mouth.

"I look like a doll," complained Juana.

"Wonderful," exclaimed Arabela. "That's exactly the style. And now, the jewels."

"I hate this."

"We all have to play our role," chided Arabela. "If you think people are gossiping now, wait and see how they twitter if you don't show up." Arabela knew that she was being cheeky, but she also knew that public shame was the very worst thing that could befall a person. She was certain that Juana was too cowardly to take the coward's way out. She would face the embarrassment of going to Court in order to avoid the greater embarrassment of staying home. "Go on, Doña Juana," advised Arabela. "Go and hold your head high."

That evening, an hour before midnight, Juana and Julia were climbing into the coach to El Buen Retiro, where they would meet Don Diego. He had an elegant suite in the palace, where his servants had dressed him for the festivities. The household had barely seen him in weeks, as he spent most of his time at the palace or else traveling with the king, but Arabela was confident that tonight, he would defy scrutiny by playing the attentive, decorous escort.

A week had come and gone since the party, and people were still talking about the face in the mirror. Some serving girls had brazenly come right out and asked Julia if she knew the identity of the mysterious model, and the maid had threatened to claw out their eyes. "Why should they think that *I* would know anything about it!" she pouted. Doña Juana, on the other hand, barely spoke of it when she returned—perhaps no one had dared mention the affair to her. Arabela concluded that the outing had done her good. She seemed calmer, less edgy.

Which it had, but not for the reasons Arabela suspected. What had improved Juana's state of mind was a conversation she had overheard between a chamberlain and a Court chaplain:

"The face in the mirror . . ." began the chaplain.

"Certainly Doña Antonia's," affirmed the chamberlain.

". . . could be anyone's . . ."

"Absolutely not. The woman is clearly Doña Antonia."

". . . or, for that matter, no one's."

"What? What do you mean?"

"The face in the mirror is blurred. It gives no clue as to the identity of the model."

"So what are you saying?"

"Just that. The face is indistinct. It's a generic face, something Velázquez could have pulled out of his head. Not only that—if you look at the angle of the mirror, you'll see that it couldn't reflect the model's face. If realistically rendered, it would reflect her torso!"

"Her torso! Don't be ridiculous."

"I studied the angle carefully when I was at Haro's. The mirror is positioned in such a way that it could not possibly capture the model's likeness."

"So you're saying that the face in the mirror . . ."

". . . could be nothing more than a made-up image. Anyone's face. No one's face."

The chamberlain thought about it a moment. "But Don Diego is too good a painter to make a mistake like that!" he said finally. "He would never miscalculate the angle of a reflection of a mirror."

"Oh, but I'm quite certain that it wasn't a mistake!" countered the chaplain with a smile. "It's clear that he wanted to throw people off the trail in order to keep the model's identity a secret. He wanted to protect her. Of course it's also possible that he worked *without* a model. He could have copied the torso from an existing Italian painting—one none of us have seen . . ."

". . . and then added the face in the mirror, creating the illusion of a reflection. You're saying that the whole thing is a trick? Or a joke?"

"It's certainly possible. Maybe he wanted to mock the Holy Inquisition."

Yes, thought Juana, it was certainly possible. Whether the story was true or not mattered not one bit—as long as the chaplain was advancing the story that there had been no model for Velázquez's Venus. It would surely spread and take hold of the public imagination. The malicious gossip would stop and she could again hold her head high.

When the messenger came to the gate, Arabela was telling Bárbara about the dangerous effects of melancholia. She still remembered Juana's bouts of despair after the death of baby Ignacia, and she was thrilled that the *señora* was no longer floating from room to room like a soul in purgatory. Now that Juana was in better spirits, Arabela no longer had any interest in the identity of Don Diego's model. She didn't care whether it was Doña Antonia or the neighbor's goose.

The messenger identified himself as Don Osorio de Bogotá, and to Lidia's surprise, he asked to speak with Arabela. Lidia brought him around back to the servants' entrance. He was a strange looking man, this messenger. He wore bizarre colors—teal and tangerine, turquoise and rose—colors that Spanish men never wore. His pearl-hued, padded *coleto* was edged in scarlet, and his wide britches were tied at the knee with ribbons of outrageous shades. Even his cape, the most conventional of his garments, was fastened with an ostentatious brooch of bright green emeralds. On his feet he wore *borceguís*, slightly platformed leather shoes fastened with leather rosettes. Fortunately, thought Arabela, his ruff was white, as God commanded. Even so, he reminded her of a jester, or a parrot, or one of the *locos* from the asylum who dressed in garish colors and performed antics for the amusement of the public.

Don Osorio bowed low. In spite of his attire, his stance was cool and dignified. Still, Arabela was not impressed. She was not used to being bowed to, and his gesture was certainly proof that he had no sense of decorum. Or perhaps he was mocking her. He waited for her to say something by way of greeting, but instead she stood there glaring.

"*Señora . . .*" he began.

"I'm no *señora!*" she snapped. "You can see I'm a maid."

He raised his eyebrows and nodded slightly, as though she had just offered him a cup of tea.

"You are Doña Arabela?" he said finally.

"I am Arabela."

"I bring you a letter."

Arabela glowered. What kind of nonsense was this? Nobody wrote her letters. And anyway, she couldn't even read!

"Why do you talk like that?" she asked unceremoniously. The man pronounced his c's like s's and occasionally interjected a word she didn't understand.

"What do you mean?"

"You don't sound like a Christian."

"I've been living in America. In New Granada. I'm a gems merchant, and I'm here on business." He sounded suddenly irritable, as though she were wasting his time with her foolish questions. "I promised Don Carlos I'd deliver this letter," he added. He frowned with impatience.

"Who's Don Carlos?"

He handed her a sheet of paper folded to form an envelope. Arabela noticed fleetingly that it was quite heavy, but her attention was fixed on the man. She didn't like his cold arrogance, the way he squinted past her rather than looking her in the eye. She didn't like the way his mustache crimped along his lip, or the way his teal-colored hat feather brushed the ground when he bowed. Everything about him was odd. Why had he agreed to talk to her in the servants' quarters? If he was a wealthy businessman, a *Don* Osorio, why would he lower himself? Why didn't he just give the letter to Lidia and ask her to deliver it? Arabela squinted at the paper in her hand.

"Wait . . ." she said, tracing the calligraphy with her gaze. The script was even and professional. If she had been used to receiving letters, she would have recognized the hand of a scribe.

"You've got the wrong person." Arabela thrust the weighted paper back at the man.

"I think not." Don Osorio turned to go. "Now, please excuse me. I have other obligations."

Who was this New World upstart, Arabela wondered. This was a man with a lot of money and no taste. Those *Indianos*— she used the word in vogue for Spaniards who returned from the colonies—they all call themselves *Don*, whether they're nobles or farmhands.

"Who gave this letter to you?" she insisted.

"I told you: Don Carlos," Osorio responded curtly. He was nearly out the door. "I understand it concerns a matter of *vital* importance."

Arabela felt suddenly numb. The way he stressed the word "vital" seemed ominous. She looked at the paper and turned it over and over. She only knew one person in the Americas, and that was her son, the soldier. What if it was about him? He was no *Don*, of course, but his name *was* Carlos. Stories about the New World flooded the *mentideros*—the savagery of the Indians and the brutality of greedy, low-class Spaniards struggling to prove their muscle; honor duels, bloodbaths over landholdings, battles against English and Dutch pirates off the coast; and horrible diseases—smallpox, measles, and *el mal francés* . . . Arabela had heard about these things, but she had never given them much thought. She had her own problems, what with Don Diego's painting of Venus and Doña Juana's delicate nerves.

But now, as she scanned the folded sheet of paper in her quivering hand, the reality of Carlos came rushing back to her. The baby she had given birth to, nursed, held. The little boy she had given away. The ragged soldier who had stood before her, begging with his eyes for a tender word.

Doña Juana usually ordered that messengers be taken to the stable and given food and beer, but the haughty *Indiano* had already disappeared. Letter in hand, Arabela hobbled across the patio. She felt suddenly old, ancient. Her swollen ankles and her stiff knees ached. She stopped by the foot of the stairs. I'll plod up to Doña Juana's *estrado* and ask the *señora* to read it, she thought, but instead, she stood grasping the rail and shivering.

Arabela took a deep breath. The letter was still folded, with only the address visible. It seemed to be stuffed with something. After a while she tiptoed into the parlor, lit a candle, and gently melted the seal. As she unfolded the sheet, a fat packet slipped to the ground, but Arabela didn't notice. She stared at the writing for a long time, as if by examining the characters she would suddenly comprehend them. Although she'd never been a real mother to Carlos, the thought of losing him now shattered her. She wanted to scream, to sink down into a pool of sludge, to go to sleep and never wake up. She wanted to tear up the letter.

Punishment, she thought. This is God's punishment for my neglectfulness.

Arabela refolded the letter and walked back out into the patio. Wooly clouds blocked the sun. A flock of birds flew in formation, like soldiers moving across a field. The air smelled of roasted lamb, onions, and carrots. Bárbara would be whipping egg whites for meringues, Doña Juana's favorite dessert. Don Diego wouldn't be home for the midday meal, but Paquita might come by with some of the children, Cristina and Ana perhaps. Cristina was soon to be married, but Ana was a strange little thing, as quiet as a spider and as prayerful as a mantis. Arabela thought about all the things that filled her life and suddenly found them meaningless. She hugged the wall and wished she could cry.

And she wished she could read.

"What are you doing out here in the cold, Arabela? Come in, before you get sick." Juana was standing in the doorway. She pulled Arabela's shawl around her shoulders and nudged her inside. "What's that letter?"

"Bad news, *señora*. Bad news from the colonies."

Juana took the letter out of her hand. "How do you know it's bad news?" Juana scrutinized the writing. "It was written by a scribe," she said thoughtfully. "That much is clear."

"They've written to tell me that my son is . . ." Sticky tears rolled down Arabela's furrowed cheeks.

"Do you want me to read it?"

Arabela dropped her chin. "Carlos is . . ." Juana carefully unfolded the sheet and read aloud.

Esteemed Mother,

I pray that this letter finds you in good health. I am in an excellent state, extremely fit for my age, and with a full and robust beard. In my present position, it would be a boon to know how to read, but a man of my position can hardly sit for lessons like a schoolboy. Nevertheless, I have learned to count and do sums, which is a more important skill for a landowner like me. I have not married an Indian, as you feared, but have taken a wife from among the girls the Spanish king in his goodness has provided. Her name is Yolanda Torvisco, and although she is not a great beauty, she is strong, broad of ass, and a good breeder. She is not yet twenty and has already given me three children, two boys and a girl—blessings from God in spite of my sins. So now you are a grandmother, and you have nothing to be ashamed of because all your descendants are of Old Christian lineage as God has willed, and not only pure-blooded but also rich (Jesus be praised). Yolanda is very competent. She manages the Indian servant-girls with a firm hand and will be able to take care of me in my old age.

In gratitude for my service in the wars against the Mapuche in the south, the king granted me a tract of land, not in Mapuche territory, but far in the north. Although I am still vigorous enough to do battle, I think there is more profit to be made in farming than in warfare. A great many products grow here: coffee, cocoa, sugarcane, rice, corn, plantains, oranges, guavas, coca. If you keep goats, you can easily find a bezor stone in its gut when you slaughter the animal, I mean one of those magic stones that can cure any illness; these stones bring large sums of money, as they are much treasured in Spain. I grow plantains and bananas on my land, which is a hot, humid northern area of Nueva Granada, and do very well indeed. The markets here are excellent. We Americans would rather buy local goods than import from Spain. The Spanish impose taxes on shipping to pay for insurance and defense against pirates, which eats at our profits, so it's more economical to sell at home. I have accumulated considerable wealth here, Mother, which is why I am able to send you these gold coins.

Life can be difficult here. There is much disease and the constant threat of Indian uprisings. However, a rugged soldier like myself, bred in poverty and used to hardship, can find his paradise. Here in Nueva Granada I have property and servants; a quiet, subservient wife; and plenty of money. I work hard governing my lands, but, God knows, I am no stranger to hard work. Here I am someone—they even call me Don Carlos—while in Spain I was no one.

Mother, we will not see each other again on this earth. May God keep you and give you peace.

Your son,
Don Carlos Yepes

Arabela stared into space, her jaw moving rhythmically.

"Coins?" she said finally. "Did he say there were gold coins?"

"He did. Don't you have them?"

Arabela looked at Juana blankly.

They found the packet in the *sala*. Juana stooped to pick it up, then handed it to Arabela, who took it and turned it over and over.

"Aren't you going to look to see what's inside?"

Arabela tugged at the end of the thread that someone— perhaps Yolanda—had used to sew the packet together. It slid out easily and Arabela tucked it into her sleeve for future use. She unfolded the cloth carefully. Twenty gold ducats appeared, like glistening crocuses thrusting up through the snow in early spring. Arabela swallowed hard.

"You take them, *señora*," she said after a long pause. "I've never had money. I wouldn't know what to do with it."

"No, Arabela," said Juana gently. "It's yours—a gift from your son."

Arabela wiped her eyes with the back of her hand. "My son," she whispered. "*Don* Carlos. What can I do with this? Can I buy a house?"

"No, Arabela, but you could rent one for a year, if you wanted to."

"I don't . . . I don't want to leave you, *señora*." Tears trickled down her furrowed cheeks. "My Carlos. *Don* Carlos," she kept murmuring. "Even though I neglected him, he didn't desert his mother. I don't deserve . . ."

"Of course you do, Arabela," said Juana gently. "Keep it. You'll find a use for it."

"Use it for my funeral," said Arabela. "Give me a beautiful *capilla ardiente*, with lots and lots of candles. A funeral that would make Don Carlos proud."

It's better if you can draw from nature—that's what Velázquez always said—but my eyes have gotten so bad I can hardly see what's in front of me. The film over my pupils is growing more and more opaque every day. When Velázquez taught me to paint, he started out by showing me how to copy hands from a sketchbook. Then he made me reproduce my own hand. "Hold it this way," he'd say. Then, "hold it that way." I'd paint a fist, a pointing finger, a palm turned upward. I'd paint my elbow, my feet, my image in the mirror. I was never good at figure painting, and my self-portraits never looked like me—they looked like some statue in the church garden. What I liked to paint was flowers. I'd position my easel by a rosebush, and I'd paint every petal and leaf, keeping in mind the source of light, the angle of the shadows, just as Velázquez taught me. But now I can't see the flowers in the garden clearly enough to paint them, so I paint the images in my head. Lately I've been trying to paint the messenger—the one who looked like a parrot and brought Arabela her son's letter. The teal plume, the scarlet-edged jacket. I don't know if my picture looks like him because I never saw him. It's just an image I pulled out of my head.

An invented image, just like the face in the mirror.

17

Meninas

1656–1658

M ENINAS—LITTLE GIRLS—THEY FILL YOUR LIFE, AND THEN they're gone. Only in art can they stay small forever.

Juana knelt by the bed and intoned the verses she had held in her heart since childhood, verses she had learned from Sister Inmaculada decades ago in the Seville Carmel. The old nun had insisted she memorize them. Ever since the ban on reading the bible in Spanish, women had to stow useful passages where the inquisitors couldn't find them.

"Keep them in your heart, Juana," she always said. "It's safer than sewing them into your underwear."

Juana had chuckled at the time, but she was glad she'd followed the old nun's advice because now she needed those verses. Now, in this room darkened by drawn curtains and doused embers. Now, in this chamber of moaning and sobs, of rotting flowers no one had the presence of mind to throw out. Now, as always when death crossed her doorstep, Juana's own words failed her. Only the words of God could express her grief:

A voice is heard in Ramah,
Lamenting and weeping bitterly;
It is Rachel weeping for her children,
Refusing to be comforted for her children,
Because they are no more . . .

Arabela pressed her fists to her eyes. Her voice was thick in her throat. "Oh, God," she whispered. "Why didn't you take me instead? I'm old and I'm ready. Why the child? And why the child of the child?" She shook her head and pulled her shawl more tightly over her shoulders. Francisca's daughter Ana bowed her head and prayed. Tears dripped onto her cuffs.

The Lord gave, the Lord has taken back.
Blessed be the name of the Lord.

She swallowed saliva. "*Mamá*," she murmured, "why were you taken from us? We need you here on Earth. But it is God's will. Blessed be the name of the Lord."

Juana wanted to scream, and yet to sink into an abyss of silence. Where, she asked herself, was the little girl that Paquita had been? The hellion who tore through the house and burst like a windstorm into rooms? What lay before them was dead flesh, motionless as a stone. And the baby, the dull, lifeless baby—she looked like a wax doll with painted lips, although she was clearly Paquita's child, with Paquita's wan complexion and mousy features, her upturned lips and her tiny nose.

Velázquez stood in the doorway, his features drawn and twisted, his large frame wilted. When his daughter Ignacia had died, he had hardly reacted, but Ignacia had been an infant, without any distinguishable qualities. He had hardly known Ignacia, and besides, babies died in Spain all the time. Infant mortality was so common that no intelligent man would become attached to a young child. But this was different. Paquita had grown into an endearing young woman—bright, witty, and energetic. She was the wife of his associate Mazo and mother of his grandchildren. She gave him joy, and he loved her with tender, paternal devotion.

He surveyed the group: Juana, Mazo, Arabela, Julia, Lidia, Bárbara, Francisca's six children, their spouses, and their offspring. All of them knelt by the bed where Paquita lay, her eyes closed, her lips parted as if ready to blurt out a wisecrack. The buzz of their prayers hovered over the corpse. Velázquez knew that this scene should calm him. Francisca had died as one should; she had had what the manuals of *ars morendi* called a "good death." She had taken all three sacraments and had faded from this earth surrounded by a loving family and servants. But Velázquez found no solace in the image before him. Everything seemed askew and grotesque. There was no equilibrium in it, no beauty. Francisca was not yet forty. She had been a good daughter and a good mother. She had borne six healthy children, but this, the seventh pregnancy, had proven too much for her. This picture made no sense, and Velázquez felt his jaw harden in anger. He knew it was a sin to resist the will of the Lord, and yet he had to ask—how could He let this happen?

It hadn't been the baby's fault, the doctors said. A cancer had eaten away at Paquita's breasts. The woman who had nourished six children was depleted, and she couldn't nourish the one growing in her womb. The finest Court medics had attended her. They had sweated her and fed her expensive, ground-up bezor stones. They had bled her. But the excruciating pain was too much. Every day she grew weaker, and finally, she stopped eating. Soon after, her heart gave out, and she stopped breathing. Hot tears gathered on the painter's eyelids. God, he thought, has taken her in payment for my sins. God gave me a son, but He took away my daughter and my granddaughter. "The Lord gives, and He takes back."

Juana turned to look at him. He was pallid. He caught her gaze and crumpled against the wall.

Not two weeks after we buried Paquita and the infant, Arabela fell ill. One morning, she simply couldn't get up from her cot. Juana ordered that she be brought from the servants' quarters to a room in the main house, but Arabela gripped the wooden frame and refused to let go. "I'm too tired and too weak," she rasped. "With God's grace I'll soon be in eternity with my little girls—with baby Ignacia and little Paquita. I'm sure that in heaven she looks as she did when she was eight."

Juana sank to the ground next to the woman who had raised her, comforted her, guided her, and protected her. The woman who had been a mother to her. She dissolved into sobs. "Please, Arabela, no."

"It's time, Doña Juana. I'm an old, old woman. I must be over eighty."

Juana caressed her hand.

"But don't forget," she added. "I want a nice funeral. I sewed the money into my blanket. If there's anything left, give it to Lidia for her daughter, Jael." Lidia had named the child for the biblical heroine who seduced the enemy of her people into her tent, then murdered him by driving a peg through his temple. This was exactly the kind of story Lidia liked.

Juana was certain that no other servant had ever had a funeral as sumptuous as Arabela's. The cortège stretched from Velázquez's house to the Plaza de las Palmas. Juana gathered servants from the houses of all of her friends and paid the Franciscan orphanage for forty boys with excellent mourning skills, who moaned and wailed as though they had just lost their very own mothers. The luxurious *capilla ardiente* that Juana assembled in the chapel was fit for a princess. Buckets of tallow had gone into making the hundreds of candles that flickered and danced in the shadows. Laid out in her coffin, old Arabela seemed to smile at the endless stream of mourners who filed by to bid her farewell. "I may be a maid," she seemed to be saying, "but my son Don Carlos paid for a hell of a fancy send-off."

A sumptuous feast followed the burial. Even though the neighbors said it was absurd to spend such a fortune on a funeral banquet for a servant, they eagerly partook of the fine meats and pastries that Juana provided.

Juana followed Arabela's instructions scrupulously except for one thing: she did not use Carlos's gift. Juana had inherited money from her father, and even though Velázquez controlled it, she could use it with her husband's permission. It was she who supplied the mourners, the candles, and the rivers of mutton stew. She saved Arabela's ducats for Jael's convent dowry. Within three weeks of Arabela's death, Jael entered the Carmel of San José de Madrid.

Velázquez stayed away. Home was too gloomy. The loss of Francisca had left an abscess in his heart, and Arabela—well, Arabela had been the pillar and mast of the household, and without her everything seemed unhinged and shadowy. Objects melted into space and paintings seeped into the walls. The family cats bumped into furniture and lost interest in mice. Nothing was where it should be. Juana disappeared into her *estrado*, and the maids forgot their routines, drifting from room to room like feathers in a midnight breeze. Faces merged into one another, and Velázquez forgot the names of the gardener and the laundress. Colors looked dull. Everything looked dull—everything, that is, except the image he held in his mind of the bright, bouncy girl who had been Francisca.

Velázquez took up permanent residence in an apartment in the Treasury House next to his atelier. His rooms, which were connected to the palace by a passageway, gave him easy access to the familiar bustle and bickering that he thought would moor him to life.

As for Juana, she was too immersed in grief even to notice that Velázquez had disappeared. It wasn't until months later that she began to emerge from her stupor. She picked up a paintbrush and swept it across the canvas. First a vase of roses. Next a basket of lilies. Then a slow, gradual resignation.

"I thought Court life would occupy my mind," Velázquez told Juana when they could both finally talk about it. "I thought the endless chatter would ease the chill of the nights without you and of the days without Paquita." He dropped his chin as though holding his head on his shoulders were an unbearable burden. He sighed and went on: "But then I realized that the Court is nothing but an illusion."

And now the Court was completely disintegrating. Queen Mariana, whose boisterous girlishness had delighted Spaniards upon her arrival in Madrid, was turning sour and demanding. The dwarfs and jesters no longer amused her, and she no longer found pleasure in the theater and balls. One miscarriage followed another, and those children who survived lived only briefly. The king was miserable, and so he did what he always did when he was miserable. He drowned his melancholy in the charms of chambermaids and prostitutes, and he forgot all about the wise advice of Mother María de Ágreda.

Meanwhile, Queen Mariana's bitterness grew. Her husband was old enough to be her grandfather, and yet as profligate as ever. She hated Spain and everything about it. She hated Haro, the king's chief advisor, and most of all, she hated María de Ágreda. Everything Spanish was abhorrent to her: politics, mutton stew, rioja wine, *mantillas*, farthingales, *juegos de caña*, bullfights. If it was Spanish, she loathed it. She began to wear only black, to surround herself with Austrians and Germans, to speak German, to demand *schnitzel* and *apfelstrudel*. She became inseparable from the confessor she had brought from home, the sinister Jesuit Johann Eberhard Nithard, who had a face like a goat, with a long bony skull and eyes sunken deep in cobwebby sockets. The queen included Nithard in everything—council meetings, social gatherings, children's lessons. Rumor had it she was plotting to get rid of Haro and replace him with Nithard as the *valido*.

None of this made any sense to Velázquez. The Court life that he had coveted was a perverse lie—as strange and disorienting as purgatory. There was the Spanish queen who wouldn't speak Spanish; the penitent king who spent his nights in the gutter; the goatish Jesuit who prayed in Latin but skulked in the shadows like the Devil; the flamboyant Court with an empty treasury. The festivities in the majestic salons of El Buen Retiro continued, but salary payments to cooks, carpenters, and coachmen had once again been suspended. Velvet capes were patched and re-seamed. Brocade skirts were mended on the underside. After the parties, gold jewelry was returned to the pawnshops. The ducat had been devalued to the point of worthlessness. Everything that appeared elegant and fine was putrid to the core. It was a game of mirrors, reflections of reflections that left you dizzy. Mirrors like the mirror of Venus, whose reflections you couldn't trust. You never knew what was illusion and what was real.

So Velázquez plunged into his painting. To be sure, the duties of *aposentador mayor* were important, but only laying color on canvas gave him solace. The king had asked for a portrait of his daughter, the Infanta Margarita Teresa, an exuberant five-year-old with golden blond hair and an ivory complexion, and Velázquez was glad to oblige.

Velázquez tottered in front of his easel and struggled to get his bearings. He thought about Paquita, his own little girl. She had never been a pretty child, but her spontaneity and verve imbued her with charm. Like all little girls, she was candid and shrewd at the same time. She could disarm you with a smile and twist you around her little finger. That is what he wanted to capture in the infanta: her artful artlessness, her vivacity, and her magnetism. And when do little girls display such traits? In the company of other little girls. He would place little Margarita Teresa among her playmates, the *meninas*, her maids of honor. This would not be yet another stiff rendering of a porcelain doll in a shellacked farthingale. Instead, he would capture the child's bloom and sparkle.

A knot formed under Velázquez's sternum. It was as though his viscera had forgotten their function and huddled together into a ball. He had never paid enough attention to his body—or to Paquita—and now his body was irritated and she was dead. The pain he felt in his chest was the work of seditious organs collaborating to bring him down. Hot drops splattered onto his hand.

¿Está bien vuestra Merced? Mazo stood in the doorway. When did young Mazo get to be a middle-aged forty-four-year-old with graying temples? wondered Velázquez. For a man who had just lost his wife, Juan Bautista looked strangely serene. Instead of mourning clothes, he wore a dark blue doublet adorned with nightingales. Rumor had it that he had already set his sights on a replacement for Paquita: the buxom, dark-haired Francisca de la Vega.

Estoy bien. Gracias, Juan Bautista.

Mazo remained motionless.

"I don't need your help," said Velázquez evenly. "You may go."

Velázquez holds his breath. The king has seen the painting at different stages, of course, but who knows how he will react to the final version? Will he think it's a caprice—or worse, a joke? A shrewdly realistic rendering of Court life or an insult?

He has painted a domestic scene, with little Margarita

Teresa center stage. Wearing a wide farthingale, her blond hair thrown over her shoulders, she looks out at the spectator, child-like yet strong-willed and imposing. She is surrounded by her ladies in waiting, a nurse, a bodyguard, and the dwarfs Maribar-bola and Nicolasito. The large brown mastiff that lies beside her looks friendly, but is clearly powerful enough to take off your head if you bother his little girl. Everyone is frozen in the midst of the hum and buzz of a typical afternoon.

The painting offers more questions than answers. Velázquez has incorporated his own image into the canvas, but is he looking at the viewer or at King Felipe and Queen Mariana, reflected in a mirror behind him? And where are the king and queen, anyway? Are they outside the picture space like the viewer, or are *they* the viewers? Are they posing for the painter or just watching him paint? And that mirror—does it show the king and queen, or is it actually a painting of the royal couple? What is real? What is an illusion? Is royal authority an illusion? The faces of the royal couple are blurred, just as the face of Venus is blurred in my painting. Is the very notion of the ideal monarch nothing more than a deception? Is the very notion of ideal beauty embodied by Venus nothing more than a sham?

Velázquez waits for the king to speak. But kings must always be opaque. They are symbols of authority, icons of the Empire, and they can never reveal their true thoughts. Don Felipe stares at the painting, at the painter in the painting staring back at him, and says nothing.

Velázquez closed his eyes and concentrated on the sensation: the liquid felt warm and soothing on his back. Pareja's hands moved deftly, splattering orange-scented water over his shoulders. Velázquez felt the droplets dribble down his spine to his buttocks, down his arms, down his chest. He had never expected to feel such serenity. He had thought he would be nervous, fidgety. But now that the glorious day had come, calm enveloped him.

Don Ávaro de Zúñiga, tenth duke of Escalona and Grand Master of the Order of Santiago, looked on as Pareja dried Velázquez with perfumed linens, and then slipped a white tunic over his head.

"White, to symbolize purity," intoned the grand master.

Purity? Velázquez thought of Antonio. How could he, who had fathered a bastard son in a foreign land, claim to be pure? He bit his lip and remained silent.

Escalona held a red robe out to him, and Velázquez slipped his arm through the armhole.

"Red, to symbolize nobility."

Nobility? The words "artisan," "plebian," "tradesman" ran through the painter's mind. He had been called those names all his life. In spite of royal support, the commission on lineage refused to dispense with the usual investigation. Both Velázquez and Juana had to prove they were Old Christians, free of Jewish or Moorish blood. There were endless questions, endless petitions, endless interviews with courtiers, neighbors, maids. Did the Velázquezes have the house cleaned on Friday? Even if they weren't crypto-Jews, it could be a custom inherited from some ancient ancestor, who scrubbed and polished on Fridays to get ready for the Sabbath. Could Velázquez produce five witnesses

who would swear that for six generations there had been no
gente non sancta in the family? That there had never been a
moneylender or a carpenter or a baker? After this barrage of hu-
miliations, the commission refused to clear him. He was an artisan of artisan stock, they said. In the end, the king himself had
to intervene on his behalf, arguing that Velázquez was not only
an aristocrat, but an influential courtier. Furthermore, as the
royal painter, stated the king, Velázquez could hardly be considered a "tradesman"—obviously, he did not sell his paintings.

"Black, for death," declared Escalona. "For we are mortal
and to dust we shall return. Blessed is he who gives his life for
the one true faith."

Death. This time Velázquez had no doubts. He knew he
would die, and suspected it would be soon.

"You have completed the ritual cleansing of the body," pro-
claimed the grand master. "Do you swear by Almighty God that
you would die in defense of the Immaculate Conception of
Mary? Are you prepared in mind and spirit to proceed to the
royal chapel for the night vigil?"

"I do," murmured Velázquez, "and I am."

The grand master moved down the corridor like a triumphant hunter, his robe trailing behind him like captured
prey. Velázquez kept his eyes lowered as he followed the duke
to the chapel. Slightly behind him came the count of Ordóñez,
followed by Pareja. Velázquez heard the shuffling footsteps as
though through a light drizzle. He felt his newly washed skin
tingle in the frigid palace air. He wondered what he would do if
he should need a chamber pot in the middle of the ceremony,
but shoved the thought out of his mind. He could hardly believe
this was happening.

Once in the chapel, the grand master placed a sword and shield—symbols of the Order's warrior origins—on the altar. Velázquez felt the weight of fraud on his shoulders. He had never been to war or defended the faith against Moors. He had never killed anything but rabbits and ducks. Nevertheless, he knelt before his weapons and bowed his head.

His escort left the room, and the vigil began. He had cleansed his body with the ritual bath, and now he would cleanse his spirit with ten hours of prayer and meditation. He was utterly alone. The candles in their silver candelabras flickered, sending eerie shadows along the walls. Christ hung on his Cross—head bowed, hands and feet bloodied. The Virgin stood in her corner and smiled tenderly. She would keep him company. Beams of blue streamed through the stained glass. The vows of the sacred Order of Santiago constituted a solemn commitment. He bowed his head and swallowed.

The next morning, we all flooded into the chapel to witness the dubbing. I wished Paquita could have been there to see it. She would have been so proud of her father. It was hard to believe she'd already been dead for three years. By then my eyesight had already started to falter. The tapers and the gleaming sword were gobs of light surrounded by mysterious auras.

The chapel reeked of incense and candle wax, perfume and sweat. The air was close and heavy. The priest's smooth pate was hardly visible over the heads of the congregation. The celebrant faced the altar, his Latin consumed by the crackling of the tapers. Then Velázquez made his vows in Spanish. I only remember fragments of what he said—"not trafficking with traitors . . .," "serving the Lord faithfully . . .," "protecting the faith . . .," "respecting all ladies . . .," "observing fasts . . .," "hearing mass every day."

The priest blessed the sword and shield that lay on the altar. Then the grand master and the king rose and took their places on either side of him. Both wore the black habit of the Order, with a red cross of which the lower part forms a sword blade—the mark of the warrior. Escalona solemnly took the weapons and handed them to the king.

Velázquez, still in white, knelt and swore his allegiance to His Majesty. His voice and his hands were steady. His cheeks were damp with tears.

The king unsheathed the sword and laid it on Velázquez's shoulder. Then he said the words: "I dub thee Sir Knight of the Order of Santiago." Finally, he raised the sword and struck Velázquez's shoulder with the flat side. Escalona slipped the white tunic over Velázquez's head and dressed him in the black habit of the Order. Velázquez turned toward the congregation to display the red cross. Women cried and men cheered right there in the chapel.

The celebrations lasted three days. The bankrupt king invited the entire Court to join him in an orgy of feasts. Once again, endless platters of food paraded into the banquet halls, and musicians stationed on the mezzanine entertained the guests with music and song. There were *juegos de caña* in the afternoon, and balls at night—all in honor of the painter Velázquez, favorite of the king.

Las Meninas, as Velázquez's game of mirrors came to be called, had hung for three years in a salon off the main corridor of the palace. But, a month after Velázquez had been dubbed a knight of the Order of Santiago, the king ordered that it be taken down and brought to the same room where it had been painted. Don Felipe himself supervised the move. When the workers had placed the huge painting in its original position, the king ordered that they go to the studio of Don Diego de Velázquez and fetch a pot of red paint. The king checked the color for shade and consistency. Then he called for Haro.

The *valido* was astounded to find the painting standing in the oversized easel that had been constructed for it. A spark of satisfaction probably flashed through his mind. Finally, Haro must have thought, Don Felipe had tired of the painter. Perhaps His Majesty had finally realized how much the absurd celebrations for the man's knighting had cost. Now he was taking down his paintings to send them off to some rarely visited *sitio real* or to sell them.

"Have Velázquez brought to me."

Haro bowed deeply. "Yes, Your Majesty. Right away, Your Majesty."

Haro hobbled to his office and called for a secretary. "The king wishes to see the painter Velázquez in the mauve salon."

By the time the secretary called for a page and the page brought Velázquez, the red paint had begun to thicken.

"Don Diego Rodríguez de Silva y Velázquez, Knight of the Order of Santiago," announced the page.

In an instant Velázquez took in the scene. Beads of sweat formed on his forehead. The pressure in his chest became unbearable, and the color drained from his face as he knelt before the king. His knees were stiff, and when Don Felipe told him to rise, he had to struggle to straighten his legs.

"Check the thickness of this paint," ordered the king.

Velázquez stirred the paint with a stick and added thinner. He bit down on his lip to keep it from trembling. *Las Meninas* was his masterpiece, and now the king was going to order it destroyed. Velázquez had known he was taking a chance when he depicted the royal family as a play of reflections. It had taken the king and courtiers a while to catch on, but now that they had, his days of glory were over. Would they confiscate *Venus* and destroy it, too?

"Is the pigment ready, Don Diego?"

"Yes, Your Majesty," whispered Velázquez.

"Good."

Don Felipe took the pot of red and stood before *Las Meninas*. While Velázquez looked on horrified, the king dipped the brush in the paint. But then he thought better of it and turned to Mazo, who had been standing unnoticed in a corner.

"Here, Don Juan Bautista, you do the honors."

Mazo took the brush from the king. Then he reached up and drew the red cross of Santiago on the black garment of the image of the painter Velázquez.

"Now," said the king solemnly, "the painting is complete."

18

Revelations
1660

VELÁZQUEZ TOUCHED MY HAND, AND I FELT A FRISSON—A shiver of fire. It frightened me, and I looked away. I didn't want him to see the foreboding in my eyes.

"Is something wrong, my dear?"

"No, of course not. It's just that I'll miss you, that's all." I caught my breath. He called me "my dear" more frequently now.

"I've been away before, sometimes for more than a year. This will be a short trip, just a couple of weeks."

"More than a couple. His Majesty isn't scheduled to meet the French king until June. It's only the beginning of April." I forced my lips into a smile. Something about the way he shifted from one foot to the other was making me nervous.

The valet appeared and bowed. "Maestro, we will be leaving shortly."

"Yes, yes of course." Velázquez looked around absentmindedly, waiting for the man to exit the room. Finally, he said, "You may go now."

The valet bowed again.

Six days earlier, Luis de Haro had commanded Velázquez to pack his bags. If Velázquez had qualms about traveling, he didn't show it. He took a deep breath and ordered his staff to ready his wardrobe. I knew he was exhausted. I could see it in his eyes. We women are observant creatures, and when you love a man, you're sensitive to his every groan and twitch. And yes, I did still love him. He was fading now—we both were—and we needed each other. He clung to me, even though he didn't allow me to cling to him. And so I clung on to the memories of our life together—our intimacies, our disappointments, our tears. No matter what he had done with other women, I was still his best friend, his lover, his Venus. Sometimes he'd sink into a chair and doze off in the middle of the morning. When we shared a table, he'd close his eyes and catnap mid-bite. I'd take the morsel from his fingers and try to lead him to bed, but then suddenly he'd open his eyes and wrest his arm from me.

"What are you doing? Let me go!"

"Take a little rest, Diego," I'd coax. "For just a few minutes."

"I'll do no such thing! Why would I? Do you think that I'm a doddering old man?"

"No, not at all. But I do think that you need a break."

As *aposentador mayor* and a knight of the Order of Santiago, he had responsibilities. He had to show His Majesty that he was worthy of his titles.

Haro had been precise in his instructions: Velázquez would travel with a small party of assistants to prepare the way for the king's journey north. The hostilities with France had ended at last, and the truce between the two countries was to be signed on the Isle of Pheasants, which has always been considered neutral territory. Haro would represent Spain and his

French equivalent, Cardinal Mazarin, would represent France. To confirm the agreement, King Louis XIV of France was to marry the Spanish Infanta María Teresa.

Velázquez seemed nervous, but perhaps it was because I was looking at him so intently.

"I feel like a theater director," he said finally, "creating a massive spectacle on twenty-three separate stages."

"Maybe it's too much for you, Diego. After all, you're no longer . . . young."

I shouldn't have said it. He didn't like to be reminded that he was now a man of sixty, with pains in the chest, aches in the knees, swelling in the fingers. I saw his jaw tighten and waited for him to snap at me, but instead he stroked his beard and looked down at the diamond-studded medallion with the red enameled cross of Santiago he had placed on the secretary.

"Very stylish," I whispered, stroking his wrist. "You'll be more elegant than Don Felipe himself."

Velázquez picked up the medallion and turned it over in his hands. The skin around his eyes was thin and crinkled. He already looked exhausted, and he hadn't even set off yet.

The present assignment was an enormous undertaking. Velázquez was to plan the king's journey from Madrid to Fuenterrabía, situated on the west shore of the mouth of the Bidasoa, in Basque country. In order to get there, the king and his party would have to make twenty-three stops along the way, and it was up to Velázquez to prepare every single one of the royal habitations that Don Felipe would visit. Was the decor dazzling enough? Were the sheets silky enough? Would the roses be in bloom in the gardens to provide a proper vista for a king? Velázquez had to attend to every detail.

"I wish you could devote more time to painting . . ."

Velázquez grimaced. He was a statesman now, a true confidant of the king. He constantly met with important officials and even participated in state meetings. As it was up to him to organize ceremonial visits and audiences with his Majesty, he was privy to all kinds of secrets, and from time to time, he even had the opportunity to express an opinion. Paint was the last thing he wanted to do.

"You seem more relaxed when you're painting . . ."

"I don't have time for that now," he said curtly. "I serve the king. I speak with him regularly. I even . . ." He puffed out his chest as if to emphasize his importance. "I even give him advice." He paused. "When he asks for it."

I couldn't help but smile. Velázquez had never been an arrogant man, although he was ambitious. Now, he was clearly proud of how far he had come.

A stocky young man accompanied by three uniformed attendants entered the room. He gave the order, and the others finished packing the few last personal items that Velázquez would carry with him. One took the diamond medallion and placed it in a locked coffer, which he nestled in a trunk full of velvet and fur. They hoisted one of the trunks onto their shoulders and disappeared. I imagined that the procedure would be repeated until all the trunks were in carriages, but I didn't wait to see. Instead, I accompanied Velázquez down the corridor toward the main entrance. We ducked into a small parlor to say our good-byes in private.

"I'll miss you," I whispered.

He took my hands in his and kissed me gently on the fingertips. "Keep painting."

"Oh, I'll never create anything worthwhile."

"It doesn't matter. It's good for you. It keeps your mind occupied."

"Paquita was better at it than I."

"Yes," he said. He looked for a moment as though he were going to cry, but instead, he bent down and kissed me on the lips. "Good-bye, my dear, my Venus."

"Good-bye," I murmured. "*Dios te acompañe.*"

He walked through the door to the train of vehicles lined up in the entrance yard. I made my way back to Velázquez's apartments and gathered up my things. I had decided not to stay in his rooms at the palace while he was gone. I could have, but the noise and gossip of the Court got on my nerves. I would be more comfortable at home, where I had an easel set up in the studio Velázquez still sometimes used in the house on Convalescientes Street.

Velázquez's quarters in the Buen Retiro felt vacant and lonely. The heavy walnut secretary stood devoid of clutter, and the armoire languished open and empty in a corner. Without Velázquez's commanding presence, nothing made sense. The curtains hung forlornly along the window frames—they seemed to be the wrong color. In the atelier the easels stood like three-legged monsters looming in a weird and ethereal sunlight. Although I had every right to be there, I felt as though I were defiling a sacred space. I gathered up my things, called for my carriage, and left the Court. I was an old woman now, and so I rode alone, without an escort. I opened the curtain a bit so that I could enjoy the fresh April air. Not enough to compromise decorum, but enough to feel the sun, warm and comforting, on my brow. The street smelled of jasmine and cinnamon and garbage. Tiger-striped gazanias and geraniums of every hue bloomed on balconies. The sounds of carriages and carts filled the morning. Somewhere, a *buñolera* hawked her sweet, sticky fritters. *"Buñuelos!"* she cried. *"Compre buñueeeelooos!"* Somewhere else, the throaty croon of a drunken soldier. The sounds of the street brought me back to that time, long ago, when I had lazed on a maroon sheet that would someday turn charcoal-colored, posing for Velázquez.

Once home, I retired to the *estrado* to rest a while and change clothes. Then, I sat down at my easel. It would be hours until the midday meal. I should take advantage of the morning light, I thought. Meticulously, I began to arrange objects on a table—fruit, a vase with flowers, a book, a squab. I put on my spectacles and dipped the brush into a pot of crimson.

Stories of the meeting on the Isle of Pheasants reached the Court soon after it took place. María Teresa—now called Marie Thérèse—was married by proxy while she clung to her nannies and her ladies-in-waiting. Terrified that she'd produce a French heir to the Spanish throne, Haro made her renounce all rights to the succession for herself and her children, while Mazarin required an enormous dowry that never got paid. After the papers were signed, His Majesty accompanied his daughter to the waiting diplomats, who ferried her off to France.

I can imagine the little infanta, now the queen of the country that until the day before had been the archenemy of her own. I see her huddled in the carriage with her maids, bumping along, tears rolling down her cheeks. She knows she'll never see her father or her homeland again. She'll be married in Saint

Jean de Luz, and then her new life will begin. The French royal custom of consummating marriage in public must weigh on her. She must wonder what it will be like to be undressed by her ladies-in-waiting in front of spectators, and then disappear under the covers with a husband she doesn't know. Fortunately for her, her new mother-in-law, Anne of Austria, will dispense with this heinous convention at the last minute and allow the infanta and King Louis to celebrate their wedding night in private.

But the infanta and her tribulations were really of little importance to me. What mattered to me was Velázquez. He was old and sick, and he was pushing himself beyond endurance. I was worried he'd collapse right into the pudding. I needn't have fretted, however. Long before he returned, people were saying that he had cut such a dashing figure that he'd actually outshone everyone else. His bearing was aristocratic; his comportment, gentlemanly. His speech was measured and melodious. His style was impeccable. Dressed in a black suit trimmed with Milanese silver point lace, he was the epitome of Spanish fashion. At his side fell a fine rapier in a silver sheath. Around his neck, on a heavy gold chain, hung a diamond- and sapphire-studded medallion with a red enameled cross of Santiago—the same one that had lain on his secretary the day he left Madrid. Gossips said that the French, in their plumes and pastels, looked ridiculous, while the Spaniards, elegant in black, looked dignified, regal. And the most magnificent of all was Velázquez.

The manservant unfastened Velazquez's travel cape and folded it over his arm.

"Shall I fetch your black silk doublet, *Señor?*"

"No, not yet."

"Naturally, *Señor*. I understand. Will you be changing out of your traveling clothes, *Señor?* Would you like to sit down so I can take off your boots?"

"No, I'll stay as I am. Give me my cape."

"Which cape, *Señor?* Surely your mercy wishes to . . ."

"For God's sake, Lorenzo! Don't assume you know what I want to do!"

"Of course, *Señor*. I'm sorry. It's only that you just arrived after such a long journey. After all, you've been away for three months, and I thought . . ."

"Call for my carriage. I'm going out."

"But like that, *Señor?* In your travel clothes?"

Velázquez turned and stared at the man with his black, decimating eyes. Lorenzo handed his master the cape and bowed. I wasn't there, of course, but Velázquez described the scene to me later that evening, both of us giggling like when we were children.

He came to me just as he was, in his dusty boots. They must have told him at Court that I had gone back to the house on Convalescientes Street. I didn't hear him enter the studio. My back was toward the door and I was concentrating on a new painting, on creating shadows out of burgundies and purples, just as he had taught me.

He stood behind me and put his hand on my shoulder.

"Juana, *mi amor*," he murmured.

Somehow I wasn't startled. I laid down the brush and smiled without getting up or turning around.

He bent over and kissed my temple.

"You're getting better," he said. It was the first and only time he complimented my painting.

"You think so?"

I stood, and he took me in his arms. I laid my head on the grimy threads of his travel cape. He slipped it off and threw it on the ground. Then he took my chin in his fingers, tilted my face toward his, and kissed me deeply.

"Yes," he whispered softly. "Yes, Juana, I think so."

EPILOGUE

M Y GRANDMOTHER JUANA ALWAYS SEEMED A MODEL OF PRO-
priety. She was a plain-looking woman with lusterless gray
hair and a rutted brow, and she wore the modest, dreary
clothing that became a woman of her age. After my grandfather
died, she entered a convent, where she lived as a boarder until
Our Heavenly Father called her away from this valley of tears. I
never suspected that she had once posed for a lewd painting
until I read the papers she left in the convent. She had wisely
kept it a secret because her shameful conduct was an offense
against God, our Holy Mother Church, and the honor of our
family.

My grandfather, Diego Rodríguez de Silva y Velázquez,
was Court painter during the reign of our most Catholic King
Felipe IV. He was a noble, a knight of the Order of Santiago, a
highly respected courtier, and a devout Catholic. He produced
many dignified paintings of our most Catholic King Felipe IV
and his family, as well as works for the propagation of the faith
such as a Virgin and a Saint John the Evangelist, both of which

hang in Seville; the Apostle Thomas; Mary and Martha with Jesus; Saint Anthony and Saint Paul in the desert; and a Christ on the Cross, which hangs in a convent in Madrid. I don't believe the horrible things my grandmother writes about our most Catholic King Felipe IV because it's well-known that he was a truly great man—a saint. Her vile descriptions are nothing more than justifications for her own bad behavior. I should say that I also know nothing about the painting of Venus my grandmother describes in her writing.

My grandfather died less than two months after he returned to Madrid from the Isle of Pheasants, where he had gone to assist our most Catholic King Felipe IV in the marriage of his daughter, María Teresa, to the king of France. Soon after he arrived home, my grandfather fell ill and withdrew to his apartments. When the Court physicians realized his time was near, they advised the king, who called for the archbishop of Tyre, Patriarch of the Indies. The blessed archbishop preached to my grandfather and helped him to enter peacefully into the kingdom. His day of Glory occurred on August 6, 1660. Afterward, his servants dressed him in the habit of the Order of Santiago and his body lay in stillness in his bedroom. The next day, he was carried to the Church of San Juan, where he was buried, while all the great noblemen and ladies looked on. It was a solemn and blessed event.

At the time, I had already made up my mind to take vows. I entered the Order of Saint Clare shortly after my grandfather passed to a better life, and I was sent almost immediately to the Convent of San Francisco y Santa Clara on the outskirts of Seville. Although I had never been to that city, I felt a great affinity for it, as my great-grandfather Francisco Pacheco had had a famous art school there, and both my grandmother Juana and my mother Francisca were born there. Besides, there is much need of convents in that place of sin, for many fallen women roam its streets. Our fathers go forth to proselytize to them, and sometimes, when the sinners repent sincerely and show signs of refinement, we take them into our holy house. It may seem unlikely that any such woman would exhibit finesse, but in this calamitous age, ladies of breeding sometimes fall on such hard times that they engage in wickedness in order to survive.

Seville is also full of *beatas,* the ghastly women who claim to have heard the Word of God but are actually frauds. We know they are frauds because they wander shamelessly through the city, preaching on street corners and promising salvation, when our Mother Church teaches that women are not to preach but must remain silent. The Holy Inquisition rounds up these false holy women and incarcerates them, or places them in convents like ours. Of course, it is repugnant to us to have them near, but we know it is our Christian duty to receive them and so we do. What I cannot believe is that my grandmother was as depraved as they.

Soon after my grandfather went to join my precious mother in heaven with God, my grandmother entered a convent in Madrid, where she spent her last days writing her life story. She passed out of this life about a year after my grandfather. Only God knows if He forgave her for her sins. Sometimes I think it was a blessing that both of them passed out of this world when they did, for they were spared the plunge into darkness of our dear homeland. The same year my grandmother died, the king's long-awaited heir Carlos II was born, and from the beginning it was rumored that he was mad or feeble-minded. Our most Catholic Majesty Felipe II went to God five years after my grandfather, and now his son sits on the throne, hidden from view, manipulated by *validos*, sterile and, from what they say, blubbering into his supper. Only God knows what will become of us. Is this punishment for the impiety one finds everywhere? For the immorality and the corruption? Alas, God has punished us all for the sins of a few, although He can't have forgotten that it was we, the Spaniards, with our blood and fortune, who protected the One True Faith against the incursions of the heretics from the north. He won't abandon us, I know He won't. He is testing us, as He tested Job, but He will restore us to our ancient glory in the end.

My father, Juan Bautista Martínez del Mazo, was the executor of my grandfather's will, and after Don Diego went to heaven, my father made an inventory of his belongings and attended to the distribution. I don't know how much my grandmother Juana inherited, but she had enough to pay her convent fees and live out her life in a house of God. After she died, her things went to my sisters and brothers, some of whom married into very fine families. As a Sister of Saint Clare, I neither wanted nor received anything. All I know is that her writings were not among her bequeathals.

I didn't see her papers until years later, when I was getting to be an old woman myself. It seems that after my grandmother's passing, her story was gathered up by a member of the convent community named Cintia—no doubt a devout and holy sister who wanted to spare my grandmother's memory the stain her scribbling would leave on it. This dear Cintia kept the shameful story of Venus to herself for many years. When she finally reached the moment when she knew that God would soon call her, too, she sewed the pages into a burlap casing and had them delivered to me by a messenger. There is no doubt in my mind about why she chose me to receive them. Like her, I am a bride of Christ, and she wanted me to know the truth about Juana Pacheco de Velázquez, so that I could protect my soul from contamination. She wanted me to purge my heart of the sinfulness of my forebears. My dear Cintia! I thank you and I bless you! May you live forever in Glory!

I have written these paragraphs in my spiritual chronicle as a sort of confession, but now I am perplexed about what to do with them. If I show them to the prioress, she might find me unworthy to continue here at the convent. And if I show them to my confessor Fray Jerónimo, as I know I should, he might tell the prioress. Even though information revealed in confession is confidential, Fray Jerónimo is known for sometimes being indiscreet. If they cast me out, where will I go? I am no longer young. Will any of my brothers or sisters have me, a lamb who has devoted her life to God and knows nothing of the ways of the world? I don't know. I just don't know what to do.

Ana Martínez del Mazo y Pacheco de Velázquez
Signed this 16th day of November, in the year of Our Lord Jesus Christ
1675

AUTHOR'S NOTE

Diego Velázquez was the most famous Spanish painter of the seventeenth century, and *The Rokeby Venus* was his most enigmatic painting. For centuries, art historians have conjectured about the identity of the model. Velázquez cleverly angled the mirror in Cupid's hand so that it does not reflect her face. Scholars have calculated that a more realistic rendering of the reflection would show the area from the left hip to the left shoulder. Thus, the woman in the mirror could be anyone . . . or no one in particular.

In *I Am Venus*, I undertake an exploration of Venus's identity and offer a playful and surprising conclusion. The book is based on years of research. The historical facts regarding the profligacy of Philip IV, the corruption of the count-duke of Olivares, the construction of the Palacio del Buen Retiro, and the details of the Thirty Years' War are all accurate. Most of the details of Velázquez's life are also accurate: his ascendance to the position of Court painter, his trips to Italy, his illegitimate child, the death of his daughters Ignacia and Francisca. Recently some scholars have suggested that Velázquez was of *converso* (Jewish) background, which may be why he was so touchy about matters of class and lineage. However, this and many other aspects of Velázquez's personal history remain in the realm of conjecture, leaving plenty of room for the novelist to invent.

Velázquez's wife, Juana Pacheco, was a real person. The daughter of Velázquez's mentor and father-in-law Francisco Pacheco, Juana was born in 1602 and died a few days after her husband, in 1660. For the purposes of my story, I have extended her life a bit. Juana left no trace of her inner reality, and so I have reconstructed her as I imagine her. Juana's friends and servants are all fictional characters, but the descriptions of her milieu are based on historical documents.

I am indebted to many researchers whose work enabled me to recreate Velázquez, his family, and his world. *Velázquez*, by Jonathan Brown, and *Velázquez: su tiempo, su vida, su obra*, directed by Jorge Montoro, provided me with essential information about the painter's life and work. *Velázquez, the Technique of Genius*, by Jonathan Brown and Carmen Garrido, contain detailed analyses of the artist's procedures and practices and helped me to describe his work. *The Late Paintings of Velázquez*, by Giles Knox, provides additional information about Velázquez's development as an artist. Another of Brown's books, *A Palace for a King*, contains descriptions of the Palacio del Buen Retiro and Philip IV's art collections. Andreas Prater's *Venus at Her Mirror* contains much relevant material about the Rokeby Venus and about the history of Venus as an artistic subject. The essays in *The Cambridge Companion to Velázquez*, edited by Suzanne L. Stratton-Pruitt, were valuable resources for data on Velázquez's formation and the Court environment. Two that I found to be particularly useful were Zahira Véliz's "Becoming an Artist in Seventeenth-Century Spain" and Antonio Feros's "'Sacred and Terrifying Gazes': Languages and Images of Power in Early Modern Spain." Maribel Bandrés Oto's *La moda en la pintura: Velázquez* gave me a good understanding of fashion in seventeenth-century Spain and helped me to dress my characters. Several general studies of seventeenth-century Spain and the Court of Philip IV were also helpful, among them *Early Modern Spain: A Social History*, by James Casey; *El rey se divierte* and *La mala vida en la España de Felipe IV*, both by José Deleito y Piñuela; and *The Count-Duke of Olivares: The Statesman in an Age of Decline*, by J. H. Elliott.

I would like to express my gratitude to the novelist Janice Eidus for her editorial comments and to my agent, Anna Ghosh, for her support and encouragement. I am especially indebted to Mark Krotov, my editor at The Overlook Press, for his excellent suggestions. I also wish to thank my husband, Mauro E. Mujica, for his patience and good humor during the writing process.

ABOUT THE AUTHOR

BÁRBARA MUJICA is a novelist, short story writer, critic, professor of Spanish at Georgetown University, and a contributor to many publications, such as *The New York Times* and the *Los Angeles Times*. A two-time nominee for the Pushcart Prize and winner of the E.L. Doctorow International Fiction Competition, she is the author of the novels *The Deaths of Don Bernardo*, *Affirmative Actions*, *Frida*, and *Sister Teresa*. In 2012, *I Am Venus* was a winner of the Maryland Writers' Association competition in the historical fiction catagory. Mujica lives in Washington, D.C.